The Gypsy Gorger

J M Muir-Coates

ISBN: 9781074708139

THE END

I could not tell if my eyes were open or closed. I knew the bright light was fierce and burning although I could not feel it. I could not feel a thing. As I floated towards the light, the silence was ringing in my ears, but it did not last long before the numbness in my stomach changed to a warm hot glow, soon turning into painful cramps. As I rolled over my head started pounding, and the taste of rum on my breath suddenly hit me along with the realisation that I was lying outside on damp grass. The morning dew had soaked through my clothes and the hangover from hell engulfed me.

As I lay on the ground shivering, too cold and hung-over to move, the blurred memories from the night before started to come back to me with renewed clarity. In the centre of the camp, a large fire was burning, the flames wild and high, crackling, spitting and hissing. The sadness and pensiveness that existed at the start of the evening gradually transformed into liquor fuelled merriment. The fiddler played and a couple of women danced whilst others clapped their hands to the beat. Good times.

Bang. There was a split second of silence as the first punch was landed in the obligatory family fight. I did not see the recipient of the offending blow, but it resulted in the whole place erupting in a frenzy of blows, shouts and screams. I was on my own in a corner of the tavern leaning against a wall with my bottle of rum and my memories. Watching through my alcohol blurred eyes, I saw bottles flying everywhere, a couple of which I witnessed surreally bouncing off heads. Mostly they smashed against the walls. It wasn't only bottles that were being thrown, barstools were being grabbed, thrown and smashed over people's heads like a scene from a wild west saloon. I had a subdued chuckle to myself as I remembered little Jim alias 'Wee Man' hurtling through the air at speed. He was caught midair and tossed back across the room, and fortunately this time he had a soft landing. However, it was not so fortunate for the woman he sideswiped, knocking her to the floor then landing on her. Why these family fights start is a complete mystery. How to choose sides is a dilemma but stopping the fight is a bit more straightforward. Most ran out the door as soon as the opportunity arose, some got knocked down and stayed down as this was the safest place to be, unconscious or not. The bigger mystery was I knew I had spent the whole night at the campfire, so how the hell did I get to the tavern.

I had to move. The feeling of cold intensified as I realised that I was shivering uncontrollably, and I could feel the liquid contents of my belly swirling round and round like a whirlpool. Suddenly there was noise, lots of noise. Had it always been there? Was I just blocking it out? A baby cried, women shouted and bawled at each other or most likely their menfolk, and dogs barked continuously at each other as if they were expected to be part of the affray.

'Come here you' said the soft soothing voice of an angel. My angel. 'Let's get you up and to bed' I felt her hands pulling at me, so I slowly tried to move 'Just leave me' I moaned. Thump, thump came the noise from the ground as heavy footsteps came towards me. 'Here doll we'll get him'. She never replied but I could almost hear her frown at being called 'doll'. I didn't have a clue what happened, but I was in the back of the wagon sitting on my bed. 'Thanks boys', 'No bother doll'. I was sitting there still unable to focus my eyes, my head throbbing. 'Let's get these clothes off' she said almost suggestively though I had no interest at the time. Undressing me must have been hard work for her as I was no help. Stripped completely naked I lay down while she piled the blankets on top of me. 'Layers' she whispered 'Thanks' was all I managed to choke out. I heard her say 'You get some sleep it's only six hours to the funeral' then she gave me a kiss on the forehead and ruffled my hair before I rapidly succumbed to sleep.

What is she on about? I thought to myself, *the funerals not until tomorrow*. 'Wee dram of whisky' a voice piped out of nowhere. I made out what must have been a face looking in the door 'Whisky! Get yourself away from here' I rasped. I then realised - six hours to the funeral, drinking all night by the campfire then a night at the tavern, that solved the mystery of how I was at the tavern.

Billy's funeral I thought, before drifting into a sleepy continuous daydream...

NORMAL

Everybody has a first memory and I was no different. Mine would haunt me all my life, the vivid nightmares, when I would wake up sweating, heart beating as fast as a March hare, head throbbing with the intense reality of the terror.

The cause of what happened that night was that I was breathing. 'Stop breathing' my brother whispered, he kept on saying it over and over each time louder and louder, 'STOP BREATHING…I CAN HERE YOU BREATHING' he shouted. That was it. My mother flew at me in a rage, smacking me in the head and face with a two-handed frenzy of blows. She then turned her attention to my brother who got off comparatively lightly with three pathetic slaps, but even with that he was crying like a baby despite being 2 years older than me. Then it was my turn again. It was too dark to see what she had picked up, but it felt solid as she battered it into my head. 'I was not strong enough to hurt you just with my hands' she revealed in later years. Such an admission but without the slightest hint of regret.

This was my every night normal for years, 'stop smiling' was another of his favourite sayings, my brother was a bully, I grew to hate all bullies, violence was my normal, the beatings were turning me into a monster, just like them.

Everybody remembers there first fight, I was no different, 'Fight! Fight!' the kids chanted as I knocked the older boy to the ground then started smashing his head off the ground repeatedly, 'Fight! Fight!' the chant continued. I did not know how to fight but the cheers spurred me on, and I kept smashing away blindly, afraid to stop in case he retaliated. 'He's had enough' a large lad said as he pulled me away 'Well done champ' and patted me on the shoulder as I walked away. The crowd disappeared and so did the memory of the fight. I was a shy, quiet little five-year-old, an easy target for bullies, or so they thought.

When my father left us, I was only three years old, and I had no memory of him. However, my mother filled in my brother and I with plenty of derogatory details about him when the mood took her, 'He's a low life, a drunken no good thief' she would say. On many occasions, my brother was desperate to meet our Dad, a keen apprentice who wanted to learn how to be a low life just like him.

My mother was a scary looking creature, thin almost skeletal, the difference being that a skeleton had teeth. 'It takes two' she would say, even though it only takes one to start the trouble. If I asked for anything, I would always get the same reply 'Askers do not get' on the other hand if I queried why my brother had got something and I had not, the standard response was 'If you do not ask you do not get'. I was always in a no-win situation at home.

The one thing that I hated the most was her constantly telling lies, even in the house of god she would lie. 'You are too young to go to Sunday school' she would say as I watched my brother go off with the other children. At the door my best friend Hiddle stood with his younger sister waving to me to go with them. They were both younger than me. but I was forced to sit in the church with my Mum, feeling utterly miserable while staring at the closed door, listening to the sound of the other children having fun.

My life was making me numb to feelings and emotions, the darkness and hatred were all I knew. This was my normal.

Another bully another fight, 'My dad is the hardest man in town' he goaded before pushing me menacingly. 'Fight! Fight!' came the cries of the other children as they circled round us. I pushed him back hard and he went flying onto his back with a crunch. As he lay there, I picked up a piece of broken milk bottle and plunged it into his forehead. Even minor head wounds bleed a lot due to an abundance of superficial blood vessels. All the kids ran, and the bully ran too as blood poured from his head, down his face and onto his shirt.

I thought I was in deep trouble when I got home and was bracing myself for what I thought would come next. My mother said nothing. Then came the knock at the door. I listened hard but could not make out a word of what was said. 'You are not in trouble; he is always battering your big brother' she said. My brother probably deserved it.

School was no better. The teachers seemed to take an instant dislike to me from the moment they came across my name on the register. 'I had your brother two years ago' one old female teacher spat. The look of hate on her face spoke volumes yet I was nothing like my brother. The prejudices were unjust, especially from people who should have known better.

Two years later aged eight a big change happened. My mother had the luck to meet a new headcase, husband number two, my stepdad. He hated us from day one. For me the good point about him was that he hated my brother and me equally.

All the years of beatings had not knocked any sense into him, still every day he would start trouble, 'You are a thicko' was his new favourite thing to say. 'Grounded, bed with no supper' my stepdad would rage. As soon as we were in bed my brother started name calling, and the result would always be a hiding from our enraged stepdad. This was nothing compared to my vicious nasty beatings. Still my brother cried, still he never learned.

We were already underfed. Bed with no supper meant no breakfast either. Dinner was often mince and potatoes, the cheapest the butcher had. If my mother had teeth, she might have noticed it was all bone and gristle. A tablespoon of that with two tablespoons worth of potatoes was all we got most days.

One winters night my brother started screaming like a girl, crying like a baby, beside himself. I however sat and watched as my stepdad attempted to kill my mother, his hands tight around her neck, choking the life out of her. In hindsight, I wish he had finished her off. It is what she deserved after all.

It took two nights of us staying with our grandparents before they made up, at which point we were dragged back home to suffer. He was a drunk, but a good one. His problem was being sober. As soon as the drink touched his lips, he would transform from raging maniac to normal person. This was my normal.

Friends came and went when I was young. My best times were with friends. The only time I felt I could be a boy was with friends. Freedom from the oppressors. The problem followed me though, and my brother would always turn up at some point when I was with my friends. Everybody hated him, there was always trouble when he showed up.

To make matters worse he would turn up when I was not there. Longtime friends were turning their backs on me because of him, 'Your brother said he does not know why you play with me, as you told him you did not like me' one friend said. How many friends had he told that lie to?

I found myself enjoying the solitude. The rain was my friend. Sitting watching the raindrops land on the loch, watching the ripples circle outwards until they fade away. Anything was better than my home life, even death was a better option, but I was not prepared to let them win.

Sanctuary was weekends with my grandparents. By the time I reached ten years old it had become my only escape from the brain-dead tormentors of home. Being fed three times in one day was amazing, not that they were big portions, but they were bigger than the portions at home. Unfortunately, this was only once a week, twice on a good week.

My gran did nothing as far as I can remember. 'Ask your Grandad' she would say, or 'Your Grandad does that'. My Grandad was the most annoying man in the world and seemed rather proud of it. 'I am the most annoying man in the world' he would often say, but an additional talent was that he was also the most prolific farter in the world. 'Hup two three' he would say as he blasted one out. Whether you think that's disgusting or hilarious, a major problem that came with my flatulent Grandad was he stank of stale farts, and the smell hung on him like cheap cologne. Unfortunately, he never smelled any different, even after a good wash.

'You are my favourite' my Grandad would utter to my older brother, always making sure I was in earshot, 'This is my favourite Grandson and this is the other one' he would say as he introduced us to company, always with a nasty scowl in my direction. His cruel attitude towards me changed as I got older, but his was the only one in the family that did.

I must have been twelve when my next fight came in the form of a boy called Peter, 'Keep away from Fiona' he growled at me. I knew who Fiona was, but his accusation was bizarre. I had never spoken to her or been anywhere near her and I concluded that he was trying to court her in some macho, egotistical way.

We were the same age, but I was a good bit bigger than him. I pushed him away thinking he would have more sense than to pick a fight with me over nothing. 'I want a fight after church' he demanded. A fight right there and then would have suited me better although I did not want to fight him but turning down a fight was not an option.

All the kids from town seemed to have gathered to watch what was going to be a very unfair fight. 'Come on then' he provoked, keen to get the fight underway. One punch later he was on the ground holding his face. 'Jump on him' came a shout. It was the same person that had pulled me off the fight before and I did jump on him, but not the way everybody expected. I jumped high then landed with both feet on his leg, his femur making a horrendous crack.

The fight was over so quickly that the crowd had not even begun their usual chant. 'My dad wants to see you up at camp' the mystery boy announced. I was told on many occasions not to have dealings with the gypsies, therefore going to their camp would have been a big 'No'. I went gladly.

My brother watched on furtively, spying on me from around a corner of the church building, 'I'm telling Mum' would have been his words if he were not such a coward. 'We are your second cousins, you're no gorger even if you do live in a house.' Really? My heritage was gypsy? This was a revelation. Billy continued 'I am Billy, and this is Callum, Alex, Warren and Thom'. This was news to me as my Mum had done nothing but bad mouth them to us, not that I was surprised. She was good at that.

The conversation during the walk to camp was full of interesting and surprising information. 'We were born on the road. I was born just outside Dundee then a month later you were born at Bigger' Billy informed me. This was a completely different place from where I had been told I was born.

Billy strode up front, we all followed. It was clear who was in charge. 'We are all family connected in one way or another, if not by blood, in kinsmanship' he said. Thom was looking up at me beaming. He was a slightly smaller version of Billy, and all four were, slim and athletic, with the same prominent, aquiline nose and a good suntan.

I was in awe of the camp when I saw it for the first time with its wagons, horses, people cooking on open fires, children running around playing and the sound of laughter. We were heading over to a group of men at the far side of camp. 'Here he is Pa' said Alex, as a large man in all regards stepped forward. 'So, this is the wee pipsqueak' Pa said as he looked me up and down, 'He is knee high to a grasshopper' one of his friends joked. They all laughed. 'Hold up lads, he's a proper wee fighter this one' Pa said, as they all chortled with laughter again.

It was not a nice experience initially and I felt quite unnerved. 'You can come here anytime as long as you're not going to turn out like your Da and Ma' Pa sneered, then spat on the ground in disgust. 'Tell him about what they did Billy' said one of the men, who also spat on the ground in disgust. 'Come and sit over here with your Uncle Billy'. I was confused. Then I realised - Uncle Billy was Billy's Pa.

All the men gathered around, they were keen to hear the story, and probably not for the first time either. 'You see we all watch each other's backs around here, but not your Dad' Billy's Pa began. There were a few calls of agreement from the gathering. 'Things started going missing. Nobody knew who it was. It had been going on for months. Then one night, we caught your Dad rifling through Bert's wagon and stuffing things in a sack'. All the men hung on to every word Billy senior said, not that I knew who Bert was - any one of these men could have been Bert. 'We banished him from Galloway. Your Ma knew what he had been up to but did nothing about it, so she had to be banished from our community as well' Billy's Pa said, spitting once more. The tale of my parents went on, most of which I believe to be true. 'Stealing from friend and kin is the lowest of the low' said an old man shaking his fist in the air angrily. They certainly had nothing nice to say about my parents.

It was getting late by the time I left the camp. 'Say hello to your Grandparents for me' Billy's Pa said. I just nodded my head in agreement, knowing that I dare do no such thing else risk the wrath of my family at home when they found out. Thom and Billy walked me back to town. 'Pa likes you. He never talks to anyone he doesn't like' said Thom. 'Your brother is not welcome at our camp' said Billy. To me, this was good news as his presence at the camp would no doubt cause friction for them and trouble for me. 'Are you coming up tomorrow?' Thom asked. 'Of course he is, you are one of us again' Billy said before I had the chance to reply. He was correct in his assumption. There was nowhere in the world I would rather be than there with them. It felt friendly and safe, like home should.

As soon as I parted company with my newfound family, my annoying brother appeared. He must have been spying on us all this time. 'You are not allowed to play with them, I'm telling Mum' he snarled. His plan was to torment me all the way home but a quick punch in the face had him scuttling away. 'I am telling mum and you'll be for it' he shouted from a safe distance. As I entered the house, she was waiting for me. 'You are not my son. What will the neighbours think' she said, her sneering face contorted with disgust as she took a swipe at me.

For the next two weeks I would run up to the camp first thing in the morning. Billy always had errands to run for his Pa, sometimes just messages. 'My Pa wants to see you today' he would say, or he'd deliver messages to various recipients such as 'You have two days then there will be consequences if you haven't paid up'. At other times he collected money. It was only very occasionally that he would give money away. There were also the mysterious packages which would be picked up then delivered elsewhere. When the afternoons came it was our time. Time to climb trees, build dens and throw stones into the Druid Loch or the river…time to just be kids.

After one of Father Jack's particularly boring services was mercifully over, the slow process of escaping the church began. The long, slow walk to the church doors was as tedious as the service itself. Father Jack always stood at the door. 'Thank you for your attendance' he would say to every parishioner.

Once finally outside I spotted Callum. He was on his own waving at me and beckoning me to go with him. I ran off immediately without looking back at my enraged family. 'Tell him Mum' my brother squealed. 'Get back here this minute' she roared angrily. I glanced back then ignored them. Just as I almost reached Callum, he ran off behind the church. Billy was waiting.

We headed off to Whyte Loch. 'See tonight, tell your mum you are staying at your Grandparents for a couple of nights' Billy insisted. I agreed without asking why and we spent the rest of that Sunday just being kids. It was great to just be allowed to feel free and content. 'Be up at camp at first light' Billy said as we walked back to town.

WORK

The first thing I became aware of was the banging. My eyes flew open and my heart raced. I had slept in. I jumped up hurriedly and had my clothes on in a flash. When I sheepishly opened the door, there was a reddish hue in the morning light. 'Come on you, we'll need to run to catch up' said Billy and run we did, fast and far. We caught up with them just in time to see three wagons turn into a hay field.

Each wagon belonged to a family group, all of whom were there to work, men women and children. The two Billy's worked the scythes, while the rest of us raked the hay into flat rows to dry out in the sun.

The farmer provided lunch which consisted of watery soup, with a big wedge of bread. The best and possibly only way to eat it was by soaking the bread in the soup. 'You all right son?' Billy's Pa asked when it was near the end of day. It was plain to see that I was anything but all right, as my eyes had puffed up so much that they were reduced to slits that itched almost unbearably. My nose was very congested, and I sneezed continuously. I could only breath through my mouth. Even my throat and chest were affected causing me to struggle for every breath.

Billy's Ma had a good look at me and concluded 'It is the fever; you need to go to Meg. She will have something to help sort you out.' 'Can you ride a horse son?' Billy's Pa asked. I had sat on a horse which was led along by the reigns. 'Yes' I said unconvincingly. *There can't be that much to it* I thought. 'Take this blanket. Do you know where to go?' Billy's Ma asked, to which I answered 'Yes'. I had been to visit Meg once before with my Grandad years ago when I was very young. 'Eat these magic straws, they will cure your vomiting' Meg had said. They were just dandelion stems, but they had worked nonetheless

Riding old Ned was made easy by his slow laid-back plod. The cool night air coupled with being away from the offending field of hay helped ease my breathing. It only eased my mouth though as my nose was still swollen. The nasal secretions seemed to be endless, no matter how often I blew my nose. My eyes only got worse and I was on the point of being almost blind, the itch driving me wild.

There was a chill in the air, and if I described myself as feeling exhausted it would be an understatement. For me, stopping for a nap was a not an option in my current predicament. Wrapping the blanket tightly around myself we plodded on, and the warmth of the early morning sun helped keep me cosy. It was going to be another hot day.

The fever had calmed a little by the time we arrived at Meg's late that afternoon. Meg was in her multi coloured garden which appeared to contain every flower, plant, herb and vegetable I could think of plus hundreds more. 'Hello son. Don't you look a picture! Come along with me to the well' she said. I followed closely, 'Watch your feet' she warned just before my foot went crunching down on an unsuspecting frog.

Meg filled up a whisky jar with fresh well water, and demanded 'Drink all of this, every drop'. I did as Meg instructed. As I drank the water, I could feel it coursing through my body and it seemed to accelerate through my system at an unnaturally fast rate, desperate to escape. 'Drink all of it. If you do not eat and drink properly you will dry up. It is a slow and unpleasant way to die' she informed me. Apart from the overwhelming urge to urinate, the remedy was instantly working. *What on earth is in that well water?* I wondered, too self-conscious to ask.

It may not have been the magical potion that I was expecting Meg to concoct, but rather a basic life skill - eat and drink or die. 'You bed yourself down for the night in here' Meg said, showing me to her bedroom. There was only one bedroom with one bed, but my tiredness overtook my insecurity at her joining me in bed as I fell into a deep, dreamless sleep.

The aroma of food frying filled the air as I woke. 'Come and eat this' Meg beckoned 'You need to keep your strength up'. The plateful of hot, delicious breakfast was immense, and was washed down with another whisky jar full of well water. 'If you leave now you should be back before dark' said Meg. 'Thanks' I replied 'And I will see you soon son and remember to bring me a thousand fairy caps come September harvest' she instructed. I had never heard of them before, but Billy would surely know.

Meg was correct in her prediction and I was back with the rest of the group just in time to see the finishing touches being made to the haystacks. Old Ned made lighter work of the downhill journey back. 'You look cured already' Billy shouted as he stood on top of a haystack, stomping the hay down. He was right. I felt healthier and more invigorated than I could ever remember feeling before.

The next harvest was turnips which the women and children picked. 'I will do the baskets' said Billy, but his Pa embarrassed him by saying 'The men do that, get over there with the women and kiddies'. Billy was furious and I could almost imagine steam come out of his ears as his face turned dark red with humiliation.

The work that day was back breaking. 'Mind fill your pockets; the farmer expects us to. It is part of our wages' Thom said, still smiling away. The turnips were far too big for my pockets, I managed to find three smaller ones by the time we had finished for the day. As I looked around at the others, I couldn't help but notice that their pockets bulged ridiculously.

The farmer ignored the obvious pilfering. When I received my meagre wage, I began to think that Thom was correct about the turnips, but it was still more money than I had ever had in my life before. Once the farmer was gone, a sack appeared, and everybody placed their produce inside.

The camp was bustling when we returned, and everybody was keen to see what they could swap. Different groups had each attended a different harvest, and the bartering for carrots or peas had begun, 'One turnip for ten carrots' Billy's Pa announced but nobody bartered with him, he was the chief of the clan, he kept everybody in line.

September had arrived, and with it the September rains. 'What are we harvesting next?' I asked, hoping fairy caps was going to be the reply. 'Apples, up the colonel's orchard' answered Alex. The disappointment must have shown on my face. 'What's wrong with apples?' Billy asked, but I just shrugged my shoulders.

The apples turned out to be large cooking apples, not the Cox's or Russets I was expecting. The sharp, acidic taste of the apples was overpowering, and just sinking our teeth into one made the bitter juices flood our mouths. Naturally, we all had to try a bite, followed by throwing the apples as far as we could. Billy, who was always out to impress and wanted to be the best at everything had to throw two. His competitive nature came to the surface when my apple landed further away than his.

It was on the second day of constant rain that Billy pulled me to the side 'Tomorrow we are going mushroom picking' he whispered, his four brothers were not paying any attention, 'They are not coming shh' he continued. I was not sure why Billy wanted to keep the mushroom picking a traveller.

The morning was overcast but dry, 'Perfect weather for Mojos' Billy said. I was about to ask what Mojos were when Brian and the boaby turned up. He was referred to as the boaby rather than just plain Boaby because of his unfortunate ability to irritate and antagonise practically everyone but his mother, who seemed to think that he was a good and loyal son. 'Come on then lads' shouted Billy as he sped off. We chased after him, and the boaby really struggled to keep up. We didn't wait for him and just left him behind. I would have preferred it if it were just Billy and me.

Billy arrived in an open field of cows, panting from exertion after running there as fast as he could. The grass was still sodden from the previous day of rain. 'Over near the marsh reeds, that's where the witch's nipples grow' Billy said, as he rushed about excitedly looking down at the grass. 'Here they are!' exclaimed Brian. Billy was obviously not happy at not being the first one of us to find them.

There were loads of them, all growing in groups of between four to eight. 'Are these fairy caps?' I asked, looking down at the innocuous little mushrooms. Brian and the boaby erupted into hysterical laughter 'That's right, although I prefer witch's nipples' Billy joked. 'Meg wants a thousand' I said. 'A thousand, that'll be right! She will just have to want' said Brian laughing at me once again but Billy overruled him with 'No bother, we will pick all day if we have to, wont we lads', making sure Brian and the boaby understood who was in charge.

After an hour we had collected what looked like a vast amount of fairy caps. 'That must be enough now. I want to take some' said the boaby. Billy turned to me saying 'You'd better just take fifty for your first time', and the other two laughed once more as we all took a handful. Who could know how many we took? Some of the stems stuck to my tonsils when I tried to swallow them, causing me to gag.

Nothing seemed to happen at first, so we picked and consumed more fairy caps. I was afraid to cross Meg as she was a formidable woman. Some say she is a real witch, but she is a rather nice old woman if you ask me. It's difficult to guess exactly how old Meg must be, but you can tell that she must have been a real beauty in her youth with her curvaceous figure, piercing green eyes and a mane of long dark, now greying hair cascading down her back, and a demeanor that could comfort and terrify people in equal measure. 'Look' shouted Brian, as I looked up from the grass and noticed the sky had changed colour. The rainbow sky gave way to a field of throbbing grass covered ground, the faces of the other three were pure white, it was no longer a grey day, it was dazzlingly bright, but the sky was still laden with clouds. We all started laughing uncontrollably for no reason.

It felt as if the effects of the fairy caps lasted for the whole day while we were under their influence, but once the effects wore off it felt as if the experience had only lasted for five or ten minutes. 'We need to heat an empty pot to dry them out' Billy said. 'I can get one, my Gran won't notice' said Brian rushing off to retrieve the pot. 'Let's get a fire started. Where is the boaby?' asked Billy looking around. We found him leaning against a tree stuffing his face with more mushrooms.

Once the pot had warmed up, we put in exactly one thousand mushrooms, and there must have been the same again left over. 'It will take a few hours for them to dry out. The pot must be kept away from the heat…dry them not cook them' Billy said. 'Let's take some while we're waiting' suggested Brian, 'One hundred this time, coz you need to double up each time or they won't work' said Billy. They tasted like soil, but we were all keen to eat them regardless of the taste.

It was dark before the effects came on. The sound of the wind was haunting, stones glowed bright purple and orange, and blood was coming out of Billy's mouth. As it dripped from his fangs, we ran away from him, but he ran with us. Billy's eyes glowed menacingly as we laughed, 'Where has the boaby gone, he's no here' I said. This made us laugh even harder.

We ran around for hours before we bumped into Billy's Pa. Enraged, Billy's Pa punched Billy square in the face knocking him out with a single punch. 'You get yourself home' Billy's Pa shouted at me. Brian was nowhere to be seen and had disappeared quicker than a fart in a storm.

Billy arrived the next morning, with two horses, a broken nose and two black eyes. 'Mind and wrap up well, we'll need to camp out tonight' he said. Billy was in a foul mood. We never spoke until we reached the Grey Mare's tail. The horses had a good drink of water from the burn as we sat on boulders watching the waterfall. 'There is another Grey Mare's tail near Moffat, one in Ireland too' Billy said, breaking the silence.

Billy reached into his pocket. 'Half each' he said. There was two hundred and thirty-one each, and at this rate we would be eating into Meg's thousand if I was not careful. Walking through the forest when you are hallucinating is not a good idea. The place was alive with different sounds - the howling wind, the rustling and creaking of trees, insect, animal and bird sounds. Everything seemed to be moving, even the ground throbbed and undulated as if it were breathing in and out.

The rain came on suddenly and became heavy very quickly. Lightning flashed through the sky. We felt euphoric. As the thunder rumbled, we could feel it through our bodies. The realisation that we were soaked through to the skin, freezing in the cold night hit us just as suddenly. The effects of the mushrooms wore off. We travelled all night, my teeth chattering as the cold sank into my bones.

The smoke rising from Megs chimney was a welcome sight. Getting my frozen rigid body to dismount from old Ned was a challenge. 'Hurry up boys, come and get a heat up by the fire' came Meg's voice through the open door. We hobbled into Meg's home slowly on numb feet, happy to see the roaring fire which gave off a fierce heat that we gravitated towards. 'Soon get you two warmed up. Give me the fairy caps son' Meg beckoned. Meg counted the fairy caps into three piles. 'Come, eat these' Meg said with a cackle, just over three hundred each.

Soon the whole house was swaying from side to side. 'Hold still son' said Meg, the sound of Billy's nose crunching echoed in my ears, 'That is wild, it is straight again' I said, well I think I said that, Meg cackled again, her face was constantly changing from old crinkly skin to smooth young looking, then back again, her cackle was becoming terrifying.

I awoke the next morning on the floor in front of the fire with a blanket over me with no recollection of going to sleep. Meg and Billy were nowhere to be seen. Curling up in the blanket I fell back to sleep. 'Morning sleepy' said Billy as I opened my eyes some time later.

Meg was busy at the fire, stirring the contents of her cauldron. 'Sit at the table boys' breakfast nearly ready' she said. I was still yawning as I sheepishly stumbled over to the table where Meg had produced two enormous bowls of porridge with an 'Eat up boys'. It was a struggle to finish the entire bowl, but it would have been rude not to.

The journey home was a long, cold and miserable one. It was a blessing that the rain stayed away. 'I'm going to show him; I will take over as chief…just you watch' muttered Billy bitterly. His Pa was too large, strong and cunning for Billy to take on. I had nothing to say, it was just some bad blood between them. It would hopefully blow over soon enough.

We spent the whole of the next week in some field or another, the mushrooms still visible. 'The frost will kill them off until next year' Billy said, the effects of the fairy caps were a lot less than when we first tried them, our bodies were becoming immune to them. 'That's fine, it will give us something to look forward to next year' I said, thinking what a great escape from the everyday drudgery they were.

On the way back to town Billy stopped and announced, 'We are heading to Dumfries for winter'. It was to be a long, uneventful and dull winter on my own. 'How long for?' I asked him, the disappointment probably discernable from my voice. Billy's shoulder shrug did nothing to make me feel less despondent 'Probably be back around spring' he replied. Walking back home on my own that night was lonely. The thought of running away to Dumfries to be with Billy's group filled my mind for the next few months.

CRUEL RUNNINGS

I could hear the dawn chorus and see a chink of light through the closed curtains. It was first light and therefore time to get up. I got out of bed, gathered my clothes from the chair and sneaked past the mound under the covers of the adjacent bed from which came sounds like a wounded animal. My brother was sound asleep. I made my way quietly downstairs and dressed once I was sure I was out of earshot of the rest of the household. There was no point waiting for breakfast. That never happened. It would be the usual long wait in silence until midday when my mother would rise. Then would follow the now familiar tirade of verbal abuse which would not fill my empty belly.

A stomach wrenching stench followed me to the door. The house usually smelled of damp but the previous evening, my mother had plucked a chicken and burned off its pin feathers with a candle. The smell would take days to dissipate completely. I slowly and quietly turned the door handle to avoid detection, then eased the door halfway before edging out, quiet as a mouse. As soon as I stepped outsider, I inhaled a long, deep breath. I felt the cold, icy air flowing over my lips into my mouth, down my throat and finally deep within my chest. The air was so cold yet so invigorating.

The sky was a cloudless blue, my eyes strained for a few seconds whilst they adjusted to the dazzle of the sun. In that moment I felt the weight of despair lift and melt away, replaced with *it's great to be alive.*

I sauntered slowly up the High Street. I was in no rush as I wasn't heading anywhere in particular. Since Billy had gone, I had spent most of the time all by myself. As I walked along, I noticed the grass, some was white and some of it was just normal and damp, but the amazing part was the line of vapor that separated the white from the damp, the vapor rose no more than a foot high as the sun devoured the shade. It looked almost magical, and I wondered if will-o'-the-wisps actually existed.

The town clock hit seven o'clock, I knew nobody would be around this early in the morning, so I headed up to where the chimes had sounded. Halfway up the street my stomach gave out an enormous growl, brought on by the lovely aroma of fresh baked bread as it wafted out of the baker's shop entrance and into my nostrils. My empty stomach growled again. Even a burnt roll that had been kicked along the floor would have done, I'd have eaten it gladly. I had just passed the bakers when another stronger aroma hit me. This time my stomached cramped and wrenched, the putrid smell of the dead carcasses hitting me hard. I ran a few strides to get away quickly. Fortunately, the cold air suppressed the area of the smell to just at the door of the butchers.

This was the better route to choose as straight across the road was the fishmongers and even looking at the fishmongers from a distance would turn my stomach. There was also the back ways and alleyways, but you would have to be mad going down them, especially at this time of morning. Some homes had outhouses that stank something awful, but most had a bucket in the corner of a room that some poor soul had to slop out every morning. The thought of the buckets' contents being emptied from above as I walked past *gardyloo...*

Once I arrived at the Town Hall, I checked the time. Only 30 minutes had passed. I took a spot against a wall where I would be fully exposed to the sun's rays. I stood watching as the street got busier, and day-dreamed in wonder about where people were heading or where they had been by the time the clock struck 8 o'clock. My toes had started to tingle as the cold from the ground had begun seeping into them. I started walking back and forth just to get some heat circulating. I was getting bored. *A proper walk,* I thought to myself. That would help to warm up my now chilled body.

I glanced up the street then down. Looking down the street, I could see the slum I called home and wanted to stay clear of it for as long as possible. On deciding to walk up the street, I set off. I literally took no more than two strides when I heard a distant whistle and I instantly turned around and looked to see if someone had whistled at me. I couldn't see anyone I knew, so I turned and set off again. I got a fright when a hand suddenly slapped me on the back 'Did you no see me' a familiar voice said. Looking to one side I saw a smiling Brian, his face full of mischief as usual. I had jumped out of my skin but the last thing I was going to do was admit it to him, so I acknowledged him with a nod of my head and an 'Alright Bri'. 'Did you no see me' he repeated, chuckling. I ignored his question. 'I was hiding behind that horse all the way up' he continued still chuckling. I changed the subject by asking 'What you up to anyway'. With an arm in the air he pointed to what could have been absolutely anywhere in a vague direction he replied, 'Heading up to see Billy'. 'Me too' I lied for I had no idea that Billy was back. News spreads fast. The group tend to travel at night, so it was very early in the day for anyone to know they had arrived.

I never bothered asking where they were camped as this might give me away that I hadn't known, we just headed out of town in silence. Once the town was out of sight, we changed direction towards the woods 'Through here' said Brian. The camp itself wasn't a secret just the going's on and the who's there. The woods were almost silent, just the random drips of water hitting the ground as they fell off the trees. 'Argh' shouted Brian 'Right down the back of my neck'. It was even colder in the shade of the trees. We kept going and soon we arrived at the other side in a clearing. The moment we stepped out of the woods, the unmistakable loud booming voice of Billy said 'Well hello boys'. We looked around the place like headless chickens, then we looked at each other. Out of nowhere an acorn hit Brian on the head, then a fraction of a second later one hit me right between the eyes, then we both looked up to see Billy sitting on a branch of a huge red oak with his back against the trunk. 'Looking comfortable' I said, Billy laughed 'Yes indeed young man' he laughed again 'I am the King looking out over my kingdom' this was something that his father would say. 'Good shot Billy' said Brian in his sycophantic voice.

Next thing I knew Billy was hanging from the branch with one hand 'Me big monkey man Oo,oo,oo!' he said, following this with a fancy circus style somersault, landing on one foot and striding off in his usual manner. 'Come on boys, we're going fishing' Billy said but Brian was quick to point out 'We've no got rods Billy'. Billy chuckled 'The rock pools are showing, the rock pools boys' I knew what he was talking about but wasn't convinced it was something that really happened. Billy went on to explain 'When the river is swollen the fish swim freely into the underwater rock pools, then if they don't move as the water levels go down they are trapped until the water rises again…what could be easier than sticking your hand in and grabbing a fish with nowhere to escape?' *Hmm sounds too easy* I thought.

Before long I could hear the sound of distant trickling water 'This way boys' Billy commanded, taking long strides then he suddenly stopped, stretching his arm out in front of us to stop us in our tracks 'Listen boys' As suddenly as he stopped he took off at high speed down the slope and up the other side as we followed behind at a slow jog pace. 'There she is boys' Billy shouted back to us. 'Nice one Billy' Brian said joyfully, but I couldn't help thinking *ye nice one for finding the river that we all knew was there, right there where it always was, right where it always will be.* It's not that I was jealous of Billy, his antics always made the most mundane of days fun and enjoyable, it was Brian that annoyed me, constantly trying to curry favour with Billy it made me cringe.

The river was not far from where we now stood, 'Not far now boys' Billy said pointing out the obvious to us yet again, 'I need to syphon the big python' Billy modestly said and laughed 'Me too' said Brian lining up beside him 'Syphon the worm you mean' Billy taunted with a belly laugh which didn't amuse Brian at all. I never said a thing but stood beside them and joined in.

It’s what boys do when having a pee in the great outdoors, don't know why but it just was. ‘It's the sound of the water trickling over the rocks, gets me every time’ Billy chimed ‘Glad wee willy watcher’s not here’ I said. We all laughed; we all knew who I meant as we all stood there looking forward minding our own business as that was the unwritten rule of the outdoor pee procedure.

We set off along the last short journey to the riverbank and within minutes we were standing looking along the river, so peaceful and tranquil, but no rock pools to be seen. SPLASH! We glanced round to see the ripples circling away from where something had entered the water, ‘Did you see the size of that fish? must have been a twenty pounder’ Billy said with astonishment in his voice and an exaggerated facial expression to match. A five pounder I thought to myself or a stone thrown by Billy. ‘Up stream boys’ he said then strode of again with us tagging on behind as usual. Along the riverbank we went as it twisted and turned. Once again Billy stopped with another over dramatic gesture as he pointed across the river to the rock pools, loads of them as far as we could see. The rocks were smooth with pools that were no more than puddles, ‘Come on boys’ I heard Billy shout from the other side. I thought he was still standing next to me, but he'd crossed silently and stealthily. The river was deep so walking across it missing our footing on the rocks would be a dangerous and freezing mistake. I ran two steps then jumped fearlessly, landing firmly, both feet planted on the safety of the rock, but Brian held back ‘I'll no make it’ he said ‘Come on, I'll catch you’ shouted Billy. The exchange went on for a while before Brian finally took a long run up to the edge of the riverbank then jumped, arms flailing through the air frantically as if he was trying to swim across. Lucky for Brian Billy did grab him, or he might have fell back in as his feet landed right on the edge of the rock.

‘Let’s get fishing boys’ Billy chirped. Billy seemed to use the word *boys* a lot when talking to us. Because he was a few years older than we were I think he had an air of superiority and liked us to know our place. The first five rock pools were empty, not that I was disappointed as I expected as much. Billy had a determination about him, 'Blasted minnows' he cursed 'I've got one' he said reaching down into a pool, then before I got a chance to move out of the way, a handful of freezing water hit me in the face. As I turned away, I just saw Billy throw a small fish, hitting Brian in the face. Brian wasn't amused 'Where's your good shot this time' I said as Billy and I had a good laugh at Brian's expense. 'Bri, get it and put it back in the river ' Billy commanded. The next pool was the widest yet, about seven feet wide and almost a perfect circle. 'Look, look there's fins in the middle' I calmly pointed out 'Calm down' Billy said, *cheeky git* I thought, Billy always wanted to steal everyone's thunder and be number one.

As the fish came into view 'Two rainbow trout' Billy smugly said as he walked into the water bare footed with his trousers rolled up 'Come give us a hand you pair'. Brian and I looked at each other, wondering how Billy had managed to take off his boots and roll up his trousers so quickly without us noticing. The rock was ice cold 'It's not cold once you're in' Billy said smirking. Brian and I entered the water together and Brian screamed at the top of his lungs. Billy guffawed with laughter and shouted 'Bri you scream like a girl' but I was too busy holding in my own screams as the icy water felt like a thousand needles jagging into my soon to be numb feet. 'The quicker we catch the trout, the quicker we get our feet warmed up' Billy said, sounding annoyed. Billy and I were close to the fish while Brian slowly edged his way closer. I bent down and grabbed one, but it slipped out of my hand 'You got to grab it real tight' Billy said. I tried again, this time I had it. Lifting it out the water I walked out of the rock pool 'Smack its head hard on the rock' Billy instructed, as he followed behind with the other trout.

Our feet were frozen, almost numb as the rock we were standing on felt like ice. 'Jog on the spot, it will warm and dry your feet' said Billy. It worked up to a point but getting our socks on with damp feet was a struggle, although it was nice to have them back on.

Soon we were ready to head back down the road 'Ready boys?' Billy asked as he bent over to pick up the fish. Suddenly, our ears were filled with the most horrendous high-pitched squealing noise 'Quee, quee, bree!'. I was rooted to the spot and my hair felt like it was standing on end. Without a look or a word spoken we were running away, running as fast as we could as if our lives depended on it. My body was in a state of sheer terror, or a state of extreme excitement, perhaps a combination of both as it was hard to tell with the adrenaline pumping so hard. My heart was beating out of my chest, my breathing heavy. The squealing was getting louder 'Quee, quee!' we ran and ran. I was hot on Billy's heels but every time I drew alongside him, he would pick up his pace, there was no way he would let me pass as Billy always had to be the leader. I inhaled deep breaths as the pace started to slow down, but the chilling squeals continued 'Quee!' After what seemed like miles, Billy rasped out 'The farm' .

We were exhausted, but our feet were no longer cold, they were roasting. We had slowed down from a run to a fast walk, when I spotted 'the boaby' standing alone besides the pigsty laughing like madman, 'What is that dick doing here?' I said, not expecting a reply. His name was Gary, but everyone called him 'the boaby' as he behaved like one complete and utter dick. Even Father Jack called him 'the boaby' which is most unusual for a man of God. The boaby was the lowest of the low. He even got caught with his thieving fat fingers in the church collection box, the contents of which were to help the poor and hungry of the parish. This action let to Father Jack announcing the following Sunday that 'The boaby is banned from entering the church and the church grounds'. Nobody apart from the boaby and his mother had any objection.

Even as we approached, the boaby continued to laugh hysterically. Billy hurdled the pigsty fence, and at that moment I noticed the pig had an object stuck into its right shoulder. The unfortunate pig was squealing wildly, jumping, running and bleeding badly. It was a knife, the boaby's instantly recognisable knife with the bone handle. Billy cornered the pig, then pounced onto its back and swiftly pulled the knife out of the pig ,and with one smooth action slit the poor pigs throat, ending its suffering. An eerie silence followed; the squealing ended so suddenly, along with the boaby's crazed laughter. I breathed in and out deeply trying to calm myself.

'BANG!' the splinters sprayed into the air as the shotgun pellets exploded into the fence beside me, 'Run' Billy shouted although I was already on my way running as fast as I possibly could with a refreshed adrenalin fuelled energy supply. Billy was somehow in front once again; he had grabbed the boaby by the scruff of the neck and was forced-marching him along at running pace. The boaby wasn't a runner and I'm sure his feet were barely touching the ground. They were slowing quickly so I went past them, still running like the wind. I must have run a mile or so before stopping. I was on my own, *have they been caught* I thought. I jogged on slowly until I reached the woods. After checking behind to see no one was there, I walked through the woods.

There was a smell of fresh smoke lingering in the trees that hadn't been there in the morning which got stronger as I neared the other side of the wood. When I got there, I saw the flames leaping from the fire with a solitary soul sitting on a log besides it. I slowly edged forward, *Billy? No, it can't be* I thought. I stepped out of the woods to the sound of Billy's voice 'Hello there, you took your time'. I looked at the fire where Billy was cooking the fresh fish *but how?* I though. 'It's just me, I thought the other two were with you' I said 'Take a wee seat, these won't be long' he replied. I had a lot of *questions How did he get here before me? How did he get the wood and build the fire?* but instead I said 'You weren't long getting them fish gutted' I probably should have asked when he returned to the rock pools to collect the fish as well.

Billy turned the fish one last time before handing me one 'Get fired into that, it's the best fish you'll ever taste'. He was right, fresh fish cooked on a smoky fire was delicious. 'Shhh' Billy whispered, it was the clip clop of horses' hooves. Before we knew it, the horse was upon us, 'Well hello Miss Wolf' Billy said. She dismounted shotgun in hand, then pressed it to the back of my neck. I sat motionless without a care; I had always had a morbid fascination to know what was on the other side. 'Will you join us for a bit of supper' Billy said with a cheeky innocent smile on his face. 'A bit of my own poached fish?' Scarlett replied with a certain calmness in her voice 'You'll be offering me my own roast pork next' she continued sarcastically. 'Now, now, it's not like that at all' Billy said, 'Just let me explain'. Scarlett tapped me on the head with the barrel of the gun before running her fingers through my hair then pushed my head away with a chuckle. Scarlett then sat down on the other side of Billy.

I did not fancy Scarlett in the least, but I was struggling with the lust demon, *the smell of female* it gets called. This happens to all teenage boys when a female comes within twenty feet of them, they get frisky with desire. 'You boys are in trouble' she said, to which Billy replied, 'We just were putting the poor wee thing out its misery' she shook her head 'I saw what happened, but Brian is grassing on all of you'. Brian had a reputation of doing and saying anything to get out of trouble 'The boaby is in a ditch, he jumped out of my way when I was galloping towards him' Scarlett said. Billy poked the fire with a stick before saying 'We will give you a good price for the pig and your dad can keep the meat' he said to Scarlett, then he threw the stick onto the fire, 'I know you will' she laughed. They continued to talk into the night while I just sat thinking about her hand running through my hair. 'Right, I'm off' I said as I stood up and slipped away without them noticing. They were too busy canoodling.

The next morning, it was frosty again. I was out of town and heading to get Billy when Miss Scarlett Wolf appeared on her horse looking upset and teary eyed. Before I got a chance to speak, she thrashed her riding crop across my face. I did not seem to notice too much pain, in fact I kind of liked it. I was distracted though, my mind fixated on her ample bosom. When Scarlett had leaned over to strike me, I thought her breasts were going to pop out of her jacket and hit me in the face. I wanted so desperately to stick my head in between them. I was clueless as to what I would do but that is what I felt like I wanted. She went to strike me again, drawing her arm back, then she checked herself and rode off without saying a word.

I ran fast as I could to get to Billy, but when I arrived at the camp, they were all gone with the exception of the three old men that stared at me. The whole camp was barren as if they had never existed at all. Even the fires had been cleared of ash and a fresh layer of soil had been used to hide the blackened earth. Slowly I headed back to town. On the way I spotted Brian. We exchanged looks as I walked past him. Brian's parents would be away with the rest of the travellers, but they never took him, leaving him to look after his gran. 'Whack' I was seeing stars. 'Get home now, you are grounded with no supper'. I could not see what solid object my mother had hit me over the head with. I headed home.

CHANGES

Life dragged on slowly for the next few months. Brian had teamed up with my brother for a crime wave that plagued the town, sneak thieves stealing from everyone no matter how poor they were. 'Nobody likes a grass' Brian said, the same thing he had said on many occasions. 'Grasses will get a kicking my brother said backing Brian up, always acting like a big man, but on their own they were both scared of me. I was ready to start punching, *I'd take them both out easily* I thought. Brian reached into his pocket, pulling out a fishing priest, 'Anybody that grasses on me are getting clobbered he said whilst hitting the priest into the palm of his hand. 'Nobody likes a grass' my brother repeated this went on and on. I'm not sure if they were trying to accuse me of grassing or trying to brainwash me. Even two to one and armed with the priest they seemed still more scared of me than I'd ever be of them.

I made up an excuse and left them to their nonsense. I knew for fact that they both were liars, thieves and grasses. Walking through town people stared, pointed and scowled at me, constantly whispering. They knew who was doing the break-ins but had failed to catch them and being unfairly discriminated against for my brothers' actions was unfair but nothing new. In the past, friends had stopped talking to me because my brother had told them untruths and alleged that I'd said them. I was lost for what to do, but I liked it on my own. I headed out of town. After what seemed like hours, I became aware of a horse clip clopping behind me. 'Where is he?' it was Miss Scarlett Wolf. I looked at her then shrugged my shoulders. It was true I had no idea where Billy was or when, if ever he would return. 'You owe me for the pig' she said as she gave me a smile. A nice big friendly smile. 'Come and work at the farm, we can sort something out' I said nothing in reply, simply nodding a *yes*. 'Come to the farm at first light tomorrow' said Scarlett. I nodded again 'Toodle-pip' she shouted over her shoulder as she cantered off.

The next day I woke up nice and early, struggled out of bed and splashed cold water on my face before slipping my boots on and heading out. It was a drab, wet and misty morning. *When actually is first light?* I thought as I rushed along to Wolf Farm. I had only been to the farm once, but I was sure the shortcut I was taking should have been shorter, unless I had got lost in the dark and gone the wrong way. The uphill walk was quite a trek. As light began to break, I spotted the farmhouse, the door of which was opening. I sprinted the last bit, managing to meet the farmer halfway to the barn. Mr Wolf was a short well-fed man, rather egg shaped with arms and legs sticking out. 'You the boy?' he asked as he walked on not waiting for the obvious answer. Stepping into the barn he kicked a tin pail towards me 'Use that to fill all the troughs, there's five of them' he said. I looked at him expecting him to say where I would find the water, but he walked off hurriedly.

I looked around for the five troughs first. That was easy, but finding the water was not so easy. After looking around, I spotted a large well right outside the farmhouse, which must have always been there. I was mystified as to how I managed to run past it on three occasions without seeing it. The day was turning out nice. As I walked to the well, I noticed the mist had not gone, but rather I had walked up out of it. I was amazed to see that the town and the whole valley were invisible, shrouded in the white mist.

Being up early and working away from home felt great. The first three troughs took ten pails of water each, and the small hole at the bottom of the pail was making the job longer than it needed to be. *I finished the trough in good time,* I thought but the same cannot be said for the next trough and by the time I had filled the fourth I was struggling. I dropped to the ground, sitting with my back against the well wall, exhausted and starving, and I just wanted to curl up for a sleep. 'C-r-e-a-k' went the door to the farmhouse. I almost jumped to my feet but thought better of it. I had worked hard and needed a rest. Stepping out of the door came a small round woman with the rosiest cheeks I'd ever seen. More importantly was that the tray she was carrying was laden with food. 'I bet you are a hungry young boy' Mrs Wolf said. She smiled constantly, in contrast to Mr Wolf who never appeared to smile. I nodded a *Yes*, 'It's all fresh, I baked the bread this morning and it's still warm' she continued. It was all so nice, a feast fit for a king. 'We make our own cheese' she beamed proudly. Such creamy cheese, and the tankard of milk was fresh and creamy too. 'It's no before time we had help, you are doing good. It takes the three of us to fill those troughs, and it's not as if Scarlett can help much now' said Mrs Wolf, smiling away. She continued chatting as I ate. 'Come and see me before you go' she said, then turned and went back into the farmhouse saying 'Toodle-do the noo'.

I had not noticed anybody approach. 'Have you finished yet' I heard Miss Wolf say. Turning to face her I said 'Almost, Miss Wolf' she smiled, her fiery red hair floating gently in the light breeze, crinkled her nose 'Call me Scarlett'. She made me feel nervous in an excited way 'Alright Miss Scarlett Wolf' I muttered, she laughed 'Just Scarlett If you stuff the hole with mud it won't leak for a little while anyway', I did what I was told 'That will be dried hard by morning. Come with me' she said walking off. I followed close behind, staring mesmerized at her behind, each buttock moved independently, rising, falling, bouncing and wobbling, yet looking firm. I had never seen a woman in trousers before, only skirts and this was the closest I had been to seeing a naked woman. I liked looking and I would have followed Scarlett around all day given the chance. Suddenly she turned, so I quickly I averted my gaze, embarrassed that I might have been caught. Her eyes twinkled and she smiled a cheeky knowing smile, as if she knew and liked me looking.

Scarlett pointed over at a wheelbarrow and shovel 'Clean everything out the stable and pigsty and dump it over there. You'll find fresh straw in the barn' she walked off leaving me to it. I couldn't help watching again as she walked away, and she flicked her head round so fast and my face exploded with heat as my face turned red, 'Get a move on' she shouted over in a softer breathier tone 'The quicker you start, the sooner you'll be finished! Toodle-pip'.

There were two beautiful horses, one brown and white and the other jet black. The Grim Reaper himself would have been proud of such a dark majestic creature as this. I rubbed and patted their necks one at a time, making sure they were friendly. Taking my time, I slowly opened the stable door just wide enough to enter with the wheelbarrow, entering apprehensively in case I scared the horses. 'There, there' I said softly, petting them again. Five sizeable piles of dung were quickly shoveled into the wheelbarrow. With fresh straw in its place, closing the stable door I smiled at the horses 'Good job my friends' I said to them. The black one neighed as if he were answering me, 'That should be yey' I replied laughing, before having a look around for in case anyone had witnessed my madness.

I looked at the pigsty 'Pigs in shit' I said to myself sighing. It was everywhere, but unlike the horses dung it really stank. I got on with clearing the pigsty as fast as I could, but my already exhausted body was giving up. Although I was only halfway through the sty, I started feeling dizzy, my eyes were stinging from the fumes. Using the shovel to steady myself, I stumbled half blindly to the well, where I splashed cold water in my eyes. Hearing footsteps from behind I turned and saw the welcoming friendly smile of Mrs Wolf as she approached which lifted my spirits. 'Just put the things back then that will do for today' she said, I smiled and nodded, and she passed me a muslin bundle 'It's a bit of ham and a teacake' she said still smiling 'Toodle do the noo'.

Placing the bucket almost exactly where I had got it, I looked around the barn. There was plenty of straw. I looked out of the barn door, checking nobody was about in the now half dark yard, I closed the door quickly. I lacked the energy to travel home.

Walking to the left side of the barn in the dark I stumbled, tripped then fell into a pile of straw. I sat up and devoured the piece of tender boiled ham, then holding the large teacake in both hands I took a large bite 'Mmm' it was the tastiest thing I had ever eaten. I sat and finished my feast in the dark before laying back. I pulled some straw over myself in a half effort, the smell filling my nostrils. I had followed Megs instructions, drinking water all through the day, the sound of mice running, and scratching filled the barn, a hoot from a barn owl came had a haunting yet soothing feeling to it, I was asleep in seconds.

I woke up startled and disorientated. It seemed like only a short time had passed since I had lay down, straw I thought, then remembered I was in the barn. I could see the brightness from outside. How long had I slept? Footsteps where coming towards me and I lay still not knowing if I was visible in the straw. *Whack* went the riding crop on my buttocks, 'Morning my sleepy' Scarlett said 'Morning' I replied not letting on I felt the sting of the crop. *Whack* again she whipped me, this time a lot harder 'Who said you could sleep in here naughty boy' I raised myself onto my hand and knees 'I felt that' I said in a calm casual manner. I stayed in the position, provoking Scarlett with my cheeks pointing high. Turning, I saw the anger on her face. Her hand was raised high, then she thrust the crop towards my raised buttocks with all her strength *Whack* I really did feel it this time. Doing what came naturally I burst into an uncontrollable bout of laughter. Scarlett stormed off in a rage. I jumped up and brushed the straw off myself with my hands and rushed after her, but when I looked out of the barn doors she was gone.

I walked slowly across the yard towards the well, feeling the welts that were raised and inflamed on my backside. Then I turned back towards the barn to get the pail, as I headed towards the well for a second time, Mrs Wolf greeted me 'Here's some breakfast before you start' she said 'Thank you very much, it looks delicious' I replied taking the food from her, a boiled egg, bread and a tankard of creamy fresh milk. After eating every scrap of food, I felt energised and got to work finishing my tasks before retreating to the barn once again exhausted. To my surprise and delight, there was a blanket in the barn. The Wolfs and I had not talked about any agreement or payment for my labour, but I was more than happy working all day for food and a place to lay my head at night in peace.

After about a month I was thoroughly enjoying my new life. Scarlett and I had become the closest of friends. She flirted and teased me all the time, but we just laughed. I was so sure her buttocks looked larger than ever and, looking at her bosoms, as I often did, they had definitely grown from more than ample to enormous. 'Eating too many new potatoes' Mrs Wolf said one day as she watched Scarlett cross the yard.

Scarlett summoned me over one evening after I had finished my work 'Can you ride a horse' Scarlett asked. 'A little bit' I replied. Old Ned was an easy horse to ride 'Come ride with me' she waved me to follow her to the stable 'You can learn to ride on Cookie, Dark Lord needs a confident handler. I stood by her as she showed me how to put the horses tack on. The last item to be put on was the saddle and turning quickly she knocked her left breast into me. I looked down at them, then at her, and we started laughing, but then Scarlett's face contorted, and she burst into tears. I put my arms around her, her head tucked into my shoulder, 'Shh' I said to comfort her, rubbing my hand across her upper back and shoulders. I was confused, sniffing her hair, thinking about her bosoms pressed against my chest, I was trying not to, hoping she would not notice my rising embarrassment. 'I'm pregnant' she cried. I did not know what to do or say, I just comforted Scarlett until she said, 'Come on, get on'. As I placed my foot in the stirrup, then went to hop up, Scarlett placed her hand on my backside, pushing me up. We smiled at each other.

She took Cookie's reins and led me out of the stable 'Watch your head' she shouted back a bit late. If I had not already ducked, I would have cracked my head on the stable lintel, 'Just move with the flow of the horse' she instructed as she led me round the yard. After a few times round the yard we stopped. 'You are a natural' she smiled, handing me the reigns, 'Hold them with a bit of slack, pulling to the left turns the horse left and right to go right' she said. Cookie moved a lot faster than old Ned. I was not quite ready for this and to my relief she took hold of the bridle, leading me around the yard a few more times. I dismounted, then clapped Cookie to the sound of cheers I had not noticed the spectators, Mr Wolf and two Mrs Wolf's, 'Come and meet my sister, we are twins' Mrs Wolf said, 'What both of you?' I joked with a cheeky surprised look on my face, the four of us laughed, while Mr Wolf just stood with his regular dead pan look on his face, then interrupted with 'There's someone coming'. Looking down the road I could just make out a figure moving in the distance.

DARK TIMES

The five of us watch the figure grow larger as it approached. 'Go inside' Mr Wolf said commanding the three females to get in the house, following them closely behind. He returned with his gun, 'We don't trust uninvited visitors' he announced 'Get behind me lad' he said. There was no rush, we had a long wait ahead of us before the distant figure arrived at Wolf Farm. I spotted Scarlett peering through the window. She waved me over, then motioned her head to the door. As I got to the door it opened a little, 'Here, it's just for show ' she said as she handed me a gun.

Ten minutes later the door opened once more 'It's Billy' Scarlett shouted as she rushed over to her Pa. Her eyesight must have been superb, as I still struggled to make him out. Billy approached the farm with caution, then raised his hands in the air shaking a purse of coins. Billy stopped at a safe distance 'Why have you come here' Mr Wolf asked. 'Well hello sir' Billy politely replied 'I'm here to right an injustice that has been bestowed upon you' Billy shook the purse of coins in an attempt to prove his intentions. 'Is this him' Mr Wolf said to Scarlett 'Yes Pa, that's him' she replied her face awash with tears. 'Get in the house' he said to Scarlett, then turned to me 'You too'.

It was the first time I had been in the house 'Take Pa's seat by the fire' Mrs Wolf said 'Would you like a scone with jam and cream' her sister asked 'Yes please' I replied licking my lips. Scarlett sat staring out of the window never budging as her Pa and Billy talked into the night. Then it struck me like a lightning bolt, Billy was going to be a father. The night I'd left them sitting at the fire must have been when it happened. *That makes sense* I thought to myself, Scarlett was furious when Billy disappeared, and for good reason as it turned out. Billy had a lot more explaining to do about that than the pig situation.

It was so warm and cosy at the fireside. I felt myself drifting off to sleep and had to fight it so as not to be rude. I raised myself from the chair to my feet, and stood beside Scarlett, watching Billy wave his arms around, making hand gestures and pointing around as he so often did. Scarlett sobbed even harder when Billy turned and walked away, with Mr Wolf's gun still pointing at his back until he was almost out of sight in the half dark. Mr Wolf strode towards the house. The door flew open, and the bag of coins just missed the fire before it landed on the floor, in the few seconds it took me to look at the bag Mr Wolf had left through another door slamming it behind himself. Scarlett took my hand, pulling me towards her 'Get Cookie back to the stable' she said I nodded then rushed out. *Cookie could be anywhere* I thought. I checked the stable first, hoping Cookie had just wandered home but I could see from a distance that the door was closed.

I ran around frantically, desperate to find the horse before the night got too dark. 'Cookie!' I shouted a few seconds later 'Cookie, Cookie' went my echo. 'Bloody Billy' I mumbled to myself, we were just boys starting out in life. A baby changed everything. 'Cookie' I shouted, again my echo replied 'Cookie, Joabwah' I paused, I must have just heard it wrong, walking towards the direction of the echo 'Cookie, Cookie, Cookie', 'Joaby, Joaby, Joaby' went my echo which was strangely coming from the stable. I ran over and peered in to see Billy hanging up the saddle, 'You lot want to be more careful, this wee beauty might have run away' he said.

I was pleased to see that Cookie was safe and sound, but my feelings about Billy being there however were both pleased and angry, 'You will get us both shot' I said, Billy clapped the horse 'Just doing a good deed for the father-in-law' he replied looking pleased with himself. '18 and a man of the world, going to have a wee Billy Junior' he boasted proudly. Billy was not 18, he just had not learnt to count yet, at this my mind went to the purse of money. It had sounded rather a lot. 'It could be a girl' I said, pointing out the obvious 'Oh no way, it's a boy for sure'. Then Billy proceeded to go on about this and that, and I thought he would never leave. Finally, he said 'Tell Scarlett I love her, and I will see her soon' then he went off into the night 'Right' I said after him 'I will do the right thing, you will see'.

The days were passing quickly, Billy had not returned, I had looked down the road many times in a day to no avail. I was busy mucking out the stables when I heard the voices. Sticking my head out of the stable door I saw my worst nightmare. Standing there was my mother and step-father, 'Right you, home' she shrieked'. I looked around confident someone at the farm would stop them, but no one did. 'Black affronted so I am, you canny just disappear' she went on. She was always *black affronted*, 'Grounded, with no supper' my stepfather growled. It was a long miserable walk home; my new life being left behind just as I was feeling settled and happy for a change. We were almost home when I saw Brian. He opened his long coat as we passed, revealing the horned handle of a knife. His smarmy expression made me think that perhaps he grassed me up to my family.

I had never felt as famished in my life until now. Years of hunger had falsely numbed my hunger. I always had a full stomach on the farm, but now I suffered. I promised myself that next time I am never coming back to this hell. It was weeks until I met up with Billy again 'I'm really sorry, I thought they knew. I'd never mention seeing you if I knew' he said sincerely. It was fair to say I never asked him not to say anything to my family about my whereabouts, but it did irk me that he'd spoiled things for me at the farm. It didn't help that the company he was with was the boaby and Brian. Brian pulled his new knife out holding it in the palm of his hand, 'Carved the horn handle myself he boasted' it was lovely 'It's an eight-inch blade' 'he said. I reached forward to have a closer look, but he snatched it away 'You are no man enough to handle it' he laughed then proceeded to slash the blade close to my face playfully. I was not in the mood, so I stepped forward and clattered my head into his face, he stumbled back, raised his hand to his bleeding burst lip. 'What did you do that for, I might have stabbed you' he said in a shocked bewildered voice. *He'll think twice about bullying me again*, I thought. Even with a knife he now knew I was not afraid, we stared at each other, until Billy said 'Come on you two' then laughed.

Brian spent the whole day showing off his new knife. We hung about all day bored, it wasn't like Billy to not have ideas to keep us occupied. When Billy got an opportune moment he jerked his head, signaling me to come over and stand beside him so he wouldn't be overheard by Brian and the boaby 'I'll be moving into Wolf Farm within the week, you should visit' he said I was not overly delighted at this news. I was desperate to go back and stay at the farm forever, even just in the barn. 'Yes, Scarlett says her Pa is struggling to manage all the work, so he'll soon be begging me to come'. I left their company that night feeling empty, not just my belly but my heart and head too.

The autumn rains came, a daily deluge that seemed never ending. The hours of daylight were now too short to travel to the farm on foot. There was no sign of Billy or any word about the impending birth of Scarlett and Billy's baby, not until Christmas Eve at home when the door flew open, 'Little Billy junior has been born' Billy shouts. He was right, well it was a fifty-fifty chance he would be 'Come on we need to wet the baby's head'. We entered the tavern to cheers and congratulations, 'Two bottles of rum, please my fine man' he said slapping a few coins down on the bar 'Everyone fill up'. Two bottles of rum for this drunken rabble wouldn't go far. I got myself a tankard and filled it half full, 'To wee Billy' the whole tavern toasted in unison, the rum hit my empty stomach, instantly warming me and giving me a buzz. The partying went on into the wee small hours of the following morning, not that I remember much but Billy was smitten with the new arrival, mentioning him countless times.

It snowed on New Year's Eve, ending the year bitterly and the snow didn't clear until March. I hadn't managed to get to see wee Billy, but I planned to as soon as the roads had cleared. Billy turned up on my birthday 'Birthday drinks birthday boy?' I was a big fourteen and it was time for change. I could tell something was up with Billy.

Billy knocked back a whisky, another followed quickly and by the third, I sat quietly supping my rum wondering what was bothering Billy, 'I have decided that farm life is not for me' he said. 'Why, what's up with it, it has only a few months' I quizzed him, 'I have made up my mind, it's the army for me, I'm going to make my wee Billy proud' he said. I felt he was trying to convince himself as much as convince me. 'There's a few things I that need sorting before I go' he stared at me 'Are you with me? You are going to be my batman'. I was not sure if he was asking or telling me, 'I don't fancy joining the army' I replied 'No, I didn't mean that. I want you to be my right-hand man while I'm gone' he said in a serious voice. 'Ah right' I said, feeling relieved but none the wiser. Billy knocked back another snifter of whisky 'Keep an eye on the goings on, visit my wee Billy and stuff' to which I nodded a *Yes.* 'When I get back there's going to be big changes afoot, no more crime just legit business. From now on its the straight and narrow for me' he said convincingly as he started ranting on the subject for what seemed like ages 'We can deal with those who don't follow suit'.

I watched as another whisky disappeared 'I can't take her anymore, it's all too much' Billy said with a sigh. The alcoholic tongue loosener that is whisky is starting to work I thought with a smile, 'I work all hard all day, then she wants to romp in the hay all night. You'd think she wouldn't have the energy with a newborn' he said looking glum 'It's not just that, it's the bloody riding crop, my backside is all bruised I'm not a horse' he continued knocking back yet another whisky. 'Giddy up boy she says, while whacking me across the bum.' I was finding it increasingly difficult to hide my internal riotous laughter, 'It's no right, it's just no normal is it?' Billy said with a completely straight face. I shrugged my shoulders while shaking my head from side to side, my jaws clamped shut to try and prevent a snigger from bursting out.

Billy knocked back two more measures of whisky, then stood up with a bit of a wobble 'Meet me Friday at dusk, on Whinnie Way Road. 'What's the hurry?' I asked. 'I just nipped down; I couldn't miss your birthday'. It sounded a bit like Billy had sneaked down from the farm to escape, the big hen-pecked idiot. I walked Billy out, thinking about all he said, the only good part was the Wolfs would need another helper around the farm once Billy left. I watched as he mounted Dark Lord, and the anger swelled within me, I hadn't spotted Dark Lord in the dark. I hated Billy so much at that moment, he had everything, yet he was running away like a coward. 'Bring the boaby on Friday, he has to be there' slurred Billy before he rode off into the darkness before I could reply.

I stayed in bed all morning on the Friday, it seemed like such a long day with the looming meeting with Billy later that day. I wanted to spend as little time with the boaby as possible. *I suppose I have to find him first* I thought as I headed along the High Street, I blew out a big sigh, as I spotted the boaby. I couldn't believe how unlucky I felt but there he was standing at the butcher's window, pulling faces at the butcher. *What an idiot* I thought. As I passed him, I nudged him hard from the rear knocking him up against the glass 'Oi you' he shouted at me angrily. I walked on quickly, he followed just as I hoped, 'Oi he shouted again, I looked back and gave him a *come-on* wave, trying not to be seen with him as we reached the end of town.

The boaby finally caught up with me when the town was quite a bit behind us. 'You got any money?' I asked, 'Yes loads' he replied shaking his pocket full of coins. 'That's good. Billy needs all he can get his hands on for the baby' I lied. I needed something to tell the boaby in order for him to come with me. Conversing with him was not something I had done before or wanted to do now 'Is that for while he's away in the army?' I nodded, replying 'Yes, that's right, he could be away for a wee while' I replied. The boaby smiled 'I am going with him; my Mum gave me the money for promising to go. She's fair proud of me' he continued, talking drivel.

The daylight was fading into twilight. 'Let's get a move on' I took off at a normal pace then slowed to match the boaby's. 'Where are we meeting him' he asked 'Just come on' I replied, I'd had enough of him by then as we joined Whinnie Way Road, 'There he is up ahead' I said. Billy was carrying a huge sack. It became dark quickly as a small cloud obscured the moon, then light. Looking up at the sky, there were a lot of small clouds moving through the sky. Billy greeted us with 'Well hello there boys, grab the end of this for me will you'. We rushed over, taking hold of the large man-sized sack, 'I'm just taking all my rubbish to the shit pit before I leave'. The shit pit was what looked like a bottomless pit where everything that was thrown in disappeared. There were rumours of about 50 sheep walking into it in one night, disappearing never to be seen again. The sack was heavy, 'Quick as you like boys' said Billy. The contents of the man-sized sack were suspiciously man shaped. 'How much further' the boaby complained as he puffed and panted along to which Billy replied, 'You walk up front, we can handle this'. On hearing this d let go of the sack but I wasn't ready, letting the sack thump onto the ground. A voice from sack said 'Ouch!' and Billy quickly said 'Ouch, that bent my finger right back' pretending that he had made the sound.

It did not take us long to carry the sack to the shit pit. The boaby only slowed us down ever so slightly. 'Put the sack down here' Billy said. 'Ah!' said the sack. The boaby turned as if to take off in fright but Billy stepped in front of him 'Where are you going little piggy?' he asked the boaby, 'Please Billy, I'm no wanting involved' the boaby replied nervously, his eyes darting around looking for an escape route. The sack started moving, then it ripped open. A blade glistened in the moonlight and out climbed Brian wielding his knife with a wicked smile on his face. 'Hello little piggy' he said as he stabbed the boaby in the thigh. The boaby fell to his knees and Billy put his foot on his shoulder forcing him onto his hands. 'We can't have you running around causing trouble, now can we. Squeal little piggy' Brian held out his knife with handle pointing towards me 'Let's see how hard and manly you are then' he smirked. Taking the knife, I swiftly stabbed Brian in the side of his neck. He held the wound with both hands, and as the blood ran through his fingers it looked jet black in the dull moonlight. The noise the boaby made was terrible and Billy was shouting 'That was not the plan, that wasn't what was meant to happen!'. The boaby was screaming in pain like the sound the pig made on the night he stabbed it on Wolf Farm, but the noise I was listening to was the gargling of blood and the rattle of his windpipe as his lungs continued to suck in air and collapse.

The moon disappeared behind another cloud and barely anything was visible in the darkness. The unnerving sound from Brian eased off slowly, then there came a last gargling, rattling breath and he was still and silent. The boaby was still squealing in the dark, then as the cloud uncovered the moon, he stopped in terror then let out a blood curdling scream 'No! Help me, no!' Brian had managed to crawl right in front of the boaby, before taking his last breath. I kicked the boaby hard, right on the blood-stained patch on his leg yelling 'Shut it!' Billy stood frozen to the spot. Walking over to him I passed the rear end of a stinking pig, it smelled really awful. Was that why they call it the shitpit I wondered how many others had come to a smelly end here.

I took Billy's knife out of his belt 'Here, snap out of it, put him out his misery', Billy's hands were shaking as he took his knife, 'The plan was to scare him out his wits, no this' he said, the boaby was whimpering, 'Plan D, no witnesses, pretend he was a fat piggy wiggy' I said, I knew Billy needed to do this, one for one, equal leverage over each other. Billy grabbed his hair, pulling his head back there came the blood-curdling sound of the knife as it sliced through his throat.

I grabbed Brian's legs, 'Get his arms' then we swung his lifeless body into the shitpit then the same with the boaby's. The stench was eye watering. The thin layer of water barely made a splash. The mud under them would give way to their heavy bodies, 'It is not working' panicked Billy, 'Just wait, it takes a while' I said with a lot of hope which he did not have. Billy leaped onto Brian's back, then jumped up and down like a madman, 'He is going down!' he shouted, the body was thankfully going under. 'Stop! Check their pockets, the boaby has a stash of cash' I exclaimed. Billy rifled through every pocket on both bodies, 'He is almost gone, do the boaby'. I said quietly as Billy jumped up once more. On landing his feet gave a splash, he leaped high landing on the boaby 'Parrp!' I started to snigger 'It is not me farting' I joked 'Parp parpp paaarp!' we were in hysterics. Billy jumped off, 'Hope that will do' and the water bubbled and gargled as both bodies disappeared.

Before we parted the cash was split between us. Billy said 'Give me his knife' I looked at Brian's knife, reluctant to be weaponless, and looked quizzically at him. 'Here, you take mine for now' Billy said as we swapped knives. I was a bit cautious, it bothered me all the way home, why did he want Brian's knife?

THE STRAIGHT AND NARROW

I woke up refreshed after sleeping like a log. An early start. *I'll head up to Wolf Farm* I thought to myself, *Billy would still be there for another week or so.* Stepping out of the house it seemed strangely quiet, as if something was going on. I felt the urge to rush to the High Street, and when I arrived I could see that there was a gathering at the other end of the street, a real hubbub ensued. I'd join the search party and make a day of it. It's not as if the two of them were going to be found 'In fact tell everyone that I'll check up at Wolf Farm to see if anyone's seen them' I said out loud then checked nobody had heard.

I joined the back of the group unnoticed. There was someone at the front speaking, but I could not hear a thing initially, then there was a murmur from people in the crowd as they repeated key words such as 'Murder' then 'Knifed.' A small boy waved his cap in the air 'They have got Billy at the camp' he shouted, and my cold heart sank as realisation set in. *We'll hang before the weeks out* I thought miserably. My body was freezing as the colour drained from my face I must have looked as white as a sheet. I struggled to move but managed to sneak away from the crowd and out of town towards the camp. Even walking slowly, I was out of breath. I wanted to lie down and curl up into a ball.

I approached the camp cautiously, keeping myself concealed in the bushes. When I neared the camp there seemed to be a lot going on women crying and wailing, men shouting and balling. Getting down on my hands and knees I crawled the last hundred yards or so. The first thing I saw was a large group of women, to the right of them was the even bigger group of men. Alarmingly most had their guns in hand and they were congregating outside Billy's dad's wagon. *Billy must be held captive inside* I thought.

The wagon door opened, and there he was, Billy stepping out with Brian's knife held up high. I wasn't near enough to hear what Billy was saying but his gestures were clear said it all, waving the knife around then making stabbing motions with it. The crowd was jeering 'Let's get him' one shouted, 'Let's hang him' shouted another. A few of the men at the back were talking amongst themselves and nodding away to each other. I crawled closer just in time to hear someone say, 'I hear Billy's put up a handsome reward for whoever catches him'.

Turning away from the camp I sat there hidden in the bush, *my word against his* I thought dejectedly. *He's won, he has everybody convinced* I thought as I put my head in my hands It was too late to run but I had no choice, and nowhere safe to run to. I decided to hide where I was until it was dark enough to slip away unseen. My brain was in overdrive running through everything that had happened and how I had ended up in this predicament. Why has Billy done this?

A woman's worried voice became clearer as she approached 'Has anybody seen my wee Boaby' she said. It was the boaby's mother. The men at the camp scoffed at her 'Away you go, there's more important things going on round here than looking out for that wee scallywag' one of them said getting the crowd to laugh at her.

The fear inside me was turning to hate and anger. 'How could he betray me? I HATE HIM!' I whispered to myself. My breathing was like a raging bull's 'Kill him, use his own knife' feeling the horn handle I agreed with myself *Yes, lets even the score.* Jumping to my feet I circled the camp until I was no more than five hundred feet from my target, Billy the backstabber. Hiding behind a tree crouched onto my hunkers I looked round to see Billy still standing there with Brian's knife in his hand, and with all the people surrounding him I stood no chance.

I sighed heavily; I'd have to wait. A twig snapped behind me, then in a split second a hand was placed on the back of my neck, I froze, 'Let's be having you' he said grabbing my arm and helping me up, 'You're a good-looking boy I must say' he said. It was creepy old Gregory from town, he kept a hold of my arm, 'I'll pay you the same as I pay your brother' he said disturbingly. I pulled away from him then realised I was out in the open.

Turning swiftly, I saw Billy striding over, looking back the old pervert was gone. Resigning myself to my fate I stood my ground and fumbled for the knife. This was my last chance to get Billy, 'He's killed my Pa' Billy shouted. He didn't need to shout he wasn't very far from me. With his foghorn voice people in the next village would be able to hear him. Grabbing me in a manly embrace Billy whispered, 'Plan K, just follow my lead'. I felt confused, bewildered and still panicky *What is this all about?* I thought.

Turning to the crowd, Billy continued, 'Right the boaby was seen last night heading north to Ayr, so that just confirms Brian used his own knife to kill and rob my Pa'. Billy's words hadn't properly sunk in the first time I had heard them, but now I understood. Billy had killed his own Pa using Brian's knife, so framing him would put us in the clear. 'Right men hunt him down. He's gone west, and mind and bring the blackhearts body back to claim the bounty'.

We were on a killing spree but when would it stop? Once everybody had dispersed, Billy ordered 'Come into the wagon'.

Following him in, the first thing I saw was a large pot full of money. Billy sat down on the bed 'Take a seat' so I sat on the only chair. I felt uneasy as I noticed Billy's Pa was still there in the bed. 'Right so we had a whip round this morning, that money is for my Pa's funeral with the rest going to buy the small bakery at Creetown' Billy announced rather more cheerfully than one would expect. 'So I see' I replied eyeing up the pot. 'While I'm making the arrangements, you will need to go and tell Scarlett the news. I probably won't have time to see her before I go'. Frowning at Billy I asked, 'Are you still leaving to join the army?' Billy paused before answering 'I'm signed up now, I can't not go. I'd get into trouble'. I didn't believe him. Useless parents are useless parents, no matter what excuses or lies they use to cover up the fact. My mind and eyes were back on the money 'Extremely busy morning you've had, that's impressive'. Billy smiled 'I just got on with what needed doing. There's been a lot to sort out and get organised. My Ma can't travel on her own, it's just not done' he said.

I half expected a hostile welcome as I approached Wolf Farm, but the opposite happened. Perhaps Mr Wolf had mellowed since finding out who slaughtered his prize pig, 'Hello Mr Wolf' I said. 'You know where everything is' said Mr Wolf with a tiny twitch on the left side of his mouth, was that almost a smile?, 'Just ignore him, come get a bite to eat' Mrs Wolf said as she ushered me into the farmhouse with a big smile on her face. There she was, Scarlett in all her glory, sitting on her Pa's rocking chair in front of the fire. Her smile distracted me for a moment from the fact her engorged left breast was uncovered and attached to it was lucky wee Billy. I couldn't take me eyes off them it's not something I'd seen in person before although it's the most natural thing in the world for mother and baby. I noticed that Scarlett was giving me a devilish expression.

After informing the Wolfs of what had happened and filling up on Mrs Wolf's tasty offerings I headed out to help Mr Wolf, but he was nowhere to be seen. Looking in the stable it was clear that a serious amount of mucking out was needing done. After clearing out I stood patting Dark Lord's neck, when Scarlett appeared with something in her hand 'I brought a blanket just in case you're bunking down for the night' I hadn't thought about that 'Yes it's best I do, I've three days free if you need help?' Scarlett walked over, slipped her hands around my waist 'Come here you' she said then rested her head against my chest 'I'll miss you'.

Reluctantly I headed to the church, the place I had avoiding for the last ten years. The rain had just stopped and the fresh damp air in the warm sun smelled, well *Fresh*. The glum faces that greeted me as I walked through the churchyard were very unwelcoming, nods of acknowledgement from some and stares from others. Before I reached the church door, the sound of horses hooves walking slowly could be heard as the procession of wagons that was Billy's Pa's funeral cortege proceeded towards the church. Billy was leading his Pa's horse with his Ma sitting up front of their wagon, his Pa in the back laying in his cheap wooden coffin.

It was the usual long tedious service, but the hymns kept people awake 'The day thou gavest, Lord, is ended' and 'Morning has broken'. It was a relief once the service was over. Everybody headed back to camp still looking glum, with hardly a word spoken, Billy's Ma sat with a gaggle of woman in one corner of the camp, the men mulled around in small groups. Billy was nowhere to be seen. I ambled over to where a large bonfire had been built and stood with a few of the older men listening to their stories about Billy's Pa 'I remember back when Billy was just a toddler, I never would have thought back then somebody would end him in such a cowardly way; said the oldest of the bunch.

Out of the back of the wagon came Billy, a small keg under each arm, striding straight over to his Ma. They exchanged a few words then handed over one of the kegs, on his way over he shouted, 'Get that torch lit Thomas' quick as a flash of a flint Thomas had it lit, 'Here you go big brother'.

Billy held the burning torch high 'We will all miss my Pa'; he stopped talking, looked at his six smaller brothers, waving them to stand next to him 'We will all miss our Pa. Thanks to everybody who came to say goodbye to Billy, Chief of the Tinklers'. Passing the torch to his smallest brother Alex 'Will you do the honours little brother?' he asked, Alex's face lit up with the proudest of grins, then took the torch and threw it on the bonfire, slowly the flames started to grow as the flames took hold, 'Let get the fun into this FUNeral' we all cheered while breaking open the keg of cheap strong rum.

The whole place came alive, everybody getting liquored up. Billy was doing the rounds, thanking everybody and before long he came over to me, 'Come over here for a bit of privacy'. We checked around for eavesdroppers, 'When I'm away I want you to be my eyes and ears', I wasn't sure what he meant exactly 'Yes sure, no problem' I said 'You'll need to look in on my Ma and my wee boy from time to time'. I would have anyway. 'My pleasure' I said. 'Remember what I said, you're my main man. When I get back, I'll be claiming my right as Chief of the Tinkers'. The fiddlers started to play in the background *King of Galloway, let's celebrate* and we raised our drinks in a toast. Before long the night blurred together into drink, song and laughter.

At first light I felt a hand shaking me awake, 'I'm off, keep my Pa's horse and wagon until I get back' sitting up I replied, 'Thanks Billy, nice one'. I was still half asleep 'Mind my Ma is in the back sleeping. You will have to escort her to Creetown once she's up'. It was far too early for me to think about this, 'No problem' I said. Pulling a handful of coins out his pocket, he handed them to me 'Here take this, for the horse. Get him good oats'. The money was in my pocket before anybody had a chance to see, 'Cheers Billy, see you when you get back then' I said, Billy walked off 'Yes, see you in three years'.

The day began hours after that, but Billy's Ma never appeared until mid-afternoon, when she and went around the camp saying her goodbyes. I was keen to get going, as it would be a long journey and there wasn't much of the day left. Eventually we set off, it was a slow long journey with lots of reminiscing by Billy's Ma, 'I remember this time when Billy...' then 'I remember when…' followed by 'When I was a young girl…' repeated over and over. It was half dark when I dropped off Billy's Ma. I was going to be spending my first night in the wagon just outside Creetown.

NOTHING STAYS THE SAME

The night before had been a late and drink fuelled one, followed by an early start. The excitement of having a new home was giving way to sleepiness. I parked up, fed old Ned a handful of oats then settled down for the night. A feeling of eeriness came over me, my first night alone in the wagon. Each and every sound made me listen intently, it was different in the barn, out here it was more open. Eventually I lay back and drifted off to sleep. I awoke to the mysterious sound of someone snoring loudly, and I turned over trying to get back to sleep 'Zzz' it came again I sat bolt upright as I remembered where I was, 'Zzz' I didn't move, again 'Zzz'. I peered down at the floor beside the bed but in the darkness of night I saw nothing but black. My coat hung beside the bed, and quietly I reached into the pocket for a match; only three matches. I'd need to be quick, striking the first match I looked down at nothing but floor 'Zzz', I quickly lit the oil lamp, 'Zzz'. Someone was fast asleep under the wagon.

Sitting listening to the regular snores, I wondered if I should leave the snoring individual alone. Hopefully they would be gone by morning, or should I get Billy's knife out for a confrontation? I got the knife out, my knife now if Billy keeps Brian's I supposed, 'Zzz', it was too loud to ignore. With my oil lamp held out in front of me, knife at the ready, I looked but there was nobody there. The loud snoring continued as I crawled under the wagon, but there was no one there either. Then I looked up, and my hairs stood on end as the snoring came from above. Was it the ghost of old Billy?

Walking around the wagon the snores continued. I stepped back, looked at the wagon then walked away until the sound of the snores had faded completely. Taking a seat on the grass with my back against a tree I sat watching the wagon.

Waking with a start I sparked into life, shivering in the cold misty morning air, staring at the wagon. There was no option but to go back to the wagon, the now silent wagon. I opened the door with caution, then entered. To my relief everything was still there where I left it, undisturbed. Grabbing a blanket, I wrapped it around myself tight, then sat on the bed trying to get my head around last night's strange goings on.

The oil lamp was out of oil, and I only had two matches left. I had to decide if I was going to eat the porridge oats I had found in the wagon or the last of my cheese and bread. I was cold and tired, becoming irritable at everything. Maybe the travelling life was not for me I thought. I could not find the bread and cheese 'Damn it' I yelled out loud. The wood burner was ready to light, two chances I thought. Taking the first match I struck it down the side of the wood burner, then quickly held the flame down so that it burnt up the stick part. The burner lit straight away and the sound of crackling wood, accompanied with some welcome heat cheered me just a little. Cooking the oats in plain water made me yearn to be back on the farm having tasty porridge oats made with creamy milk.

Setting off, the plan was to head straight to Wolf farm. This time nothing would prevent me, what with Billy gone and my obligation to take Billy's Ma to Creetown fulfilled. After a mile or so old Ned veered to the side, this made the front right wheel run over a clump of grass tilting the wagon suddenly to the left. 'Ouch!' cried the wagon. Stopping the wagon, I jumped up and pulled my knife out 'Right show yourself' I shouted. The wagon rumbled then a small hatch opened in the floor. I had the upper hand and I was ready for action. Was Billy's Pa actually alive and hiding here in his own wagon all along? Nobody had seen his body properly. 'I am not going back' a young voice said as he popped his head out, 'Alex, what the hell are you doing in there' I shouted at him, his face fell, and he looked as if he were about to burst into tears.

We set off back to Creetown, the two of us gloomy faced. I would never make Wolf Farm today with this unwelcome detour. 'Thank you very much, here take this for your trouble' said Billy's Ma. It was bread and cheese. I wanted to get back on the road and said my goodbyes. 'See you boys soon'. I set off again at the only speed old Ned knew. Slow. I walked along beside him, which lightened his load a little, but this did not make him go faster, however.

Once out of Creetown I did a search of the wagon, the secret compartment had a sheet of tin stored in it, the bottom also had a trap door to the outside, after a good search I was convinced there were no more secrets, however there was a few drawers under the bed containing all sorts of things, a pair of tin snips, a cut throat razor, not that I needed that very often having never shaved.

Camp was my best choice after the slow journey. Half the wagons had gone and including mine that made seven. I got the welcoming waves and nods but only one welcoming smile, along with a couple of scowls. One of the men in particular looked then turned his back on me, but Great Uncle Dougie waved me over, 'Park up next to me' he said. I'd met him only once, when I was with my Grandad years ago. They didn't get on, Dougie liked a good drink, he was a bit of a party man, unlike my grandad who preferred a half pint and slippers. We sat having a chat with a few drinks.

A group of boys appeared from the trees, 'Well hello there boys' I said. The two at the front were the older two of Billy's brothers. They looked in charge, which was no surprise, 'My brother says you're the boss while he's away' said Thom. 'I'm not sure that's the case' I replied with caution 'Billy just asked me to keep an eye on things', It seemed that Billy had left me in charge when he wasn't really in a position himself to appoint me to such a position. 'Come on boys' Thom said walking off with his band of brothers. 'Best watch yourself' Great Uncle Dougie said, disappearing into his wagon.

The next morning, I was woken by a loud knocking and I could hear voices jabbering outside. I'm never going to get a proper sleep ever again I thought. As I went out of the wagon, I was confronted by an angry mob. 'The lads say you're in charge'. It was the same guy that had turned his back on me the day before, 'It's not quite like that' I attempted to explain. 'I'm Billy's brother, I should be in charge' he said. Old Billy had several brothers, and how many would want to claim his chief status, I wondered. This could be big trouble I thought 'Billy's got a plan, all he asked me to do was keep an eye on things' I said trying to keep the talk friendly. 'So, you are a grassing little spy' said Great Uncle Dougie, 'No, Billy wants us to lay low for a while, no more burglaries, no robberies, just keep it on the straight and narrow' well I think that's what he said. 'What about poaching?' came another question, 'It's fine for feeding yourselves but not to be selling to the town folk' I replied. There was a lot of moaning and groaning. 'He never told me what the plan was, but he said that it will make us all rich' I lied with an air of confidence.

I decided to stay at the camp for another night. I thought it was for the best, to let things settle, and see if more questions would arise. However, they didn't. The get rich plan had them suckered in, and things in camp were a touch friendlier by the time I headed of the next day. 'Hey Thom, come here' I shouted as I passed. He ran over 'What', I looked at him, he was a handsome young boy 'Watch out in the woods for creepy old Gregory' I said 'Aye everybody knows not to take his money' Thom said then ran off.

Old Ned clip clopped along at his normal laid-back speed, but I was in a hurry. I was somewhat keen to see the Wolf's, possibly Scarlett in particular. I pulled in at the spot where Billy, Scarlett and I had sat together, eating fresh fish. The memories from that night seemed so distant now. Lunch was a greasy pork pie, and I licked my lips as the grease escaped down my chin. Sitting for longer than I had planned, the thought of not being welcome at the farm had been running through my mind. *Only one way to find out* I told myself.

There was a new face in the yard working away. I had been replaced. I should have asked if I could work at the farm as soon as Billy declared his intention to leave. Realising who it was I gave him a friendly nod 'Hello Mark' but he just ignored me as if I was invisible. 'Ignorant' I said loud enough for him to hear.

Mrs Wolf's smiling rosy cheeks appeared at the door 'Hello you' she grinned, she had her arms stretched out to greet me with a nice big hug. My eyes welled up with tears, happy tears, it was a simple hug, but it was an honest pleased to see you hug, 'Come on in' she beckoned as she disappeared into the house.

The house was exactly the same as last time I visited with the fire roaring. There was just one thing missing, Scarlett, well two things really if you include the new addition wee Billy. Mr Wolf was standing at the fire, 'Come, come, have yourself a wee seat' he indicated to his own chair, 'So you got yourself a wagon' Mr Wolf pointed out, 'Yes' I replied. Mrs Wolf handed me a plate of ham with potatoes 'Eat up son', she didn't need to ask me twice. 'Did you see that sniveling wee cretin out there?' Mr Wolf asked 'You never liked my family' Mrs Wolf quickly said before I had time to answer, 'You say it yourself' Mr Wolf sighed shaking his head, 'He thinks he's here for a holiday, he will not listen to me. If you can stay a few months the boss job is yours' I nodded a *Yes* to Mr Wolf then looked round at Mrs Wolf, she was smiling nodding yes too.

Mr Wolf and I headed out into the yard 'Get over here you' he said to Mark, who looked at us then threw the pail on the ground, spilling its contents. 'This is your new boss, what he says goes'. Mark looked at me and tutted. A good crack in the jaw would do him good 'Now get shifting, those troughs will not fill themselves'. Mark turned reluctantly, and without thinking I gave him a good kick in the backside, 'Ouch' he blurted out turning to Mr Wolf, 'I saw nothing' Mr Wolf said quickly then took off into the house.

Mark was the same age as me. This was a good job, a hard job but permanent. I could not believe how useless he was though, getting the water out of the well took him forever. Taking over I got the water up whilst he was off emptying the pail, 'Hurry up' I shouted, he moved at a snail's pace 'I'm coming, give us a minute' he grumbled. His part was the easy part, it was also the quickest part, but it must have taken three to four times longer than it used to take me on my own.

As he emptied the last pail of water into the trough, I wandered off to see Dark Lord and Cookie. 'Hello, you two' I said as I gave them a good clap, 'Where the hell is he' I cursed as I looked around the yard. When I found Mark, he was standing doing nothing 'What are you doing?' I asked, 'Waiting for you' he mumbled. No wonder Mr Wolf called him a useless wee cretin; he was. 'Right come on' I demanded and he followed me to the stable, 'Were you going to stand there all night?' he shrugged his shoulders in silence, 'Do you know where the barrow and shovel are?' he nodded an unconvincing *Yes* 'Go get them then' I ordered.

It seemed to take him forever to return 'Get started then' he sighed then groaned before putting little effort into the job, 'Here let me show you' I took the shovel then hooked the shovel step to the back of his left knee, it only took a gentle shove to topple him over, the back of his head landed on a mound of horse manure.

Looking round to see Mr Wolf standing at the stable doors, I flinched, 'Stop lying about and get this place mucked out you lazy sod' he said to Mark, 'Can you nip in see the good wife' giving the shovel back to Mark 'Yes sure' I said as I hurried through the yard. It was more Miss Wolf I wanted to see. I knocked on the door then opened it 'Hello Mrs Wolf, it's just me' I shouted in, 'Come on in son' Mrs Wolf replied.

Hiding my disappointment at the fact Scarlett was not there, I stood warming my hands at the fire, 'There is something I need to tell you, its Scarlett' she paused for a moment before 'She has gone away with the baby, she will not be back here at the farm. It's for the best'. I could not believe what I was hearing 'Where has she gone' I asked 'She's away to my sisters place, that's all I can tell you, if you don't know you can't tell' she said, 'I would not tell Billy anyway she need not worry about that', I said. 'You're a good boy, I know that but just let it be for now'. Frowning at her I said 'That's fine' although it wasn't really. 'It's that Billy, he is no good. Scarlett and little baby Jamie need a good life', my eyes opened wide in surprise 'Jamie?' I said, she sighed 'Yes with Billy not being around she christened him Jamie, he is not going to know his dad' she said unhappily.

Back in the wagon I could not sleep. The first born always gets their dad's name, Billy was going to be furious. A big part of me being at Wolf Farm was my best friend Scarlett. I was glad Mrs Wolf had not told me where they were, Billy would hunt them down, it wouldn't be that difficult, somebody would tell him for sure. Then what? I was meant to be keeping an eye on things, what on earth would I tell Billy if he asked me about Scarlett and his son?

The next morning, I awoke with the same thoughts running over and over in my head. Mrs Wolf always had the porridge ready in the morning. It was nice getting to eat in the house instead of the yard. I felt more part of the family than ever, which felt nice, but the missing Scarlett left a big hole. Mark sat eating in silence, keeping his head down.

Still in a saddened state I got going 'Right you, no slacking today' I barked at Mark. He kept his attitude to himself this time, getting on with the filling the troughs, and with the mood I was in it was a wise decision. He really was useless though, and by the end of the week he was still just as useless, but at least he was trying now. The attitude seemed gone for good 'He's better already' Mr Wolf commented looking pleased.

At the end of the month I travelled back to camp for the night. It was the usual bunch hanging around, the old crew. They never travelled much these days and were pretty much settled at the camp site for the rest of their days. 'Hello boys' I said to the gang of young ones 'What's been happening since I've been gone?' I asked Thom, who shrugged his shoulders, 'Nothing much' said Warren. It was music to my ears.

Early the next morning I was up early, ready to hit the road, 'Oi' came a voice as I left camp, Warren came running over, 'Ask Ma if we're staying with her over winter will you?' good question I thought, 'Yes, will do, see you tomorrow' I replied. 'My uncle John wants to know if you are taking us'. I was trying to visit camp and Billy's Ma once a month if possible 'Yes maybe' I said, and with this information Warren ran off.

The bakery was closed when I arrived. Knocking on the door there was no reply. It was almost dark before I saw Billy's Ma, Alex and Callum coming down the street. 'Well hello, its yourself' she said 'Aye' I replied. The boys were quiet and looking rather dirty, then I noticed Alex had a proper shiner 'That's a grand black eye you got there' I said 'Oh they're always fighting with the local boys, they torment them something terrible' said Billy's Ma, 'Boys will be boys'.

I did the same for months, worked the farm, visit camp then Billy's Ma. Autumn came and went. Winter bit in hard, and I yearned for change. There had been no word from or about Billy. It could be another two years or more until he returned, it was possible he might never return. After all these months Mark was almost ready to work the farm himself.

SPRING

After tidying the hay to one side of the barn, I had rolled the wagon into one of the corners, which provided a nice shelter from the winter winds. I had built an additional piece of chimney for the wagon using a sheet of thin tin, and the small stove burned almost constantly. Burning the stove in a barn of hay wasn't the cleverest thing to do but after a few days it was clear that the chimney extension was fit for purpose.

As the days started to get longer the sun became warmer. Spring was almost upon us, and with a feeling of being lost with an uncertain future ahead, I began making plans to move on as soon as the spring solstice arrived. Mark had changed for the better. He was getting the work done, effectively making me redundant. He was no longer a sniveling wee brat; he had also matured into a proud young man. Not only did he show respect for me but also Mr Wolf.

Lying in bed, it was a thought to be leaving the farm behind. Slowly dragging myself out of bed, I noticed the sun was shining bright despite it being a crisp frosty morning. There was a sadness in my heart that I couldn't shake off. Getting old Ned fed and ready to be on our way I asked him, 'Where are we heading first pal?' From the yard came 'I hope your no just going to leave without a goodbye' came the voice of Mrs Wolf. 'No, of course not' I said although I wasn't entirely sure I meant it, I was sad to be leaving.

Creamy porridge, oh how I'd miss my creamy porridge, 'Here, get another bowl' Mrs Wolf said as she smiled affectionately at me. Mark and Mr Wolf hung about like bad smells as Mrs Wolf pampered me, 'We got oats for the horse, and rolled oats and salted ham for yourself to keep you going' Mrs Wolf said. She was smiling as always but her eyes were sad, 'Here's your wages, it's not much' said Mr Wolf but I was grateful for them all the same. Mark shook my hand as I left, 'Bye son, don't be a stranger' Mrs Wolf chimed 'I won't', I replied. Confused mixed feelings flowed around my head, a new beginning, unchartered times.

After I left Wolf Farm, I stopped off in the same place where Scarlett, Billy and I had the fish supper and the events that followed that changed the course of all our lives. It had been one of the strangest of days, and now alone with my thoughts I went over the events of that night. It was too late to go back and change things. I had no regrets regarding the boaby and Brian, justice had been served, Brian was a thief, a liar, a grass and a bully and he would have got it one way or the other. I felt it was best spending the night here. The young men and boys in camp were fine, it was the older guys especially old Billy's brothers. I felt they were still not happy with Billy's choice. I felt like an outsider.

This was my first night on the road to somewhere and it was still early when I retired to bed. Blowing out the flame in the oil lantern, I lay back looking into darkness for a few moments, then closed my eyes. 'Thump, thump, thump' came the running footsteps, up on my elbows wide awake in a split second, listening intently. 'Thump, thump, thump' it continued fast then there came a scraping sound along the side of the wagon. I banged my fist hard against the side panels, silence came back. Taking a deep breath, I thought *It must have been a deer*, which consoled my pounding heart.

The next morning, I woke up smiling thinking of the deer that spooked me the night before. First things first, light the fire, boil water, then get the porridge on. While waiting for the porridge I stripped fully and using the boiling water I took a small cloth, wet and soaped it for an all over wipe down. It was a lovely sensation, that hot, clean and fresh feeling. There was nothing like it to get you going in the morning, a routine that I intended to follow every morning religiously.

Skipping camp, I went straight to town for supplies. It didn't take long before I had what I needed and was heading out of town. I heard my brother shouting 'Where are you going' but I ignored him and just walked on leading my friend old Ned. This annoyed him immensely, then after a barrage of verbal abuse he shouted, 'I am telling mother'. *Yes, you do that* I thought, *goodbye rats, I won't miss you.*

It was still early but old Ned wouldn't make Creetown before nightfall, so we took our time. Our first stop was for lunch. Looking out across the water filled estuary, it was so quiet and peaceful even although the birds were noisy with their birdsong and the waves made a tremendous sound crashing onto the rocks.

We could have stayed there forever. The next part of the journey took us inland for a few miles before hitting the coastline again. There were spring lambs everywhere. They were so delightful, following each other around, and every so often they would randomly spring into the air. A fight broke out between what appeared to be two rival gangs, a turf war, or a sheltering hole in the turf as was more the case. I never touched lamb. How people could eat these little creatures was beyond me, although they do not stay cute for long.

As soon as the coastline appeared, and I began searching for a place to park up for the night. The coastal wind put a few nice spots out of contention. Once finally parked up, it was time for a feast of salted ham, bread and cheese all washed down with a bottle of wine. The wine tasted dreadful, like sweet vinegar. It was my first taste of wine and I was bewildered as to why people drank the stuff, although it did get better by the time I drank the last drop. I wished I'd bought two.

Turning in that night felt good. It wasn't just the wine, the whole day had been good, watching mother nature at her best, leaving my old life behind, I would always find time to return to the farm to visit the Wolfs.

It was not until my arrival at Creetown that I realised how early I must have risen that day. At the crack of dawn, the streets were still empty, but the smell of fresh bread was a good sign. The bakery door was open wide 'Hello' I said quietly so as not to wake the boys. 'Hello there' the boys replied. 'Have you boys been good, and have you been helping your Ma?' I asked. 'Of course we have, are you here to take us back to uncle John?' said one of them from the back room. 'John says it's still too chilly at night' I replied, not having spoken to John but I surmised he would have said the same. Eager to get on I shouted through 'Has your Ma got a bag of flour I can buy' there was no reply. 'Hello, I saw you pass. I was just up the road there' I turned to see Billy's Ma. 'How much flour you after?' she asked 'Just an emergency supply in case I'm stuck, I'm off for a bit round the coast' I replied.

Alex loaded a small bag of flour on to the wagon, 'Three pounds will do, Ma says your money's no good'. *Fair enough* I thought. 'Thank your Ma, see you all soon' I said leading old Ned through the village. As soon as the bakery was out of sight, I checked the secret compartment for any stowaways and relieved there were none I set off on the next part of my journey.

The road went in long curves as it followed the coastline. We passed through a couple of small villages but there wasn't much sign of life. Continuing on. we came to a river with a wooden bridge, Newton Stewart which is a busy wee town. The main street was full of hustle and bustle, with everybody going about their business. I got a few *You're not from around here looks* as we passed through, nosey ones wondering who the stranger in town was.

When we were clear of the town there was a signpost for Stranraer pointing one way and Wigtown the other. I felt lost, 'Which way Neddy boy?' I asked but as always, my horse was no help. The river would lead us back to the coast I thought. Before long the river was out of sight with no sign of the coast. Another day had gone.

Once again, I rose early. Stepping out of the wagon, the place was surrounded by rabbits. My first though was food, so with a piece of twine I set the first noose trap, then another with a solid wooden box. Quietly we sneaked off hoping the traps would do their jobs. Back to Newton Stewart we travelled. Stopping at the first stretch of the river I saw old Billy's rod was still in the wagon, everything was. Hours later I gave up, fishless, without even a nibble.

Not far along the road a man on a horseback approached, gun in hand, 'Have you been fishing the river Cree?' he demanded to know 'No, I'm just passing through' I replied not stopping, he looked at me like I was dirt. The fish are free, nobody can own them I thought. I could tell he didn't believe me, but I wasn't going to take any nonsense from a some jumped up snoot with a high opinion of himself, 'Good day to you Sir' I said ending our conversation.

When the coast was clear I pulled old Ned of to the side then watched and waited to see if the man on horseback was going to return. We took it extra slow after that, just in case. When we arrived at the traps it was all good, both traps had worked. The rabbit in the noose trap got a quick whack to the skull using the priest old Billy had thoughtfully supplied, the second rabbit wasn't so easy. Which way was the rabbit facing? Was it even a rabbit? Lifting up the box the slightly at one end I slid my hand underneath. As I felt the fur, the rabbit suddenly moved, giving me a fright. My hand was out and the box back down in a flash, *Pull yourself together* I told myself sternly. On the second try I grabbed the rabbit, pinned it down before throwing the box to the side, then whack.

Watching somebody skin and gut a rabbit is one thing, but actually doing it is quite another, a bit squeamish I slowly did the first one, then I got to grips with it, getting the second done in no time. While the rabbits were cooking, I dealt with the fur. Dried out they could be stitched together for something I thought. The rear left foot was meant to be lucky since way back to the time of the Celts but if you were lucky the person buying wouldn't know which one was lucky, *The rabbit was killed in a cemetery* would be my explanation if asked.

Sitting there with a full belly, wondering if I should move on or stay another night, I was rudely interrupted, 'Here's Lord Snooty again' I said to old Ned he replied with a 'Neigh' giving him a look 'Aye it is cheeky' chuckling to myself.

The big man had brought a friend, instead of guns they had brought wooden clubs, 'Is it not time you moved on?' he said as his friend circled round the back of me. 'Soon, perhaps', he kept nudging his horse closer, 'We don't want your kind here' he said snootily. I stepped back only for him to nudge his horse forward making me step back again. On the third time I quickly grabbed the horse's bridle, this gave me control, pushing first away then pulling back, the horse was well trained, responding at speed, back and forth. Mr Snooty was almost hanging off. As his club fell from his hand, his chum charged from behind. I turned fast, bringing the horse with me, the other rider pulled to the left narrowly missing a straight on horses head crash.

Out of nowhere came a stern female voice 'Stop this nonsense at once' which the three of us did instantly. Looking over it was a rather portly looking woman with a manly look about her, but I was more interested in her companion who was smiling away at me. Her face was quite pale, with skin that looked so smooth and soft, her hair was fair and tied back with a little black bow.

For a few moments I gazed at this beautiful creature in awe before getting interrupted, 'You two get home, instantly' she barked, they didn't look pleased but left like they had been ordered to. It was my turn next, 'As for you young man we don't allow your kind to camp on our land' I thought it best not to argue 'Yes ma'am, I was just passing through' she looked down her nose at me 'See that you do, Garlieston is more for your kind' she said before taking off. My mind and eyes were back on her companion, that gorgeous little smile on that beautiful little face, his club was now mine, I would have liked to have seen him try to get it back.

For all that remained of the day I decided to stay there one more night, setting my traps before turning in, I wasn't going to let snoots spoil things for me. Tossing and turning sleep failed me for quite some time into the night, kept awake by thoughts of meeting that lovely face one more.

At first light I was up and out to check my traps. Success! Two more good sized rabbits. I had them whacked over the head and hidden in the secret compartment before there was any chance of me being seen. We were on the move probably long before most house dwellers even opened their eyes.

Wigtown was visible in the distance. I'd be glad to get there but old Ned started walking to the left 'Hey, hey, hey, what's wrong buddy?' I asked him before checking his legs and hoofs. There seemed to be nothing visible, 'You ok old pal?' I asked 'Neigh he replied, I walked him forward a few steps. He wasn't limping but still walking to the left. Looking behind myself, I saw the problem. Carrots, an abundance of wild carrots, 'You want some of these carrots Ned?' I asked him 'Neigh' he replied 'Make up your mind' I laughed to myself. Then, looking around in case anybody was watching I swiftly harvested a large bunch of carrots. I knew perfectly well that the carrots weren't wild, but it did make me feel better about my mistreatment the day before. Ned appreciatively devoured a substantial portion of *wild* carrots.

Wigtown was a lovely little town. After having a look around, I headed down to the harbour. Initially it looked rather underwhelming, there was only a trickle of water, and there were no boats or ships to be seen. It had been a dry spring, but this was ridiculous. After parking up next to a couple of small trees, I secured old Ned.

Walking over to the edge of the pier, I glanced down and thought that it must have been at least twenty feet deep with a mud bank on the other side. *I'll have a rabbit feast then move on first thing tomorrow after an early night* I thought to myself.

I woke first thing next morning to a strange dull noise accompanied by a ding of a bell. I dived out the back of the wagon as fast as I could to investigate, 'Ahoy, me boy' shouted a man from a ship, a ship floating on air, or a ghost ship. I was not about to go any closer to find out, 'Ahoy, me boy' he repeated. This didn't make sense, 'Come on lad, a pretty penny in it for you if you unload this cargo before the tide turns'. The tide, of course, I kicked myself. It was amazing how much water had flooded the harbour with the tide coming in.

Standing at the edge of the harbour was scary. The depth of the water made me nervous, 'Five packages, for the big house', he said, 'Pass them over skipper' I said. He scratched his big bushy beard 'That's captain to you me boy!' We had them unloaded in no time. The captain walked back and forth along the deck, looking very agitated 'Here son, I'll double your money if you look after the packages until somebody from the big house comes to collect them'. Handing over the money he said, 'The tides going out, I need to go'. Five packages for the snoots. The temptation to keep the packages was strong. 'Cast me off me boy' the captain said, the ropes were chunky, wet and heavy.

Watching as the boat drifted back out to sea, it almost seemed as if the boat was dragging the water with it. The soaking wet mud left behind was alive with noise as the water drained slowly, I was mesmerized at this phenomenon, I'd have to wait until the tide returned.

Time had drifted away like the tide, the packages where still awaiting collection. I stared at them wondering what was inside. I could have bundled them into the wagon and disappeared, but a thief wasn't what I was or planned to be, no matter how tempted I was to get one over the snoots.

It was late morning before two snoots arrived, 'Here they come Neddy boy'. Their faces said it all, the displeasure of having to deal with me again irked them, 'Morning' I politely said, I got no response. 'The captain said you would pay me handsomely for guarding your packages' I announced. They wouldn't find out he hadn't said that until I was long gone anyway. 'Come to the house tomorrow, I'll have payment waiting', I watched as they loaded their cart. 'Would you like a puppy for your efforts?', I wasn't sure if I did. 'Yes' I replied, I could always sell it.

Spending the rest of the day watching the water level rise as the tide came in, then fell as the tide went back out, I wondered *where did the water go*? Or was it more where did all the water come from? Did anyone really know?

The big house was exactly that, a big house with several outbuildings around the back. A young man approached as old Ned and I slowly wandered up to the front of the house. 'Follow me' he said taking us round the back to where the barn was. I fully expected that they were going to fob me off with the runt of the litter. There she was, the fair maiden of my dreams, sitting with three gorgeous little pups.

One of the pups came stumbling over to greet me, 'His names Patch' she said with her small kissable smiling lips. He wasn't the runt after all, more the oddball. Where the other two were identical, Patch was different. He had one blue eye and one brown, one black ear sticking up one white ear, his lower jaw was a touch squint, with his paws being one black one white one three quarters black one three quarters white. To me he was the pick of the bunch, my wee oddball. He cuddled his head into my chest, *my wee cuddly oddball* I thought.

The young girl stood, 'He's three months old' she said in a silken soft voice. 'Elizabeth, get in the house this instant' came the stern voice from behind. The young girl ran off, 'You boy, you got what you came for yes?' she knew the answer, but I replied anyway 'Yes Ma'am' although there was something else I came for, a somebody. 'Be on your way then boy' the stern woman said walking off.

Elizabeth, Liza, Beth. Patch sat happy in the wooden box I'd been using for a trap, watching everything as he saw them for probably the first time. Beth. I tried to get my mind off her, but it was impossible.

Time dragged as I hung about town hoping to see Beth again. For weeks I had been watching the tide raise and fall, daily I would walk up one side of the main street then walk back to the harbour on the other side, each day stopping in front of a rather curious shop, all that was displayed in the window were books. I had never seen the likes in my life before.

Apart from a few showers, the weather this spring had been mainly dry. Summer was just around the corner; the heat was building. Then came the rain, it rained for days and days. I suddenly found myself bored and confined to the wagon.

Taking a few coins, I ran up the street to the book shop. I knew I'd get the dirty looks, some snoot looking down on me. Opening the door, I rushed into the book shop out of the rain. There were two things that surprised me inside, first the number of books, they were wall to wall, floor to ceiling, and there she was standing at the back, my wee Beth.

'Morning' we said in unison. She giggled softly as I laughed, 'What would you recommend?' I asked proudly 'How well can you read' she asked nicely. 'I've read a Dickens' I think she was impressed, 'His new novel is all the rage at the moment' she fetched it out, 'My younger brothers are still after revenge you know'. Shrugging my shoulders, I asked 'How much?' her face looked so sad 'They are going to get the locals to beat you up and burn your wagon. The book is free if you leave town', she said sadly. It was a good offer, the sensible thing to do was to take it, 'The book and a kiss for my travels' her smile returned, 'One kiss and you need to promise'.

Like a true gent I got out of town that day, with a new book and a very large smile, *it is what it is* I thought to myself, *in another life in another time.* The rains had turned the track to mud, I wasn't going far, and she never said I had not to return.

SUMMER

Old Ned walked along at his normal pace, the wheels of the wagon sliding left to right in the muddy tracks. More importantly we were gliding forward, the rain wasn't letting up any time soon. Glancing back at Wigtown I said to my newest friend 'You hungry my little pal?' reaching over to pet his head. He quickly lay down with his tiny little paws pointing skywards for a belly rub. Wigtown was almost out of sight, 'First good place we see, we will stop' I said.

Almost as soon as Wigtown disappeared out of sight, Bladnoch appeared which is a small village situated alongside the river. Visibility in the rain was poor and stopping at a bridge I pondered going across. Looking around my answer came in the form of two travellers wagons parked up behind a large malt whisky distillery.

Parking up beside them, I slowly unharnessed old Ned with as much noise as possible while Patch explored the area, sniffing anything and everything. It felt a touch strange that nobody had shown face, raining or not a quick welcoming greeting would have been nice. I thought it best not to disturb the inhabitants of the other wagons.

After eating I noticed a problem; Patch needed a bowl as Ned's old wooden pail was far too big. I still had the tin in the secret compartment, but without the knowledge or skills to fashion it into a bowl, it wasn't much good. I tickled Patch's wee belly again. A mini pail, Eureka!

The cutting, banging and cursing went on for the rest of the day, until finally I had a half-finished water bowl come mini pail for my furry wee friend to get a drink of water from before bed.

Voices. Rising quickly. I rushed out to meet and greet my neighbours, but they all just stared coldly. I stared back not sure, there was an older couple maybe in their thirties and a couple in their twenties, two children and a baby. Patch was over making friends; the young girl took off giggling and screaming with laughter as Patch gave chase.

The rain had gone, and the sun was hot, but it was Patch who melted the icy faces of the stranger, 'That's Billy's wagon is it no?' I looked back at the wagon not quite sure why, 'It was but he's not needing it just now' I replied truthfully, 'Aye we heard, dreadful business. Did they find that Brian?' Shaking my head and trying to look glum as possible I replied 'No, not yet. He's been spotted in Wales so maybe soon' he nodded in agreement 'Aye, we heard the same'. This came as a bit of a surprise as I only made it up as the word Wales came out of my mouth.

Suddenly the heavens broke, 'Catch you later' the oldest shouted as we all dashed into our own wagons for shelter, but Patch stayed out without a care in the world. The rain looked as if it was going to be on for the day, which gave me a good chance to finish his bowl.

Coming out of the wagon out to get him I realised the rain had passed. For quite a while it would seem, 'Will you join us for a bite to eat?' the older of the men asked, 'Yes, thanks very much' I replied, not that I wanted to, but it was only polite. 'I'm Edward, this is my brother Donald, our wives Fiona and Jess, and you are?' pausing I looked at the wagon, then gave him a smile 'You know who I am' I replied, everybody in the travelling community would know.

Proudly passing him Patch's new bowl 'Made it myself' he looked it over then passed it to his son, 'Here get the puppy some fresh water'. Dinner was meat free watery broth with stale bread, it was tasteless. 'I'll be waiting out the weather before I head, if you don't mind?' I don't think they were overly pleased, but Donald replied 'Oh that's fine with us'.

After refusing a second helping I scooped up wee Patch and his bowl 'Well thanks for dinner, my treat tomorrow night' I said. It was a bit of a concern that they had no meat in their broth, why did the men not fish or set traps?

When the coast was clear I sneaked out to set my traps. After that, I ran the short distance back to Wigtown. Not a soul stirred in the streets, and before long I was filling my pockets with carrots, but old Ned wasn't getting them all this time.

Next morning the sun was out, the sky was blue, and the heat was already rising fast. The two children were playing on the grass with the baby while their parents paddled in the stagnant burn that was at the back of the distillery. 'What are you doing?' I enquired, they ignored me at first, then Edward said 'We're catching leeches. You were out late', it was my turn to ignore him, 'Leeches aye, I hear they cure everything'. Edward climbed out of the burn, with what looked like ten or more black slimy slugs clinging to his legs, 'This is what we have to do to stay on the land, we can't afford you getting into trouble'. I wanted to say *nobody owns nature* but didn't 'It's nothing to worry about. Are the closest shops in Wigtown?' I said instead 'Yes' he replied.

The day was scorching hot by the time I returned with my freshly bought potatoes and of course two fresh rabbits. Edward and family were still in the burn, working a terrible job to stay poor. Looking at old Ned and Patch, 'Never have kids' I said to myself.

The ingredients were placed into a large pot to cook. Old Ned got the carrot tops. Leaving the stew to cook, I stripped off to my under shorts, then paddled into the river. The sudden cold made me gasp, but it was invigorating and a pleasant relief from the suns beating rays. Edward and his brother came running over to join me, closely followed by their wives in their bloomers. Their breasts were bouncing in all directions, and the water was only waist high, giving me a closeup of their ample bare bosoms, 'Breasts ahoy' the captain's voice said in my head, I chuckled trying not to stare too much.

I stayed in the water for longer than I intended in order to keep my embarrassment concealed, as even the coldness of the cold water didn't work to keep my boat from floating. It didn't help when the women started splashing water all over each other. I watched as the two women left the water, their wet bloomers were now completely transparent revealing their round full derrieres, 'Release the kraken' said the captain, then I was laughing both about the captain's voice in my head and the joke.

Dinner was one of the best I had ever had, rabbit stew. The children scoffed it down, 'Help yourself to more' I said to them. Edward had a long face, taking his time eating. Conversation that night was kept to a minimum. I was definitely getting out of there first thing, 'Thanks very much for dinner' Edward said before they all retired for the evening.

On the other side of Bladnoch bridge, the signpost offered two choices, left to Whithorn or right to Port William. It did not help that they were both ten miles away, 'Will I flip a coin Neddy boy?' he gave his usual answer *neigh*. Reaching for a coin I noticed Patch was already off, heading to Port William.

The summer sun was strong as we winded our way along the track. The birds sang, the bees buzzed, the flowers bloomed, everything seemed alive. It felt great, the freedom I was looking for.

Before long the track wound its way through a shaded wooden area before opening and straightening out with a view that went on forever. In the distance the land gave way to sea and sky. We pulled up for a bite to eat, while taking in the magnificent view. Patch was too busy exploring to stop for food.

Port William was a small fishing port. The place was deserted. Looking out across the water, the fishing boats bobbed and swayed as the men worked the nets. The fishermen's bungalows followed the coast. It was one of the most beautiful places on earth I thought.

Time had no meaning anymore. The seagulls soared and glided, and the coast was a combination of stones and rocks, then in the distance turned to a long stretch of sand.

There was one boat far in the distance. It was just a speck, but slowly but surely it got closer. As it passed the fishing boats, it was quite a bit larger than them. Could it be the captain? Distance on the water was a puzzling thing. The boat finally arrived in port, 'Ahoy me boy' came the familiar shout from the captain.

Throwing a rope over to me he shouted, 'Tie me up skipper'. There were three ropes, front, middle and back. 'Do you want to earn your dinner?' he asked. I looked on board, three crates were sitting on deck, 'Yes sure', he patted one of the crates. 'If you will take these three crates half a mile up the coast to my home, that is'. We loaded the crates into the wagon, 'I will get you up there, the wife is in'.

I had heard stories about the sea faring men. *Rum, bum and bacci* kept the seamen at sea, any port in a storm. *Was the captain's wife really going to be at home?* I questioned myself. He seemed to be a jolly old captain; I was sure my port would be safe.

I pulled up the wagon outside the first cottage on the edge of the village. Checking down the track it was the only property. The door opened before I got to it, and a woman in her late thirties answered, 'Can I help you son?' she asked, 'Aye the captain sent me, with these crates', I replied shyly. She laughed 'You are a bit young, you must be only half my age', smiling back 'Nearly fifteen Miss' she laughed even louder at this, 'Yes half the age of the men that normally turn up'. We both looked back to the port, 'He's trying to marry me off you know. Take your wagon round the back, he won't be long'.

Patch had disappeared. I ran to the front of the captain's house and shouted 'Patch' several times but there was no sign of him. 'Ahoy me boy' came the captains voice from the beach. 'Have you seen Patch my pup?' I asked both worried about Patch and mad that he had ran off. 'Not the way I came son, he will not be far away. Let's get the crates into the outhouse, then if your pup has not turned up, we will all search'.

After the packages were stored away, it was time to search for Patch. 'I'll just give the daughter a shout to help', the captain said. When we opened the front door, there he was tail wagging, making himself at home. 'Ahoy me boy' the amused Captain said to Patch, then he crouched down and petted Patch who loved the attention.

The captain left the door open, so I followed him in. It was a small cosy home, just a single room with a fire at one side and two hammocks at the other. The hammocks were attached to the wall at one end and to a large floor to ceiling beam at the other. There was no sign of the captain's wife and only sleeping arrangements for two, curious indeed I thought. 'Take a seat me boy', the captain beckoned. Next to a table near the fire was one chair and three stools. The chair would be the captain's I thought as I sat myself down on the first stool.

A large cauldron was hanging over the flames a roaring fire, and the water was boiling, bubbling and spitting causing the fire to hiss. The captain pulled a strange looking shelled creature out of a pail. There was water dripping from it as it moved its legs and snapped its oversized claws. 'Have you tasted lobster before, me boy' asked the captain. I hadn't, 'Not yet' I replied hesitantly, I was not all that sure if I wanted to.

Laying the cooked lobster on the table in front of me the captain then pulled another two lobsters out of the pail, 'They are poisonous if you don't boil them alive. One for each of us, me boy' said the captain. The lobsters thrashed about on the table in front of me. They were shades of dark brown, not very appetising in the least, 'Here we go, one, two, three' as the captain counted them in.

Ten minutes later the captain was lifting the first lobster out of the water with the fire tongs. At first, I thought it was some kind of magic trick, 'Look at the colour on this beauty, me boy' the captain said as he slapped the red demonic looking creature on the table. 'I'm Evelyn, you need to smash it with this' said the captain's daughter passing me a palm sized stone, 'Watch' Evelyn said as she whacked the creature hard then peeled off it's hard shell.

Pieces of shell flew everywhere as we smashed and slurped our way through our tasty bounty, our hands and faces awash with lobster juices. Just as we finished Evelyn produced a bottle of spirits, and some cheese and bread 'Have you ever tasted this lovely stuff?' the captain said as he filled up three tankards, 'This will put hair on your chest'. Evelyn laughed 'He'll need hair on his testicles first' the pair of then rolled about laughing at my expense but I didn't mind, they were good company. Taking a sniff then a small taste, 'It's lovely, what is it?' I asked, 'It's rum from the West Indies' replied the captain. I took a large swig, gulping it down hoping there was no bacci as I was no smoker.

Later the captain asked, 'Can you stick around a few days until those crates get collected, me boy?' For more rum I would have done almost anything, 'Yes I can stay for a day or two, we are in no hurry', he looked at his daughter 'It's just if I'm at sea, the man might need a hand loading up those crates'. They were a friendly pair. Later on that night, I found out just how friendly Evelyn was.

Another scorching day followed, but the tidal breeze made it tolerable. Evelyn and the captain were gone, so Patch and I took a walk down to the beach. The port was visible from there, but it was empty with no sign of the captain's boat. A bare footed paddle was as far as I was willing to venture, I had a lot of respect for the sea.

Evelyn was standing by the door when I got back, 'Dinners there. Once the water's boiling you know what to do, I need to be getting back' she said. 'Back? don't you live here?' I asked. She smiled 'No I just visit when I know my father's going to be back'. Patch was pestering Evelyn for attention. 'What about Mrs Captain' I asked stupidly. 'She passed five years ago now, but he still talks like she's still here at times' Evelyn said. The water was boiling. Looking at the lobster I thought *What if it nips me with its claw?* Plucking up the courage I plunged my hand into the water, grabbing it then letting it go, jumping back with fright as I felt it move. This is stupid I thought. On my second attempt I grabbed it tighter, hauling it out of the water. Holding the lobster at arm's length I studied the amazing creature, 'You are not so scary are you?' I said to it before I sent it to a boiling death.

The following days were much the same. The sky was the bluest of blues. Hot and happy, Evelyn was the only person I had spoken to all week, 'I'll need to be giving you money for all the food you are bringing' I said to her. Lobsters, crab, mussels, shrimps and fish I'd had them all, although I made sure mussels was just the once. 'It's fine, the fishermen almost give them away to the locals'.

The weather changed from blue to grey skies, and the sea breeze turned into full on gusts of wind. Leaning into the wind I forced my way to the edge of the beach where the tide was higher than I'd seen it before. Over in the port the sea was smashing against the rocks, exploding sprays of water that towered over the houses. There was no sign of the captain's boat. It was only midday when the clouds turned black and visibility was as poor as dusk.

Standing there for hours, I wondered if the old captain was tied up somewhere safe. Looking out to sea, the storm was building fast. Patch was in the captain's home; he was a lot wiser than me. It was now pitch black when suddenly a flash of lightning struck.

It was miles away across the water. 'Blimey' I said as the sound of it thundered across the sky. The air felt like it was shaking, but I didn't want to miss a second of this I thought as lightning struck again.

I awoke next morning feeling overheated. Looking out of the window it was as if the storm had never happened. The old wagon had survived it well. Evelyn appeared just along the track and Patch took off to speed to great her. 'Morning, you're early today' I said, 'Yes, my father will be on the next tide'. I looked out to sea in wonder. 'Can you collect some driftwood for the fire?' she asked, 'It's the least I can do' I replied.

There was driftwood in abundance, as far along the beach as I could see. Stacking it at the side of the house I soon had a pile as high as myself. 'Ahoy, me boy, that will be enough will it not?' the captain said, 'There is plenty more if you want it Captain' I replied. He pulled a bottle out of his coat 'Well suit yourself, but you might prefer helping me with this though'.

Evelyn had the water boiling for the lobsters, 'Not for me tonight' she said as the captain poured us both a large measure of rum 'All the more for us me girl' he said with a cheeky grin. 'Cheers' I said taking a large swig. 'Do you fancy learning the ways of the seas?' he asked, 'No, it's not for me' I replied. It wasn't, if truth be told it terrified me, 'That's a real shame, it's not for everybody though. He'll be collecting his crates tomorrow'. I nodded 'It's been great being here, but it might be time to move on' I said. He topped my drink up and said, 'Mind and come back anytime'.

The captain was gone in the morning, and his boat was gone from the harbour too. I wasn't sure if it was a trick to keep me there or if the crates were really being collected. By the time afternoon came I was on the verge of heading off when I spotted a cart in the distance. 'Hello son, is the captain around?' Looking at him I guessed they were his crates but how would I know 'Not today, is there something I can help you with?' I asked. 'Yes, did he leave word about my three crates?' I nodded for him to follow 'Right this way' I said. Once the crates were loaded into the man's cart, he opened one of the crates, pulled out a bottle of rum, then passed it to me 'Here son, you never saw me'. I wasn't the type of person to go blabbing anyway, but this bottle of rum would certainly erase him from my memory.

On my travels once more, well just around the next corner, where I parked up for a drink of rum, half the bottle to be exact. *We need to get a supply of this stuff* I said to myself, *I'm not going to sea no matter what* taking another swig *Aye, but it can't be all that bad, now can it?* The rum was going down a treat, *But you see how deep it was and how high the waves got in that storm.* I was tormenting myself. The next morning, I travelled on but not far. Before parking up to enjoy the new coastal view, across the water I could see land. It was a bit close, but I thought that it must be Ireland.

The Cock Inn. With a name like that the inn was either going to be full of farmers or lonely seamen. It was a relief when I noticed the cockerel painted on the entrance door. Inside there was that lovely warm yeasty beer smell of cask conditioned ale. As I entered, the place fell silent, with the six customers and the inn keeper all stopping to check out the new face, 'What will it be son?' the inn keeper asked. 'A jug of ale, with a rum chaser please' at that the inn keeper looked around the inn checking nobody was listening, 'If you go through that door, take a wee seat in the snug and you'll be attended to' said the inn keeper.

As the door swung closed behind, the inn occupants all burst out laughing and I immediately knew that the laugh was on me. Sitting down for a few moments before the door opened, with the occupants of the inn all peaking in, 'Sitting in the ladies bar looking for rum are you' one of them said as they all burst out laughing again.

Raging, I flung the snug door open, then stomped towards the exit. Everybody was still laughing when the inn keeper said 'Come on son have a beer on the house, no hard feelings'. It was an offer I couldn't refuse, 'That's a fine ale you got there, it sure beats the watery slops some other establishments serve up' I said after taking a large swig. 'So where did you get the fancy notion for rum?' the inn keeper asked, 'I just heard some sailors talking about it and saying how good it tasted' I said, not giving anything away. 'If you add on the shipping price then the tax on it is far too expensive' he motioned to his customers to make his point. He did have a point, the customers looked like they didn't have two pennies to rub together. The inn got busier as the night went on, with the ale flowing long after closing time. I had been informed that this area of Galloway was called The Machars. The people all seemed to be friendly and welcoming, and the thought of leaving was a bit of an effort.

On the outskirts of Stranraer stood a signpost for Loch Ryan coastal road, 'That's the way for us' I said to old Ned. Five minutes later I found myself at the bottom of a very windy Loch Ryan. Summer wasn't going to last much longer, and I wanted to get away from the coast before the autumn storms started. We skipped Stranraer in favour of continuing our travels north.

The wind was relentless, hitting us face on daily. The days were flying by as our progress was even slower than our normal old

Ned pace, and the only place to shelter was when the track detoured away from the coast.

Patch was now almost fully grown and was the only one that didn't seem to notice as he ran about regardless of how strong the wind blasted. Old Ned was struggling though, and on a few occasions, he opted to stop for extra breaks, refusing to budge until he was ready. It was on such an occasion that I spotted the next town 'Just a bit further today ' I pleaded giving him a pat.

AUTUMN

After finding a fisherman's boathouse at the harbour to shelter the wagon and old Ned, I headed for a look around Ballantrea. It was a nice little sea battered place, and it's single shop had a good variety of goods. Stocked up with supplies, I headed back to the harbour.

As I walked past a row of fishermen's cottages, I noticed old Ned and Patch had a new friend, a woman in her late twenties. 'Hello, are these two yours?' she asked, she looked so familiar although I had never met her before in my life 'Hello there, yes they're mine. I'm thinking about resting up here for two days if nobody minds' she smiled 'There's a storm coming, you'd be best sheltering in my father's boathouse'.

She opened the large doors, 'Put the wagon in for now, the horse can wait until later', I did as instructed. 'Will your father not mind?' I asked, she smiled again 'He'll not mind. He won't be back until after the storm anyway'.

Looking out to see I pointed out the island in the middle of the sea loch 'That's quite a landmark!' I said, she took my hand, then pulled me towards the harbour 'Come walk along the harbour wall' she said. The water was high up the wall, and splashes came over onto the wall where we walked. Holding her hand was nice, and when we reached the end she said, 'It's called Ailsa Craig or Paddy's Milestone but its better known locally as Fairy Rock'.

She was still holding my hand and I was feeling a bit nervous as anxious thoughts circled in my head. *Should I let go? It was nice. What was the proper protocol for this sort of thing?* We stood looking out to sea as the choppy water constantly changed, waves peaking as they died only to be replaced with the birth of a new wave.

A flat spot with no waves was coming our way from quite far out, rising as it came. Suddenly it turned quickly into the mammoth waves and it was too late to run so we instinctively wrapped our arms around each other. The wave hit the wall with all its force and knee-high water rushed along the top of the wall nearly taking us with it. The worst was still to come; most of the wave had been thrown high into the air and was about to land fully on us from above.

Holding my breath with my eyes closed, I held her tight, cringing as the torrent of water hit. It felt like it wasn't going to stop. The power and weight of the wave was forcing me down, then suddenly it was over. Taking a breath, I opened my eyes to see a wholly saturated stranger in my arms, water running from her hair down her face.

We were frozen there, holding each other tight as the storm raged around us, then we kissed. The excitement of the near-death experience had made us lose our wits, we kissed again, 'Run!' she shouted before dragging me by the hand. We could hardly move in our sopping wet clothes, 'Get your horse' she shouted to me frantically. I lead old Ned into the boathouse as she closed the door behind us.

The rafters creaked and groaned in the ferocious storm wind; the thunder struck in a deafening roar. The boathouse door rattled continually but it was a relief to be inside. We stood at the door dripping, taking deep breaths, slowly calming down.

We were in the dark, just able to see the outlines of things 'We need to get out of these soaking wet clothes' she said with a gasp, but this was easier said than done. My clothes weighed a ton. They were clinging together and to me. Taking my boots off then pouring the water out, I knew they would need a good wash tomorrow, the salt would destroy them otherwise.

Stripped naked I hung my clothes over the wagons front wheel, 'I'll get the stove burning' I said as I headed into the wagon. The stove was primed ready to light and while fumbling for the matches I knocked them over, feeling around for them on the wagon floor.

Shivering in my nakedness in the dark, I grasped the single match I had found, 'Please' I said to the match in hope. My preparation skills served me well as the flames started to grow, and soon the stove was burning furiously, 'Are you coming in to get heated up?' I shouted out to the stranger, forgetting for a moment we were both stark naked. As she entered, I stared at her wet naked body, then bashfully I turned to get a blanket for her, 'Release the kraken' she said bursting into laughter, she was a very friendly girl indeed.

Waking to the sound of silence was bliss. The storm had raged for hours, keeping me awake into the early hours of the next morning. I had slept late, and Patch was starting to get impatient for his breakfast. Another calm after the storm, the sun shone bright, the wind was still there blowing the heat away. I'd never managed to feel properly warm since I first started this coastal route back in Stranraer.

Having a good stretch and a good look around I noticed a boat in the harbour, a pink rowing boat. The person on board had their back to me. Patch ran over to the edge of the water then stopped with just his paws getting wet, *Sara* I said reading out the name of the boat, 'Yes? good morning sleepyhead' came the reply with a smile.

The pink boat bobbed and rolled with the eternal motion of the sea, 'Come on then, jump in' she said. Looking around for a good excuse I nervously said, 'I need to go and get something from the shop'. She laughed out loud 'Have you not been to sea? Come on I'll look after you'.

Gripping the side of the boat for grim death, I slowly climbed in. The boat was moving like crazy, 'Right sit down quick, you are rocking the boat', she was being nice about it but her constant laughter was not helping, 'What' she said as she stood up, 'Just relax, move with the natural flow' she was making the boat roll from side to side, each roll getting the boat to a steeper angle.

Sitting down beside me she smiled then nudged me, 'You need to sit on that thwart, you can do the hard work' she pointed to the seat in front. Driving the boat backwards did not make sense at first, but it soon did. 'Just use the right oar, we are heading that way' she advised. Steering was easy, the same cannot be said about rowing for hours.

On the way back to shore a drum could be heard, 'Can you here a drum?' I asked. We both listened carefully, whilst scanning the banks of the shore, 'It's stopped I said, the sound of the sea and the wind blocked out almost all other sounds.

The sound of the drums returned, 'Look! Soldiers!' Sara said pointing to shore. There were hundreds of them marching towards Ballantrea. 'Move over' Sara said taking a seat next to me, 'Let's both row, I want to find out what is happening', I wondered to myself if Billy really was in the army.

By the time we got to the harbour the army had marched off into the distance, 'Let's follow them and find out why they are here' Sara suggested. Reluctantly I tagged along but we did not get far as the track out of town was barricaded. 'Halt' said one of the three guards, while the other two pointed their rifles at us.

Sara was not having this, 'What is going on?' she demanded. The soldier barked 'Be on your way'. Taking Sara by the hand I said 'Come, we can go around them in the boat at first light' I suggested. Sara kicked the head of a daisy, 'Ok, I'll go ask around and see if anyone knows anything' she said then headed off.

Giving up on her return I settled down in bed, turning the oil lamp off just seconds before the boat house door opened. Sara, I thought to myself smiling, as I fumbled for a match something landed on the roof. I froze on the spot, then it happened again, 'Patch' I whispered, he was the most useless guard dog in the world I thought to myself.

Once again there was a noise on the roof. Opting for a safe way to find out who was playing games I opened the secret hatch, leaned in then slid the bottom open, knife in one hand. I lowered my legs through the hatch, then somebody grabbed both of my legs then pulled 'Gotcha' came the bellow from below. My heart jumped back into the wagon almost leaving me behind.

Kicking my legs free I hastily hauled them inside before slamming the hatch shut. Struggling to breath I sat on the hatch, closing my eyes, trying to calm down. My hand was shaking the knife uncontrollably.

Bang! Bang! Bang! came the noise as somebody knocked heavily on the front of the wagon 'Is anybody home?' came the foghorn voice. 'Aye come on in' I replied trying not to show that I was fuming after getting the fright of my life. 'That's a nice wee dog you got there' said Billy, 'Yes he's my guard dog' I joked dryly as I lit the oil lamp.

There he was in all his splendor, Billy in his army uniform, 'Looking rather tucker in your fancy new togs' I said, Billy saluted before asking 'Have you got any of the good stuff? I am fair parched'. Giving a sigh I replied 'No', then paused for a few seconds to see the disappointment on his face 'How about something even better than the good stuff?' Pulling out the bottle of rum, his face lit up 'Oh aye, what is this you have?' Passing Billy the bottle I said, 'Get a glug of that down your throat'.

Billy took a sniff of the bottle's contents before taking a small sip from the bottle, then proceeded to smack his lips before licking them. Looking at the bottle in silence for a moment, 'Oh aye that is a mighty fine tipple', I was starting to feel quite smug. Billy had to be first at everything, but not this time. I sat patiently waiting for him to ask, 'Just you enjoy the last' I said, after swigging every last drop he finally asked, 'Ok what is this fine stuff' smiling I replied, 'It is the RUM!'

We sat in silence; Billy studied the now empty bottle. I could almost hear the cogs in his head turning, he was about to speak 'So how's the army treating you Billy' I interjected. 'It is the best, fed and watered, all we do is march around, they marched us all the way to London', he was more interested in the empty bottle. 'So why are you all here?, I will be needing past that blockade in a day or two', tilting his face to an angle, with a serious look on his face he replied 'Oh well now, there has been a bit of really bad stuff going on around here, CANNONBALLS', there was no controlling my laughter 'The army don't half take their cannon balls seriously' I chuckled, 'It's no laughing matter, there is a whole family of them' he said seriously. I stifled my amusement, unable to speak without bursting out laughing, 'There is about fifty of them living in a cave, all mad as the day'.

He was not making any sense, then it hit me, 'CANNIBALS' I said loud and clearly, he nodded in agreement 'Yes that is what I said, cannonballs. They are attacking people then eating them'. I didn't have it in me to correct him, between cannibals and his pranking scaring the living daylights out of me sleep would be scarce the next few days.

He went on 'There are troops coming down from the north in the next day or so, then we have them surrounded for an attack on their cave'. This information did not sit well with me, where was Sara? I hoped she had not done something stupid like sneaking past the armed guards, 'The sea hides the entrance to the cave when the tide is in, and when the tide goes out it is going to get wild' he said with glee.

Having heard enough for one night I asked, 'How was London?' in an attempt to change the subject. His face lit up 'Oh let me tell you this, it is a different world down there' he paused waiting for me to ask, 'How so Billy?' before he continued 'Well there are people from all over the world. One guy from Italy puts cheese and tomatoes on flat bread before cooking it, that will no catch on over here, but get this, they sit on the left-hand side when driving the wagon'. It was not something I had thought about, Patch sat on my left always. Thinking about it he was right, everybody sits on the right, with the exception of one woman who I had seen sitting in the middle.

Billy stood up to leave 'I will need to go before the guard changes, or I will be for the high jump' he said. As he got to the wagon door he turned, reached into his pocket, then looked at me as if thinking really hard. 'Here is more money for Ned, with a bit extra in case you get a chance of a bottle of rum' he said as he pulled out some coins then handed them to me, 'If I get an opportunity I sure will'.

First thing next morning I was woken with the sound of the boathouse opening, I felt for my knife, 'Who is it?' I shouted. The pleasant voice of Sara came back 'It's me Sara, can I come in?' still half asleep after an almost sleepless night I wanted peace 'Yes come on in' I said regardless.

Sara looked pale and upset, 'I could not sleep, these cannonballs are frightful, can I lay beside you?' she asked innocently. 'Come on then' I replied lifting the covers for her, in a flash she was striped to her bloomers, climbing in beside me, 'Hold me' she demanded softly. My pleasure I thought as we lay there holding each other tight, 'Do you always sleep naked?' she asked shyly.

Sleeping through to midday, I was awoken with shouts of joy as the boathouse door opened, 'It's my Dad' shouted in Sara. Slowly getting myself together before going out to pay my regards, the wind blasted down from the North. Just one windless day would be a blessing. Sara was at the far end of the harbour wall, waving like crazy, not knowing what to expect from her father I held back, opting to feed old Ned some oats, 'Ahoy me girl' called a voice, I spun my head around quickly, once more our paths had crossed, it was the captain.

Now this was an unexpected surprise, and by the look on the captain's face it was an even bigger surprise for him to see me, 'Ahoy Captain' I shouted to him. Putting his head down he pretended to be busy with the dock lines. As I was about to call out to him again, he raised his head 'Ahoy' he replied nervously, the guilt of being caught with a girl in every port written all over his face.

Sara leaped onto the boat to greet her father with an affectionate hug. I'm not sure what she would think if she knew she had a secret sister. It certainly was not going to be me that was going to wreck the father and daughter bond they obviously share, 'Did you hear about the cannonballs?' Sara asked the captain emotionally, 'There, there, me girl, it is all over, I watched from offshore as the soldiers locked them up' the captain replied. The news was welcomed that is for sure, 'Go tell your mother to get the water boiling, it's Lobster tonight me girl'.

We stood in silence until Sara was out of earshot, 'It is not as bad as you think, it just sort of happened, it was tearing me apart loving both of them, I could not hurt them you see' he said in a panic stricken way. There was nothing I could say; it was none of my business after all. I wanted to ask how many more ports the captain had visited, but instead I asked 'So Captain how much can you get me a case of rum for?' with disbelief on his on his face he replied 'It will be too expensive, how about a bottle as a gift. You will keep it to yourself aye?' I nodded in agreement 'Do not worry my friend, hook me up with a case, I'll give you the money up front'. Holding his hand out we shook on it 'See you later, the wife is waiting' the captain said before leaving to see his wife. Before he got halfway, the captain's wife came out to greet him with a warm loving embrace.

Sitting around bored for the rest of the day, I counted the money I had in my possession. I now had both amounts that Billy had given me, along with my share of the boaby's. It was more than enough for a case of rum. I was doing well. It was over half a year and I had only used half of the wages that Mr Wolf had given me.

Wishing to get back on my adventurous travels, I waited for news. The guards knew nothing, well that is what they claimed. When the captain appeared, he was carrying a smaller case of rum than expected, 'Ahoy me boy, a case of 12 bottles for you' he said. After paying him for the twelve bottles, I shook my money pouch in front of him 'How soon can you get two more?' I asked. The captain's eyes were fixed on my money pouch 'If you can be at Girvan harbour in fifteen days' time, I will have them, me boy'.

I cracked the lid off the case of rum then took out a bottle for myself then one for Billy before storing the case in the wagon's secret compartment. Billy would be paying double what I had paid. Trying the guards again I asked, 'Is there any news of when the way will be cleared?' 'The prisoners will be getting escorted out of the area tomorrow, then we might know' the guards told me. It was not much information but at least things were starting to move. Girvan was only a day's travel, but I would give old Ned two days just in case.

By noon the next day a large crowd had gathered with excitement, now sixteen soldiers were on guard. It was hours before the drummers began drumming. The crowd cheered. 'Sawney Bean's coming' shouted a young lad who was sitting on top of somebody's shoulders. Then two drummers appeared followed by a battalion of soldiers. What followed behind them was monstrous. There was two horse drawn carts both carrying large cages.

The crowd gasped as they saw the contents of the cages. At first it looked like hairy animals, then there was the realisation that these animals were actually human. The feral creatures were completely naked, their skin was covered in ground in dirt that almost looked like a covering of hair.

It was difficult to see much from the back of the crowd. I was hoping to sneak Billy the bottle of rum I had concealed in my jacket but finding him was impossible in the sea of uniforms. The shouting and jeering were getting louder as the convoy of soldiers approached the blockade 'Hang them!', 'Burn the witch!', 'Boo!', 'Murderers!', 'Let us have them!'

The woman to my left was waving an axe in the air, screaming 'Kill! Kill!' as tears ran down her face. Looking around me, I realised that everybody was armed, even the woman and children all carried knives, axes or custom sharpened implements, the men all had their guns cocked and ready.

The crowd started edging forward. Deciding not to join them, I took up a spot just out of the firing line. This was not going to end well if things got out of hand. 'Halt!' came the command the crowd halted. 'Give us justice for the loved ones that these subhumans have taken from us' came a counter command from somebody on the front line of the crowd. The crowd cheered. An officer shouter 'These things are prisoners of the crown. Justice will be dealt to them in the proper manner'.

The crowd started chanting 'Kill! Kill!', and the occupants of the cages started howling like a pack of wolves. This enraged the crowd more, who pushed forward until they were only a rifle length from the soldiers.

A soldier on horseback came riding past the cages, 'Now, now, settle down everybody. If it is justice you want, that is what you are going to get'. 'Yea!' came the cheers, with a barrage of whistles. 'Bring us twenty-six large stakes for tying the females to, along with as much firewood as you can carry'.

The crowd dispersed immediately to go and look for the requested items. 'About turn! March!' the soldiers were ordered. This was something I didn't want to miss. Grabbing a thick plank of wood that had been lying next to the boat house, I rushed after the soldiers.

The soldiers lined the bottom of a small hill in three rows of approximately fifty soldiers per row, and there were hundreds more running around building a bonfire at the top of the hill. The subhumans sat in the cages watching, and the six soldiers guarding them stood pointing their guns at the cages. 'I will take that son' Billy said to me. After passing Billy the plank I flashed him the top of the rum bottle 'Sorted' I said to him. His face lit up as he said, 'I'll take that off your hands as soon as I get a chance'.

The bonfire was one of the largest imaginable. 'Alexander Bean, Agnes Douglas and all your family. By the power invested in me, I find you all guilty of treason, murder and cannibalism!' At this the crowd let out a deafening roar of approval. The higher-ranking soldier waited for quiet before continuing, 'With God as my witness, the sentence will be death', the crowd roared once more.

The drummers both started a steady somber beat on their drums, which was the soldiers cue to start hauling the females from their cage. Some were just young children, and once tied to a stake they were propped against the unlit bonfire. My heart felt as if it was beating in time with the drums. Not a voice from the crowd was heard. The males legs and arm were stretched out then tied with rope that was then pegged to the ground.

The high-ranking officer held his sword high above his head, and as he did this the subhumans began howling again, more agitated this time. Quickly the sword slashed downwards to signal the start. One soldier lit the bonfire burning the females alive, while twenty-four soldiers cut off the genitals of all the males then threw the genitals into the fire. Suddenly the howls were replaced by frenzied, agonising screams. The locals too were screaming and shouting. The soldiers then chopped off the males feet and hands. One of the soldiers was being sick, the females voices stopped after a few minutes, the males however lasted a lot longer as they lay bleeding to death, once dead their mutilated remains were tossed on the fire.

The smell of the putrid burning flesh was unbearable. Nothing had prepared me for the horrors of this night. Walking away from the scene, the noise slowly faded, however the smell of burning flesh lingered on all night.

Back at the old wagon, I cracked open a bottle of rum and after taking a large swig I sat lifeless for the next hour or so. Realising that I had not seen either Sara or the captain, I wandered out to the harbour, but the captain's boat was gone. Walking along the harbour wall, my thoughts were of the young girls and boys and their terrible end. From the end of the harbour wall the bonfire was clearly visible in the distance. I took another swig from the bottle.

Billy showed up with a band of soldiers on tow. As they reached the boat house door I shouted 'Billy!' 'This way lads' Billy said to his troops. We met halfway along the wall, 'Here you go mate' I said as I passed him the bottle out of my jacket pocket, 'Nice one, here get a glug of this lads'. They all held out their own cups as Billy proudly poured, 'Oh that is the good stuff alright' one of them said. Billy turned to me 'You got one for yourself I see' looking down at the bottle sadly I said, 'Yes I did.'. There was nothing more to say about what had happened that night. 'Right lads money out if you want another snifter' Billy made his money back plus he had a good few drinks himself. By the time they left, I had sold them the half bottle that was left in mine for triple what it was for me to buy, then Billy handed me his money 'Same again pal' I nodded 'No problem, leave it with me' I said. It was not that I didn't trust Billy it was more a case of keeping my supply of rum safe.

WINTER

Two days waiting at Girvan was killing me. The constant coastal wind had an icy edge to it now, and there was no sign of the captain. I had lost track of the days but was sure he should have turned up by now. Lying down to sleep that night, I tossed and turned like I had done every night that week, the horrors of what had happened to Sawney Bean's family still fresh in my head.

The journey was a strange eerie one. All along the coast Ailsa Craig was visible. It seemed almost as if it was a floating island, following me as I went. Then there was the what the locals call 'The gravity brae'. Walking up it was made more difficult as we seemed to be going backwards, then when we stopped halfway up it seemed we continued to go up hill but never getting to the top. It was a great relief to finally walk the last few steps.

My rum supplies had all dried up. Billy and all the other soldiers had left Ballantrea the day after the atrocity, but not before buying the last ten bottles. 'Ahoy, me boy' came the call at last. I had a bottle out and took a much-needed swig from it before another word was spoken.

The captain watched me closely 'Are you okay me boy?' he asked, I nodded a *yes,* but I was anything but alright. The journey from Ballantrea to Girvan was a terrifying one. Passing the blackened hill where the bonfire had been played on my conscience badly. Trying to sleep with the thought of them possibly not all being caught, I had to get away from this coast. 'I could do with more rum. I will be in touch, if that is okay with you?' he looked around before answering 'Aye that should be fine'.

The signpost was for Ayr one way or Dalmellington the other. There was no choice but to head east away from the bitterly cold coastal wind, although that was not the only reason. Billy had once told me about family up this way, fellow travellers who we were feuding with, 'When I am King, all family must follow me. We will take over Ayrshire, ending this feud' I remembered Billy saying. He had finished off by saying 'Nobody remembers what caused the family split anyway'.

Once on the east side of Dalmellington, I realised that unlike following the coast I had no clue or knowledge as to where I was heading. The severe coastal winds had gone but it was still bitterly cold. Wearing all my clothes at once, with my long winter coat and a blanket wrapped around myself had made it bearable for now.

Still going forward towards whatever was ahead, my mind was telling me to head back to Ballantrea. Sheltering in that boathouse for winter would have been the cleverest thing to do, the horrors of that place however drove me on.

Up ahead by the side of the track three wagons sat. I opened my coat in order to make sure they knew I was ready for trouble. As we approached, three strangers walked onto the track blocking the way. Patch was going crazy, howling and for the first time ever barking. Putting my hand on his back to give him comfort startled him. Patch flipped his head back then sunk his teeth into the flesh between my thumb and index finger. 'Hello young man, he is a vicious one is he not' the oldest one said as he patted old Ned. 'He is a good wee guard dog' I replied half joking half wishing he was, 'Sorry to hear about your Pa' he said as he eyed up the wagon. Being unsure of the situation I opted not to reply.

'That is a terrible thing to happen to your Pa' he said trying to get me to engage in conversation.

The strangers seemed friendly enough, but Patch thought differently it would seem. Never trust somebody your dog does not like. 'Will you join us for the night, it is no far off dark' he offered, but I said 'The dog will not settle. I will be fine stopping just up the way a bit', Patch was still barking, giving me a perfect excuse not to join them.

Once Patch had calmed down, I showed him the bleeding open wound on my hand. After giving it a good sniff, he looked up at me, his wee sad face said it all. Nuzzling his head in for a cuddle 'Good boy' I said, he knew he had done wrong, I parked up a distance away from them but still in sight. Scouting out the area as I gathered wood, there was options available for a cunning plan. After building a fire between the wagon and them I waited.

As darkness fell the light from the fire made everything outside the fire light radius extra dark. *If I cannot see them, they cannot see me* I thought. After securing Patch inside the wagon we walked across the small shallow stream. Old Ned did not mind but the icy water froze my feet and ankles. After hiding the wagon, I headed up near the strangers camp, club in one hand knife in other.

Two of them sat next to the fire, the older one was gone, 'Where is he?' I whispered to myself, waiting there in silence, watching, 'where is he?' I repeated. A twig snapped behind me, and I spun around with my heart in my mouth. Nothing was visible in the darkness. A voice came from the strangers camp, 'let's go' it was the older one, as soon as they left the fireside, they were invisible in the dark.

It did not take them long before they reappeared at my fire. 'He is gone, he cannot be far, let's get him' said the older one as he kicked the fire embers sending sparks flying high into the dark night sky. He was right I had not gone far. The footsteps ran off into the distance. Quietly entering the icy water, I sneaked back across then quickly harnessed their horses to their wagons before leading them towards Dalmellington. A few minutes down the track I whipped two of the horses in turn, sending them tearing off at speed. The third I left at the side of the track. I hoped this would send them in the right direction.

Waking with a start, it was still pitch black. The two fires were still burning, 'We will get him tomorrow, that old horse cannot out pace ours'. Watching as they headed towards their wagons I heard 'Where are the wagons' two of them ran off down the track, 'We are going to get you' the other one shouted as he looked around into the darkness. 'Jock, we got one' came a shout, but the last horse took off down the track running.

Within a few minutes old Ned, Patch and I were on the move, using the glow of the oil lamp to guide us along in the dark. There was no point checking behind, it would take hours for them to find their wagons, and even longer to figure out what had went on.

The stars came out as we slowly walked through the night, the moon shone bright, the cold got colder, morning could not come soon enough, trudging on exhausted in this endless night.

Morning came, revealing a barren landscape, white with frost as far as the eye could see. There was nowhere to hide. Looking back to where I had come from, in the far-off distance was the edge of a forest, not only that the three wagons. Even at the speed of old Ned they could never catch us, that was unless we stopped, and I was desperate to stop.

Both myself and old Ned gave up the ghost at the exact same time, there was now no choice but to rest up for a few hours. There was nothing to be seen from this viewpoint, our pursuers could be anywhere. *A heat up with my feet up then we'd better get moving* I thought to myself, and after getting the stove alight, I sat there with my feet as close to it as possible.

Waking up slowly, then suddenly jumping up to my feet, I wondered how long I had slept. Rushing out, there was no sign of anyone, and more importantly it was still light. We set off at once, still exhausted, but with warm dry feet.

Before long there were trees in the distance, and the sight of this gave me a new wave of energy, 'Come on Neddy boy not much further now', I reassured my faithful friend. Before long the track was winding through the trees, but there was no gaps wide enough to fit the wagon between the trees, so we had to continue.

The sign at the first junction we came to said Dumfries 40 M, Kilmarnock 22 M. It's always warmer down south, and even with a day or two resting up we should be in Dumfries within the week I thought to myself. A horse and carriage tour passed by at speed, then a horse and cart and it was a great relief as this passage was far busier. We pulled in as the trees ended, I knew we would be safe here as long as the bandits do not spot us during day light hours.

Resting for just one night, we were on the move again. It was too cold to stay in one place for long and it was hard going. Old Ned was struggling with the hills, and the cold was starting to affect his old bones. It took two days to reach Kirkconnel.

Purchasing some much-needed supplies that included coal, 'It is good coal that son, straight out of the mine' the merchant said, and I believed him. I had watched the miners digging it off an expanse of open land. 'Does a mine not have to be underground?' I asked, 'Well usually, but this is an open cast mine' he replied. The expanse was pure black, as were the men working it. I parked up for two days enjoying the luxury of heat.

Poor old Ned, I knew it was best to get to lower land before the weather deteriorated further, and after purchasing another two bags of coal in Sanquhar we were on our way again. The track in front of us was downhill for a good few miles. This was a good sign, but the weather however was not so good. The rain started heavily, and before long it turned to sleet. Down the track ahead of us were trees that would give us some shelter from the elements.

The trees were still far off in the distance when it turned to heavy snow, visibility was down to a few feet, old Ned plodded on regardless. The wagon however was sliding from side to side, this would be trouble if we slid towards the banking. Patch ran around like a maniac, not a care in the world, excited to see his first snow, his thick fur keeping him warm as a layer of snow built up on his back.

At last reaching the tree line safely we parked up along the bank of the river. We had no choice as the track ahead sloped up hill, one false move and we could find ourselves taking a tumble into the River Nith. The snow kept on coming as dark fell upon us, we were stuck here until it thawed.

Lying in bed watching my breath as it exited my mouth as mist, my body was toasty warm with all my clothes on, buried beneath the blankets. My nose and chin however were so cold I could not feel them. The stove burner was out, and it was a massive effort to move.

It took only minutes to get the wood alight then topped off with coal, my face started to itch as the numbness left my nose and chin, Patch wanted out, poor old Ned needed feeding, I just wanted to stay next to the heat.

Opening the wagon door, Patch jumped out and disappeared into the snow, leaping up he appeared again, he loved it. The deep snow was just above my knees, and after feeding Ned, then a toilet stop I was back inside the wagon warming up again. It was going to be a long few days. After a big pot of porridge, it was time for a tot of rum to keep my innards from freezing.

Ten bottles of rum later I realised I was almost out of supplies and only one full case full remained. I would die here if I opened that case. Over the last few days the snow had slightly thawed by day then frozen by night, and now the top of the snow was a solid crust of ice.

Sitting eating my second bowl of porridge of the day I said out loud to no one in particular, 'That coal will not last more than today. After this bowl of porridge, I will chop that small tree down' I replied to myself, 'Then what, starve?' I will check the traps then catch a fish' I said, laughing at myself 'The traps have been empty since we got here, you are useless at fishing'. On hearing this I began getting mad at myself, 'I will show you' I said then stomped out armed with the axe and fishing gear.

Was there even fish around at this time of year I wondered, 'At least we are going to be warm with all this wood' I said to myself, 'Patch get away from that bush' he had been barking at it for hours, biting branches off with his razor sharp teeth, 'It might be food' I advised myself, sliding over as fast as I could I checked under the bush.

There it was a tasty little meaty hedgehog, 'Get some clay from the riverbank' I told myself. My hands went numb as I dug into the freezing riverbank collecting a large ball of clay, splatting it down heavily on one of the rocks, then bashing it flat with the butt of the axe, I know had a sheet of clay.

Sliding the axe under the bush, then hooking it around the hedgehog before slowly rolling it towards me, I said 'Do not look at it whatever you do, just get the clay wrapped around it then put it in the stove to bake'. With hunger pushing me on I had it wrapped in a flash, 'When the clay dries out just crack it open, the spikes and skin will come off with the clay'.

With the ball of clay in hand I slid towards the wagon, 'It is cruel, I know. I will probably kill the poor wee thing then not eat it'. An argument with myself was about to kick off again, 'Yes but you are starving, it is about survival'.

Panicking I slid down to the river, frantically washing the clay off hoping the hedgehog had not suffocated. As I pealed of the last of the clay I had nowhere to hold the spiky wee critter. Still curled up in a ball I just left it there, later on catching a glimpse of it as it disappeared under the bush.

There were enough oats left for a small bowl of porridge tonight then one in the morning. After that I was done for, and my only option was to take our chances on the ice laden track. As I watched the flames flickering on the stove, I asked myself out loud, 'Do you know your problem?' then answered 'Yes, you are my problem'. Laughing at myself before replying 'You have a bad case of wagon fever, just listen to yourself'.

With a belly half full of porridge, we set off on the upwards slope that led into the wood. Patch slipped banging his chin on the solid ice, 'You okay my little friend?' I asked but he was back on his feet before I got the words out, wagging his tail as he walked on. Old Ned would not walk unless somebody had the reins. This made keeping the wagon in a straight line even more difficult. The front of the wagon only slid marginally where as the back end was all over the place.

Once we were into the woods the track levelled off to a more gradual incline and the relief was immense. Exhausted, and still slipping and sliding around it was only the beginning of a long hard day. Everywhere the sound of water droplets splatting as they hit the ground could be heard, and the chill as a droplet splatted on my head then slowly ran through my hair. Looking up into the branches for signs of a thaw, then splat! A freezing cold droplet hit me dead centre in my left eye.

I felt joy as we rounded a corner to see in front of us that the way ahead was downhill. The back end of the wagon swung away to the left and hanging on I slid with it. Then it swung back to the right with such momentum that I was just a sliding passenger. My back was facing the edge of the bank, and knowing it was coming did not help me any. In the blink of an eye I was hurtling down the banking towards the river below, the left side of my face and head scraping across the ice as I plummeted, hands and feet scrambling to find a purchase to stop myself or even just slow myself down.

Feeling my right leg scuff against the trunk of a tree, I frantically put my right arm out to catch hold of the tree, but it caught me right on the elbow. The impact sent me spinning around, and I could now see the river zooming towards me. There was a thin ledge of mud that levelled out just before the river, and I hit it hard. The mud was solid, and the icy cold water rushed past my eyes as I lay there listlessly with my legs stretched upwards.

I was braced for the wagon to crash on top of me any second but the only sound I could hear was the rushing water of the river. Easing my body around so I was laying on the muddy ledge, I looked up the long steep bank. The back end of the wagon was leaning onto a tree. If old Ned walked forward one or two steps the wagon would be down here with me.

My face and hands were stinging, numb, hot, yet freezing cold, right arm throbbing with pain from when I had hit it off the tree. It was a desperate situation. Going back up was my only option, but crawling was impossible never mind walking. Rolling onto my side I dug my elbow into the ice, then one leg at a time I brought a knee up before digging my foot in. All I had to hold on to were the small indents that I managed to make. Over and over, elbow, foot, foot. The route was zig zagged as I went from tree to tree, having a short rest at each one.

The last part was the steepest, resting on the last tree, I was giving up, my body had no more, sleep was coming, as I rested my eyes, 'Where is Patch?' I whispered to myself, my eyes sprang open, 'The knife!' I shouted to myself. Quickly I had the knife in my hand and was cutting foot holds in the ice, this was far better than small indents, eventually reaching the top, crawling over to the front wheel of the wagon, grabbing the wheel, hauling myself up with every last ounce of energy before collapsing to the ground. It had all been for nothing.

My breathing was rapid, I was shivering like mad, as I lay there rolled up in a ball all I wanted was to sleep, the feeling of warmth swept over my body, so nice, so sleepy, the horses hooves and voices were not going to spoil my sleep.

When I woke, I was floating, the voices were all around, but I could not hear them. The next thing I knew I was that I was in bed, and the wagon was on the move. I must have fallen asleep. I was floating under an archway, blanking out again only to wake up in a large red room where there must have been a dozen candles burning.

KING FOR A DAY

Shiny blood red bed sheets covered my naked body. Running my fingers over them, I had never felt a fabric so thin and soft. The glow from the red candles barely reached the distant ceiling. Raising myself off the bed was a struggle, swaying as I tried to balance myself, listening as I walked slowly and quietly around the room. The only sound was the open fire burning fiercely. Beside the fire were two red velvet chairs, I had never sat on a velvet chair before and it felt lovely on my naked body.

The glowing heat from the fire felt wonderful, but drowsiness was taking over. I sat wondering where I was and who this magnificent room belonged to, the reality of this place was hard to fathom. More importantly where were all my belongings, were Patch and old Ned alright, where was my clothes and who had stripped me naked.

Opening my eyes, I could see between my knees that there was a maid, she was just feet away from me, she had built up the fire and was now cleaning the fire surrounds. Over at the bed another maid was busy making the bed, they both wore identical dresses, sleek black shiny material similar to the bed sheets.

It was almost as if they had not noticed me sitting there naked, 'Breakfast sir' a voice came from a third maid as she approached, laying a tray on my knees, then saying to the other maids 'Come girls', they scuttled out of the room closing the door behind them, it sounded like they locked the door.

Breakfast was the best I'd ever had, sausage, bacon, boiled egg, toasted bread, butter and honey, I scoffed it all down, then regretted it as my tummy felt so full and heavy. Just how long had I been here? When did I last eat?

With the curtains opened, the light shone in to reveal just how large this enormous room was. The sheer size of the windows themselves was astonishing. At the bottom of the walls were wooden panels, above the panels the walls were red, and each wall had a life size painting of some gent riding a horse in the countryside.

The room was majestic. A huge red rug covered almost all of the wooden floor. The silver candle sticks had been cleaned with new candles inserted ready for use. My clothes were nowhere to be seen. There were three doors in the room. Leaving the door that the maids used until I checked them all one by one, they were all locked but one, a fancy inside lavatory, as I sat making full use of the facilities, it felt slightly familiar, this room was a matching red.

The draft from the enormous windows sent shivers all over my naked body. The courtyard outside was empty and the long tree lined driveway was deserted. Off in the far distance were the snow peaked hills I must have travelled through, and after looking out for as long as I could tolerate the draft, I grabbed a bed sheet then sat myself down on a velvet chair.

The noise of the door woke me, the candles were all burning once more, 'Dinner Sir' a maid said as she handed me a tray. 'How long have I been here for?' I asked half expecting her to say weeks, 'Just last night, we bathed you, then laid you to bed' she replied, who all was we, the door locked behind her.

The bath was familiar after all, the memory of it flooded back, three maids had stripped me, then shaved the fluff from my chin before fully washing me in the bath tub, their giggles echoing in my head as I remember how the soapy water was not deep enough to hide my embarrassment, the only part of my body it seems that was not limp with exhaustion.

Soup, bread and a big jug of milk, it went down a treat. Five minutes after finishing, two maids entered, one took my tray then left, the other handed me a fresh tray. This time it was beef, carrots and potatoes all topped off with gravy. The maid stood in silence over at the side wall until I finished.

Struggle that it was, I finished the lot. 'The master wants to know if you want a job labouring for three months?' the maid asked as she took the tray, 'Yes' I replied before thinking too much about it, I would do almost anything to stay here 'Get a good night's sleep, you will need it' she said before disappearing out the door.

The hearty meal brought the sleepiness back, and as I relaxed beside the hot roaring fire, feeling my head roll to the side, I jerked up in the chair, realising I must have slept for hours. The fire glowed red with hardly a flicker of flame. Only three candles had been lit that night, and they had burnt down to small stumps. I was half awake in the large, quiet, dark room and there was nothing for me to do but go to bed where I lay tossing and turning.

Footsteps came running into the room in the darkness, the curtains flew open letting in dazzling morning light, the bed sheets where whipped off, leaving me laying there naked for all to see. It was the three maids 'Hurry, you need to be out at the front of the house in ten minutes if you want that work' one of the maids said as she pulled my under garments on. Porridge was being shoveled into my mouth by the oldest looking maid while the youngest looking one held out my clothes ready to put on.

The youngest one smiled at me 'I am Emily, this is Pamela and Susan' she held forward a shirt and winked, my trousers were up before I knew it, 'These undergarments are not mine' I said 'They are made from the purest of silk, do not let anybody see them' said Pamela. They were so light and delicate, it almost felt like wearing nothing at all.

Fully dressed and fed Emily grabbed my hand and we all ran through the house together, the maids all giggling. As we reached the open front doors, they pushed me out, then closed the doors behind me. 'You the new lad then?' said a man with a fully laden hand cart.

The man took off 'Grab that cart and get a shift on, the master will be home anytime'. It was a struggle for me to keep up, the cart was heavy, it also favoured veering to the right, 'Call me Dave' said the man. My mind was on the grandness of this modern styled castle, with its countless windows, the detailing was amazing. The crowning glory was the clock tower which had a large crown carved out of sandstone.

Dave supported the front of the hand cart as we worked our way up hill. 'This will do fine; we need a trench dug from here straight to the stream up there' Dave said as he pointed further up the hill with a spade. The earth was soft, and the spade made light of it, 'It will need to be knee deep' Dave said as he unloaded the hand cart 'What is it for?' I asked, Dave held up a piece of clay pipe 'We are building a water cascade, these pipes will bring the water from the stream'.

Halfway through the day Patch showed his face, 'Where have you been pal?' he was full of cuddles, 'Did you miss me buddy?' Dave came over to see him 'He is a lovely looking boy; he has been in the stable with your horse'. I had been too busy to think about these things, my mind was still in a bit of a stir, 'That is great news' I said now wondering if anything would be amiss.

As dusk loomed Dave showed me around the stable yard then into a huge kitchen. It was a lively kitchen to say the least, bread and a bowl of soup was dumped in front of us, 'They won't speak to the likes of us' Dave said, looking around the kitchen I noticed they never even lowered themselves to look at us. It was a relief to be out of there, the heat and the constant noise of chopping, pots rattling and dishes clink clanging together was just too much.

Dave walked me back to the stable that housed the wagon, 'Get your breakfast in the kitchen then head up to meet me at the cascade' Dave said with a wave before marching off. Tired from the days toil I retired to bed. Everything in the wagon looked untouched, but there was however a secret compartment playing on my mind. Getting out of bed I quickly opened the hatch, it was still there safe and sound, my precious case of rum.

Sunday was the only day off work we got, this would give me a chance to look around the vast grounds. The views were spectacular, the distant hills with their snow-capped tops, the riverside walks, the various ponds. The swans were particularly impressive. Five of them flew over my head then glided around in a half circle as they descended, just before there webbed feet touched the water, they pulled their wings vertical to act like brakes, all of this was done perfectly synchronized with each other.

Three ladies on horseback approached. In keeping with my place in society I kept gazing at the pond, they rode their horses right up close. One of the riders placed a hand on my head then ruffled my hair, giggling as they went, they all rode off, 'So you like to play games' I said, not that they would hear me for the galloping horses and wind whistling past their ears. I had been played, the three maids were actually ladies of the manor, not that I minded. My time in the red room along with the fact they probably saved my life more than made up for any fun that they had at my expense.

Later that night as I lay reading my book, footsteps sounded outside on the cobbles. The footsteps were accompanied by giggling, it was the three teasing maids or as they are better known in these parts, the Duke of Drum's daughters. 'Hello' said Emily, peering out of the wagon I said 'Hello ladies' with a smile. The three of them were dressed as maids again, 'Can we see inside your wagon?' Emily asked 'Come on in' I said invitingly.

In the time it took me took have a quick look to make sure nobody had been watching the three maids had made themselves at home, by means of getting into my bed with the covers pulled up to their chins. 'You three will get me hanged' I said to them, but they just giggled regardless. 'Please come and sit, tell us about your adventures' Emily said as she patted a small space beside her.

Knowing better did not stop me, there were always stories about deadly accidents that happened to workers in these kinds of places. The three of them looked so beautiful tucked up in bed, smiling at me with anticipation. 'Well one stormy night when I was in Ballantrea' I looked at them, they were far too innocent for that story, 'When I was in Ballantrea the waves were as high as a house, there was me and a pirate called the captain, nobody knows his real name. We were bobbing up and down in his pink boat' at that the giggles started, the story and the giggles went on into the night, 'I wish I could run away with you' Emily said bashfully.

An owl hooted, 'Right we need to go' said Emily, they all got out of bed, then curtsied towards me. I bowed respectively back, 'Why the outfits?' I asked, Emily smiled 'Nobody can see us if we are dressed like maids' they all giggled as they left, I was left wishing they would all run away with me, better still I could be the lord of the castle.

Next day a gun went off, it made me almost jump out of my skin, 'Sorry old chap' a snooty voice came, 'Mind your manners in front of the Duke' Dave whispered as a horseman rode up, 'Almost took your head of there, thought it was a pheasant', he probably meant peasant, was this a warning shot telling me to keep away from his daughters I wondered.

He turned his attention to Dave, 'Nearly finished I hope', I had never heard Dave stutter before 'Yyyes ssir, end of wwweek sir' he said. The duke looked it over 'See that it is' he said before heading off.

Before breakfast next morning Dave was standing waiting for me, 'That is you finished, you have to be on your way' he said before handing over a pittance, I looked at it in disgust, 'Is that it?' I asked, 'Food for you and the horse, plus full use of the stables', pure and simple, I had been ripped off.

Thornhill was only four miles away; the river walk went all the way there. The wildlife seemed to be coming out to greet me. A herd of about thirty deer, a slow worm, a common lizard, then for the first time ever I saw a white furred red squirrel. It was running along a branch towards me, then sat there at the end as the branch as it swung gently, the speed and agility was something to see.

Halfway to Thornhill a furry creature appeared on the riverbank. I had never seen the likes of it in my life, three feet long, one foot wide, with a thin long tail, from where I was standing no legs, feet or face were visible. Wanting a closer look, I edged forward with caution, was it wild and vicious? The creature disappeared into the river only to reappear as a slim sleek otter. I chuckled to myself for being silly, it never had occurred to me what a dry otter would look like.

My new furry friend swam along the river for around two miles, always keeping pace with me, stopping when I stopped, only disappearing when the bridge that lead into Thornhill appeared.

Thornhill was a nice little town. I did not stay long, spending my hard-earned money on supplies and a newspaper. April the first was the date according to the paper, over a year had passed since leaving on my adventures, this called for a celebratory drink of rum.

The rum made me feel sad and lonely for the first time. Being on my own was the greatest, there was nothing better than spending time with the wonders of nature, especially with Patch for company. Some things in life are for sharing though, like rum with a bit of friendly banter.

Before reaching Dumfries, I had the pleasure of the company of a young man called Robert. He was a nice although rather peculiar chap, 'You will find a place to park up on the Whitesands Dumfries, I will show you' he said, 'That will be good', 'My pleasure young man, there is often wagons parked there'. I was not sure what to make of it when he started going on about haggis, then something about a mouse, everyone to his own.

The bridge across the river looked rather new, 'Buccleuch Bridge and that over there is the old bridge' Robert pointed out as we crossed. After parting company with Robert, I headed towards the sandy river front, 'Hello, we have been looking everywhere for you, everybody has'. Looking over to the right there was a man standing next to three wagons, waving me over.

As I wandered over to him two other men came into sight, none of the faces looked familiar, they all seemed friendly, 'You never looked where I was though' I said, they all looked at one another, 'No we never thought to look there', we all laughed, then one of the wagon doors flew open, 'What is all the laughter about?' said a stout woman with a beard.

There is an old saying, 'You never forget the first time you see a bearded lady' this is true, she was a sweet woman as it turned out, 'Is that you is it? Have you got any of that rum we have been hearing about?' She was quick to ask, big mouth Billy, 'Aye it be me, and yeah I have the stuff if the money is right' The money was right, three times what I paid. The men bought one each, then we shared it between the three of us 'That is good stuff' one said as we partied into the night.

Reluctant though I was, the time had come to head back to Galloway. Gatehouse of Fleet would always be where I felt at home. Stopping off several times on the way back at Castle Douglas then Kirkcudbright. A storm was brewing by midday after leaving Kirkcudbright. Hoping to make it to a sheltered spot I knew of I pushed on. The storm broke, the rain was torrential, the wind gusted hard from the right, and using old

Ned as a partial wind break, we plodded on. Patch was taking it easy in the back of the wagon.

Just up ahead a man appeared from around a bend. It was hard to see through the heavy rain. As he put his hand up to touch old Ned on the head, I realised it was Mr Wolf, 'Hello Mr Wolf' I shouted to be heard over the storm, but he never answered. Walking towards me, he patted me on the shoulder, and the precise moment he did this, the ground began to shake. Up ahead there was an almighty rumble.

Old Ned tried to turn back as it rumbled on, and by the time it stopped and old Ned had settled down, Mr Wolf was gone. Leaving the wagon where it was, I rushed around the corner to see what had just happened, Mr Wolf was very fortunate indeed, then I realised, if Mr Wolf had not made us stop for those few seconds, we would have been under all this. There had been a massive landslide, trees, rocks and boulders double the size of the wagon. The way ahead was blocked, and we had no option but to stay there for the night.

Next morning, I was awoken early, the noise of horses, people chatting, and the clanking of pickaxes and shovels being used. Almost everybody that wanted to get past was chipping in doing their bit to get it cleared. There must have been fifty people working hard from each side. By late morning there was only the biggest boulder left to move. Five horses and ten men all giving their everything, 'Push!' shouted the biggest of men. There was no movement, I was almost flattened by this I thought to myself, 'We will need to chip it away with the pickaxes until its smaller' somebody suggested.

The boulder was big enough for four people to work at a time, 'Ten minutes each' said a guy with his watch out, thirty minutes later, the boulder was tied to the horses again, this time it shifted, and the crowd cheered wildly. 'Well done', 'Congratulations', 'Jolly good show', all types of people had helped, no matter their background.

Mr Wolf had not stopped when the land slide occurred. I felt it was a bit strange. I would go straight to the farm to thank him. From a distance the barn looked different. Getting closer to it revealed just how different it was, all that remained was a burnt-out shell of a building.

Waiting by the well was Scarlett, with her little toddler, Jamie. Her face was so glum. I was hoping for a better reception than this. Rushing over to me, she threw her arms around me tightly, lucky for me she did or those large breasts of hers would have bounced me off my feet.

We held each other for what seemed an overly long time, then I realised she was crying, 'I knew you would come when you heard the news' she said. I thought she was being a bit over dramatic about the barn, 'The little one's getting big' I said, 'The funeral is tomorrow' she sobbed, so that is why Mr Wolf was there last night, but that was not making sense, why had he not taken a horse, he could have made funeral arrangements closer to home.

Still holding each other when the door opened, Mrs Wolf's face appeared looking just as rosy as ever, her smile however was gone. Mark, I thought, the poor sod must have perished in the barn fire, 'Will you no come in' Mrs Wolf shouted over.

The first thing I noticed upon entering the house was a wooden coffin, 'It is all that rat Mark's fault' Mrs Wolf said, probably was I thought to myself, he paid the ultimate price though. 'Dad just was not young enough to run the farm after he got rid of Mark' said Scarlett, 'Got rid of him?' I asked, I would not think Mr Wolf would do such a thing, 'After Mark burnt down the barn, Dad thought it was deliberate, so he sacked him' Scarlett said, it seemed the more information I knew the less I knew.

Peering into the open coffin, there he was, Mr Wolf, the hairs on my arms and neck stood on end. I had seen him last night with my own eyes, 'Three months he struggled on for, then a week ago today we found him sitting slumped over the trough by the pig pen' said Mrs Wolf.

Standing in silence I tried to take it all in, Mark would be getting a visitor real soon. 'The landowner has given us another week to get off the farm' Mrs Wolf said, 'It is for the best, we need to move on'.

After the funeral I stayed at the farm. The week went fast. Little Jamie was a handsome boy, 'We are going to my Aunties' Scarlett announced, 'That will be good for your mother' I said. 'Can you fit our belongings in your wagon and take us?' she asked, 'Of course I will. What is happening with your livestock?' I asked, 'The pig and chickens are going to the butchers later today, we will need to find a buyer for the horses' she replied.

They never had much in the way of belongings. The wagon was still half empty. Mrs Wolf sat on the wagon looking after young Jamie, and Patch looked proud as he sat with them. Scarlett walked with me and the horses, 'Will you come visit?' she asked. Smiling at her before looking back at little Jamie 'Yes, always' I replied, she struggled with a glum smile. 'Please do not tell Billy', I winked at her, then said 'I will make sure he does not bother you'.

Leaving Dalbeattie I was now the proud owner of two beautiful horse, paying a bit over what they were worth. It felt right and fair, I probably would have paid even more for Dark Lord if Scarlett had asked.

Life was good in my fancy silk undergarments, not one but two great horses, then there were the bottles of rum that I would sell back at camp, not to forget my best pal Patch. There was no rush to get home. From Dalbeattie I would take the coastal road home.

On the third day I passed a wooden man that must have been over twenty feet tall. I had heard about these wicker men. The sound of Sawney Bean's family being burnt alive still echoed in my head. Old Ned walked faster when he was free from pulling the wagon. This was now a job for Cookie. We would not be stopping until Kirkcudbright, there was no way I wanted to hear the screams of some witch or human sacrifice, or worse I could end up being the sacrifice.

SUPPLY AND DEMAND

Strolling into camp felt good. The old ones still blanked me, with the exception of my Great Uncle Dougie, but I knew what he was after, he was a disciple of the drink. The younger generation gathered around, 'Have you got any of that rum' were the first words to be spoken, 'Yes if you have the money' I replied, 'Let's all chip in' throwing their money together, before passing it to me, 'Here lads six bottles, party on'.

Great Uncle Dougie had been holding back sheepishly, 'Have you any left? I am fair parched you know'. Pulling the second last bottle out of the case then showing him it 'This is the last one, might just keep it for myself', I proceeded to open it, pouring myself a drink, his face was a picture, 'Here give me your money' I said, 'You are a good lad' he said looking pleased, 'There might be more soon' I said, his loyalty was to the drink, that could be handy for me.

The mood in camp was good that night, 'So what has been happening around here then Alex?' I asked, 'Oh not much' he replied, I was not expecting him to tell me much, 'What do you know about Mark that was working at Wolf Farm?' I asked, taking a more direct approach, 'Mark is with your brother' he said, 'He is no brother of mine' I replied, he never had been I suppose, 'They have been breaking into old folks houses. Mark got caught, your brother sneaked off and left him' said Alex. *That sounds about right* I thought to myself.

Keeping my stay short I headed off to Creetown to check on Billy's Ma, then off towards Port William to catch up with The captain. On the way I stopped at Wigtown, 'Hello Elizabeth' I said as I entered, the lady in the book shop turned, 'Elizabeth does not work here anymore, did you know her?' it was more a case of I wanted to know her, 'A little, have you got anything new in?' I replied, 'We get new books in all the time, which genre were you after?', I was not sure to be honest, 'Just browsing, I like all sorts' I replied. After a while she pulled a book out of the shelf, 'You should try Frankenstein. It's by Mary Wollstonecraft Shelly, it's not new but you will enjoy it', the cover was red with gold writing, 'I will take it' I said.

That night I had the spot at Bladnoch to myself, which suited me fine. I was keen to get settled down to read my newest purchase. At first, I was not sure whether I had made a good purchase or not, why would I want a book of somebody else's letters? I read on regardless.

The port in Port William was empty, but there was no rush. I could stay here endlessly I thought to myself. After parking the wagon behind the captain's home, I ventured off down to the beach, with Patch leading the way enthusiastically.

On our return there was a man acting suspiciously, sneaking around the back of the captain's house. Spotting me he strode over in an aggressive manner, 'What are you up to?' he shouted angrily, 'What business is it of yours?' I asked, but this just aggravated him more, 'Get your things and be gone with you'. Walking past him I disappeared into the wagon, 'I am staying here until you are gone' he shouted, I ignored him, 'Did you hear me, I am not going anywhere', after waiting ten minutes I peered out, 'You still here then?' I said then laughed, 'You will be laughing on the other side of your face in a minute' he raged. I was getting bored of this ignorant idiot now 'When do you think my old pal The captain will be back?' I asked. That put him in his place, not that he was going to apologies for his dreadful behavior, 'So you know The captain. Just so you know I will be keeping an eye on you' he said before storming off.

There was no sign of The captain. As the days went by, I got into the routine of a daily walk into the port where I would sit reading the fascinating *Frankenstein*. It was on one such day that Evelyn appeared 'Hello stranger, I hear you met my sister', I was surprised to say the least. 'Your sister?' I asked trying not to sound surprised or give anything away, 'Yes you know Sara, do not worry we have known for years, it is not as far by land as it is by sea' she said smiling. 'Is he due back?' I asked, 'Yes back on today's tide'.

Evelyn and I walked back along the shore together, 'Aw they are beautiful, are they yours?' she said as she petted the horses, 'Yes had them a couple of weeks now, take a ride on Cookie' I said, with much excitement she was off along the beach.

Sara began boiling the water for the lobsters, 'I brought you a lobster, Mr Sharky told me about your run in with him' Sara said chuckling, 'He was just being neighbourly' I said chuckling with her.

As the water started to boil, the door opened, 'Ahoy me girl, we got company I see, welcome me boy' came The captain's voice, 'Perfect timing for dinner as always' Sara said as she plunged the live creatures into their watery death, 'After dinner can you use your wagon to shift a cargo?' The captain asked, 'Always a pleasure to help' I replied curious about what the cargo may be.

The port was deserted by the time we got there. On board the ship lay four long rectangular shaped cases, any larger and they could be used as coffins, 'Seventy-two bottles per case me boy', I liked the sound of that. 'I've only got the money for half a case, unless you let me pay the other half later' I said even although it was a big ask. How much trust did he have in me, 'It is yours for the horse I spotted my lass on down the beach', holding the pouch of money out towards him, 'Make it two cases for horse and the money, I will leave another horse for collateral', The captain scratched his bearded chin as he thought it through, 'You got yourself a deal me boy' The captain said with a big cheeky grin on his face.

The cases of rum were too large to fit in the secret compartment of the wagon. I only had one of the smaller cases left. If I only had known I would need them I would not have burnt them, filling then placing the case of twelve into the secret compartment I covered the two cases with a blanket, I would need to be on guard, with such a large cargo on board.

Sara said her goodbye with a big hug and a kiss, 'Thank you so much, I have dreamed of having my very own horse all my life', The captain had already disappeared on the night tide. Dark Lord pulled the wagon like a champion. Journeys took less than half the time than they took with old steady Ned.

Dark Lord pulled the wagon all day. The miles were passing quickly, even so it was nearly dusk by the time we reached Gatehouse of Fleet. Stopping of before reaching the camp I hid the two large cases on the bed, then brought the small case to the front for everybody to see. My reception was the same as ever, the older generation were waving one of the younger ones over.

I had hardly enough time to park up before a group of eager faces crowded close to me, 'Have you got any more rum?' a voice came, 'What not even a hello?' I replied as I opened the wagon door, making sure they had a clear view of one case in an empty wagon. The business was flowing well, even Great Uncle Dougie got his without prejudice, 'Four bottles please' I looked at him, then at the older generation. Apparently, I was not good enough to talk to, but they will buy my goods, 'No problem sir' I said. Their money was as good as anybody's.

Joining them around the fire I finished off the dregs of my own bottle that I started days before. It was a nice group, friendly, happy to share too, unlike the older generation who sat among themselves, holding their bottles in a tight strangle hold.

Before things got too lively, I asked, 'So what has been happening?', there was a bit of a hush before Thom answered, 'Mark killed himself up at the graveyard', the words 'Killed' and 'Himself' were good to hear, 'Anything important happen?' I asked hopeful of news about Billy, 'Nothing' Thom replied, the rum flowed well, the girls in the camp giggled constantly as they got tipsy.

Leaving camp next day, I felt there was too many eyes upon me although his could have just been paranoia. Although I was sure none of them knew about the rum, I had made a fair old penny or two in sales. I did not trust banks, they were run by upper class gents, upper class thieves if you ask me. Trusting people was hard. Finding out the hard why I could not trust my own mother left me with a lot of distrust issues.

A gun. If everybody knew I had a gun, they would think twice about trying to rob or intimidate me. There was a gunsmith in Dumfries, but it was a good two days trek even with Dark Lord's motivation and power maybe even three. They were a desperate lot at times, but were they desperate enough? Billy had left me to watch over everything, would they go against him I wondered.

Watching behind as I left town that nobody was following, the relief settled the paranoia to the back of my mind, for the time being at least. We were Dumfries bound but a detour to see Scarlett would work in nicely. Stopping off for a brief lunch gave me time to refill the small case. A hundred and thirty-two bottles left, what was I thinking when I purchased all that.

Before reaching Dalbeattie a couple of friendly faces were parked up by the burn, 'Well hello, Bob, Terry' I said as I approached. I had met them at tattie picking. According to Billy these two old wanderers had been to every town and village in Scotland, 'Well hello son, I heard you were out and about on your travels these days' said Terry, 'That's a terrible thing that happened to Billy, we were in Auchenbowie when we heard' said Bob. Terry shook his head in agreement 'Terrible, I hear that Brian is in Ireland now'. He does get around that Brian I thought with a bit of a silent head chuckle, 'Can I interest you lads in..' before I could say the word they Bob blurted out 'A bottle of rum per chance be it?' they were both grinning like Cheshire cats.

They bought one bottle between them, which they shared between the three of us, 'That is as nice as the rumors say it to be' said Terry, 'Oh it is that Terry' said Bob. At that they started acting rather suspiciously, they looked at me as if sizing me up before nodding to each other. I was on standby for trouble, their whispering really got to me, then Terry jumped to his feet. Reaching quickly into his pocket, one step forward and it's go time I thought as I stroked my knife handle, ready to whip it out my jacket if need be. Terry pulled out a pouch of money, 'How much for five bottles, a special deal for your old friends?' feeling relieved, the deal was done and dusted, still with a good profit margin for me.

As I approached little Jamie and Scarlett were out the front chasing each other around the garden, 'Hello' I said as I pulled to a stop. Patch took off to join in the fun, Scarlett bounced me with her bosom hug, before I knew it there was an extra set of arms around me, it was Mrs Wolf with her smile firmly back in place.

It was nice to feel wanted, 'You will be staying for dinner?' Mrs Wolf asked, before I had time to answer they were pulling me towards the house, 'Tell us of your travels, you never mentioned them when we last were together' said Scarlett. She was right I had not, the timing was not right with the loss of Mr Wolf. They listened intently while I told them an edited version of my travels, 'That sounds so nice, all that travel, fascinating' came the voice of Scarlett's aunt from the kitchen.

Leaving there was difficult. There was nothing and nobody nicer in the world than the Wolfs. Mr Wolf, the patron saint of travellers, well this traveller anyway. Before long I was on the coastal road to Dumfries, the coastal breeze made the hot day just right and after parking up for the night at Douglas Hall, I got myself stripped of for a naked refreshing dip in the sea.

After supper I noticed the water had receded of into the horizon, leaving a mudflat that I squelched on, around the corner was another sandy beach, I had noticed the wooden poles protruding the water earlier, now the tide had gone out revealing netting.

Going over to the nets to have a better look, there were what looked like three fish flapping about. Beyond that a solitary figure was heading in my direction, I splashed my way over slowly, timing it so we reached the nets at the same time. I greeted the stranger with 'Good evening', he returned the greeting with 'Hello, it's been a nice day today. I'm just collecting my supper', now at the net I could make out the fish, three tasty flounders, 'That is a handy way to catch them' I said, he tossed the first two into his pail of water, then tossed me the last one 'Have one yourself son', the fish landed almost in my hand. Not being able to grasp it quick enough it landed on the ground, flapping and flipping in an attempt to get away.

The stranger was in a chatty mood indeed, 'Have you been in the Piper's Cave yet?' he asked, 'Where is that?' I asked, 'Come, it is just around the corner' he replied, he was right it was just around the corner, 'I just live along the beach at Port Ling, now that is the Needles Eye' he said as he pointed to a natural rock arch formation, 'Why do they call it the Piper's Cave?' I asked, he chuckled at this before telling me 'Well many years ago a young piper went in with his bagpipes, and he was never seen or heard of again. Are you going in?' he asked chuckling, 'I'll go in so far, but I might need to fetch my oil lamp first' I replied, 'They say if you put your ear to the ground you can still hear him play, even as far away as Barnbarroch four miles away'. The information was music to my ears, now I knew that caves were not occupied by cannibals but were probably occupied with lost ghosts.

Not sleeping well that night, I was happy to be on my way in the morning. The drizzly rain continued into the afternoon. Parking up beside a loch with lovely sandy shores at the bottom of a hill the locals call Criffel, I set about fishing, Hours later I gave up, all over the loch fish were jumping, having themselves a good old time while teasing me.

Far and wide everyone knew of New Abbey, with the romantic old derelict Sweetheart Abbey. Rounding the corner, it was such an eye-catching ruin. In the grounds were five wagons, parked up in a circle around the campfire, 'Billy wants to see you' a gruff voice said. I did not like the look of him or this situation, Patch was barking deafeningly and very unsettled. Entering the circle, I said 'Where is Billy?' I asked. A hand pushed me forward from behind, 'I am Billy. So, you like strutting around in my cousin's wagon, do you?' he asked. William seemed to be a favourite family name, 'I got it, a case with six bottles, that dog is all bark no bite' came a voice from behind, 'Aw he is going to cry' said one of the others.

Laughing as menacing as they could, they took a bottle of rum each. Billy smirked as he handed me the empty case, 'Now get out of here boy'. Turning I walked away without saying a word, 'Yes get out of here' said the younger of the group as he kicked me in the behind. I gave him a good look over; I was not going to forget his face.

Leaving the village as fast as we could, heading for Beeswing, we were along the track a good distance before I spotted a good hiding spot. Now armed with my wooden club, I rode Dark lord bareback, it was no time until we were back at Sweetheart Abbey, waiting in the dark.

The group partied on at my expense, laughing and cheering the night away before staggering away to sleep in their wagons. An owl hooted in the silent night. The drink would subdue their minds, sleep would take them quickly. Still, I waited on for a good while just in case.

My silent approach was easy on the soft grass. Listening outside each wagon for any sounds, Billy's wagon was the first I entered. He was lying facing the ceiling with his eyes closed. The light from my oil lamp was turned down to the minimum so as not to disturb him. Standing over him felt good, I kicked him, but he never woke. I kicked him harder, this time he opened his eyes,

'What the...', I swung the wooden club into his face with all my might three times as blood poured all over him and splattered up the side of his wagon. After finding his money I was out of there.

I had watched which wagon the one that kicked me went into, but I thought better of it. Instead I took the five horses slowly and quietly, sneaking away like a thief in the night. I did not see myself as a thief though this was payment with interest.

Travelling through Beeswing then onto Dumfries was a nonstop journey. Changing horses frequently to maintain a good pace, first stop was the second loch at Lochmaben, Castle Loch, the fishing was fruitless once again.

I doubled back to Lochmaben, 'Excuse me sir what is the quickest way to Moffat?' I asked the first person I met. 'If you go left at the town hall there, then straight through Templand you will be there before the day is out' he replied, 'Thank you very much good sir' I replied.

He was not far wrong. I arrived at Beattock just before dark. Parked up on the hillside I could actually see Moffat which must have been only a mile away. I had completed the journey in two days. Billy and his gang of cutthroats should still be in New Abbey I thought to myself, I just need to find the legendary Frankie the horse trader.

Finding Frankie was easy. The first person I asked about him turned out to be him, 'Well I never, I have not seen you since you were a wee nipper' he said as if pleased to see me. He was a big rough looking man, with gold rings on every finger, 'Hello Frankie' I said acting like I had a clue who he was. I certainly could not recollect meeting him in my younger days.

Frankie turned his attention to the horses, 'You looking to trade these?' he asked, 'Yes if the price is right' I replied. He checked them over, paying particular attention to their eyes and hoofs, he did not look very enthusiastic, 'The thing is I am not really looking for any more at the moment', he was going to offer a rip off price, 'Fair enough, I will try the horse fair next month'. He started looking over them again, 'I could offer you a deal if you throw in a few bottles of rum', after agreeing a scamming low price for the horses, I returned the favour by scamming him on the price of twelve bottles.

Wishing not to cross paths with the horses previous owners I thought it best to head north for a while. It was a slow ascent up into the hills, levelling out only once reaching Crawford then Abington. A sign pointed to Waterhead; I was sure I had seen a sign for this place over near Sanquhar.

The sign had said six miles, but it seemed a lot more. As the wind blasted, it was six miles uphill. I never stopped at Waterhead, instead I braced myself against the wind, continuing on until we reached Wanlockhead. The village was very scenic, winters here must be ridiculously cold I though.

A little old woman was hobbling towards me, 'Are you lost son? Your friends are all down in Mennock Pass' she said. The word down was a joy to hear, the word friends put me on edge, turning back was a long trek.

As we rounded a corner the track went downhill steeply. The view was of a narrow pass through the vast hills and a small stream ran along the left side of the pass. There must have been at least twenty wagons all parked up randomly, there were loads of kids playing around, intriguingly all the men and women were in the stream.

Patch had ran off to chase other dogs, his silence was a good sign. The people from the wagons were all looking over, and the odd one would give a wave then continue whatever they were up to. 'Well hello again' said a rather cheery voice. It was a familiar face, a rather hairy face that belonged to Betty, 'Well hello again' I said smiling happily, pleased to be in the company of friends.

As instructed, I parked the wagon next to Betty's, 'So what are they all up to paddling about in the stream?' I asked, 'Oh they are not just paddling son, they are panning for gold, the purest gold in the world' she replied. I liked the sound of that, it sounded easier than catching fish.

A week later I had caught nothing. What a lot of bother for nothing I thought. Only one person had managed to fish out a small nugget of gold and it was now mine, along with most of the money. My liquid gold had been selling fast, I could not believe the seventy-two bottles I bought from The captain were all gone.

The nights in Mennock Pass had been lively. Betty had introduced me to everybody, Kilmarnock, Glasgow, Aberdeen and Edinburgh were where most of them had travelled from. The remainder came from places that I never heard of before, one was from Fort William, 'I like it in Port William' I said to him, 'No it is Fort William, way up north' he replied correcting me. 'We are all heading down Dumfries for the Rudeboy Fair, you are welcome to travel down with us if you fancy, everybody will be there' Betty said. I was not that sure if I wanted to see everybody, I was rather keen however to go to the fair, 'Yes that sounds good to me' I said.

The convoy of wagons travelled on slowly for days. Memories of last winter came to mind as we travelled past familiar places. As we passed Drum Castle, I kept an eye out for the three sisters to no avail. Sales of my liquid gold had slowed dramatically as money pouches now were drastically lighter. Each time we stopped for the night there were more wagons joining us. It was like a pre-planned convoy.

Dumfries loomed ahead of us. I intended to stay near Betty until I had seen the lay of the land. She would not put up with anybody with any kind of nonsense. She seemed to be the leader of this group, now thirty wagons strong.

RUDEBOY

At first light Betty was banging on the side of the wagon, 'Come on you, we need to get moving if we want a good spot'. It was a struggle to open my eyes as they felt like solid lead blinkers, 'Just coming' I shouted back. Looking out into the dark I realised it was still nighttime. Off in the distance, Dumfries glowed warmly as the gas lamps burnt the dark away.

It was still dark as we travelled along The Whitesands. There was a good few wagons there already with the occupants still sleeping the night away. 'This will do. We like to park as near the dock as possible' said Betty as we parked up in a neat row with the other wagons. Time for breakfast I thought although going back to bed was tempting, but the excitement and anticipation would keep me awake.

The day was overcast. It was not raining yet, but it more than likely would before the day was done. By afternoon the place was alive. Groups of youngsters passed by, lads all in their Sunday best, girls giggling away amongst themselves, all heading for the dock, families with their young ones, all walks of life.

I was around the back of the wagon when Betty said, 'You get yourself away down the dock, enjoy yourself son'. I was not too keen to be in such crowds, not on my own anyway, 'I will get changed first' I said before heading inside the wagon. After an all-over steamy cloth wash, I scraped the fluff from my chin, then pulled on my fancy silk undergarments. This was the kind of special occasion I had been keeping them for, strutting around the back of the wagon in them felt great.

The thought of the crowds was making me nervous, and after filling the small case, I took a large swig from a bottle of rum before placing it into my coat inside pocket. Dutch courage. Grabbing the case plus one extra bottle I was ready for whatever may come, 'Can you sell these, my last bottles of rum for me? Here is one for yourself' I said to Betty. Her face beamed the biggest of smiles, 'Of course I will son, you are a star'. It was a fair deal, plus it indicated there was no rum left in the wagon.

I headed back along the Whitesands first. Some of the wagons had their wares out for sale, others were locked up. The local businesses also had stalls set up. Everything you could imagine was for sale here. The most intriguing ones had signs outside, 'Meet the bearded lady', 'Meet the words shortest man', 'Meet the world's tallest man', 'Meet the words strongest man', then there was the tarot card, palm and rune reader. A familiar face came out of one of the wagons and waved me over 'I must say you look much better today than the last time I saw you' said Meg, 'I'm not usually keen on going to places where there's lots of people, but the Rudeboy Fair is a must'. 'Same here, but it's the event of the year, not to be missed', I laughed. 'Come on in and I'll read your cards', Meg said, and I followed her into her wagon. I'd never seen anything like it before. The wagon smelled amazing as there were many flowers, herbs and potions inside. Meg and I sat at the table where her tarot cards were. She shuffled one pile and set it down, then shuffled a second pile eight times then split it into three piles. She turned over the top card on the first pile and looked at me, 'The Devil', I knew you'd be an interesting one. You have lived in fear but there has been change. You need to be careful in the material world son, especially in your business dealings'. Meg then turned over the top card on each of the other three piles, closed her eyes, took a deep, slow breath and looked at me, 'The Ace of Pentacles shows you will prosper in business, money and other matters. The Three of Wands signifies travel and adventure. Now this is an interesting one, the Ace of Cups. Met someone, have you?' Meg chucked. I started back at her blankly, 'No, but I have been doing a fair bit of travelling and doing alright for myself lately.' Meg paused then said 'All will be revealed son, it's all in the cards. Here, have a sprig of mint or parsley to chew on, it's very refreshing,' then Meg stood up and said, 'You get out there any enjoy yourself son, but watch yourself,' so I stood up and left with a sprig of parsley in my pocket thinking about what Meg had seen in the tarot cards. I wasn't sure if I believed any of it, but Meg was very wise.

The thing I was more interested in was all the street food stalls, the fresh aroma of the food being cooked as I passed by was amazing. I started with a large pork sausage cooked on a wooden skewer, then a tasty fresh lobster boiled as I waited, 'Take your pick' the vendor said, 'Just any' I replied. He picked one out of the half-filled bath, holding it up for me to see before plunging it into the boiling hot water. Minutes later he pulled it out then slammed it on top of a large wooden barrel that was being used as a table. 'Ahoy me boy, you have met Mike my son in-law then'. There he was, as large as life, the captain. I looked at Mike, curiosity was killing this cat. Who was married, Sara or Evelyn? Another daughter was the most likely answer, as it was not that long since I was last in the company of the captain and Evelyn. I would have to play it cool for now, for the time being anyway. After a hearty enjoyable chat, I made a move. There was still more to explore. It's not that I was hungry, but I felt the need to finish off my dinner with roasted chestnuts cooked on the open charcoal fire.

There were several ladies with their breasts almost out, 'Would you like to be shown a good time son' one said, 'Come on son I will break you in if the price is right' said another. There was one that was far prettier than the rest, 'Cheap as you like sir' she said. Her neck had a large pus-filled scab down the left side, they were asking every male that passed. I strode on keeping my money safe.

Almost back at my wagon, a faint sound came from the distance. A band had started up in the dock area, and the closer I got the louder the music sounded. There was a proper party feeling ahead. The crowd was massive. Cutting through the small gaps in between groups of people was hard going, the band was still not in sight.

All the local inns and taverns had beer tents set up, serving up watery slops. The Coach and Horses the sign outside one said, in smaller writing at the bottom it said bring your own tankard, peering inside it was heaving. 'Right you, it is all your fault' blasted a voice I never wanted to hear ever again.

Turning around there they both were, my mother and stepfather, 'You never even turned up for the funeral, you are a disgrace' my mother screeched at me. I was not going to bother replying, they were not worth a second breath, 'It is all your fault, you should have been there for your brother'. Before I said a word, my stepfather swung a punch at me. Just in time I kicked him in the belly sending him stumbling backwards. I was not the little boy from years ago, nobody was using me as a personal punch bag. He got the message, stropping off in a mood with my mother going after him, 'Look what you have done now, black affronted so I am'. She was off before I got a chance to say it is me that should be black affronted at them. It did not matter what I did or how far away I was, it was always me that was in the wrong.

I walked over to a chestnut tree on the riverbank, watching the river flow by. Several swigs of rum later the problem of my parents was gone, and party mode had replaced it. The good old drink, the mood was festive around the smartest bandstand I had ever seen. I spotted some girls I knew from back home, Dawn, Melanie and Victoria, all dancing away like they had ants in their pantaloons.

It was my intention to go see the girls when I almost walked right past Billy's brothers, 'Hello there, how have you been?' asked Thom, 'Hello boys, you enjoying yourselves?', 'Yes that band are very rhythmic indeed' Alex replied, we all laughed. Having the company was nice, 'I thought I might have seen you at your brothers funeral' said Warren, 'He was never my brother, the loss of two of his lovers must have been too much for him' I said. This got us all laughing again.

Then it happened. I spotted the most beautiful angelic little face I had ever set eyes on. Not only that she was walking straight over to me. I was not sure if she was smiling at me or just smiling. I loved her smile. 'Hello' she said with a large happy smile on her face, 'Hi' I said back to her. She had left me speechless with her beauty. I was not sure about her hair, she perhaps slept on it funny or perhaps it just had a mind of its own, maybe it was one of them fashion fads, they never last. Instead of falling over her shoulders like normal hair, hers went up into the air. This did not matter to me, it meant I got a good look at her little cute kissable face.

I cannot for the life of me remember saying anything to her. Did her friend speak even? I was in a daze. The night drifted away as she chattered on and on. The only thing I remember her saying was 'I made this dress with my gran'. It looked new, a dazzling white dress.

She and her friend went for a dance with the others, I watched her dancing. For an age they danced, then walked off in the opposite direction, My heart sank, it could have been minutes, but it seemed like hours before they showed face again, and my heart raced once more.

She started looking chilly as the damp night air got colder. Noticing this I opened my big coat, put my arm around her shoulder to hold her warm inside. The feel of her little body pressed against mine felt like nothing I had ever experienced before. My nerves had got the better of me and I was terrified, scared even, 'What is this?' she asked as she produced the bottle of rum. Smiling up at me she was adorable. Having a sniff then a tiny sip before saying 'Oh that is nice', not that I was listening. Her wet lips were calling to me, 'Kiss us' they were saying, so I did. Her little rum flavoured soft lips felt so, so nice.

When it was time for her and her friend to leave, I was speechless like a nervous baboon. Watching her go off into the distance, I was left with all the things I did not say. They swirled around in my head, around and around, I wholeheartedly wanted to go say something to her, but I followed in a halfhearted way.

I had blown it like a fool, a first-class clown. Suddenly I realised I had walked away from the bustling crowd into a dim alleyway, 'So you like to smash people's faces in as they sleep do you' came a voice. I had made a point of waking him first, so no that was not true. Stepping backwards I felt something pressing into my back, it was the same guy that had kicked me, now thinking he was a big man with a wooden club in his hand. There were three behind, with four in front. Billy lit an oil lamp. I wish he had not as his face was such a pulped mess, two black eyes, a nose that pointed towards the left corner of his bulbous fat lips, 'Do you like your handy work?' he asked. Did he really want me to answer?

Seven to one, the odds were slightly against me, but on the other hand I had nothing to lose. Lunging forward I punched Billy slap bang in the middle of his face. He seemed to fly of his feet backwards, landing on his back but the oil lamp still in his hand exploded as it hit the ground. His screams were horrifying. I spun around grabbing the one that had kicked me, then started punching. He was defenseless as he hit the ground with me on top of him. For every punch he got in the face, I was receiving about five, they were kicking, punching and hitting me with their clubs. I felt them trying to drag me off their friend, there was no way I was letting go his collar.

Then came running footsteps on the cobbles, 'You'd better run' shouted Thom angrily. Looking up there was Billy and his brothers, 'He has had enough, you are mad picking fights on groups of people' said Billy laughing, 'Lucky for you we heard the screams and seen the flames' said Thom. 'Two down, five to go, I was still in with a chance of winning' I said laughing, the adrenaline was pumping, the pain with minimal, the body blows had all been cushioned by my thick coat.

I felt the liquid running down the inside of my shirt, 'Hold on lads' I shouted angrily, 'What is it?' Alex asked. I opened my coat, reaching inside, 'It's alright, I am only bleeding…for a minute there I was worried I had smashed my bottle of rum' I said laughing as I pulled the bottle out for a much-deserved swig, 'Here lads help yourselves'.

We headed back to the bandstand area. She was gone. I would never forget her. 'What are you doing fighting with that lot of low lifes for anyway?' Billy asked. We laughed all the way through my tale of New Abbey, 'Do you know who they are?' Billy asked, 'No but they will not forget me' I said, 'The one who's face you were smashing was John, your dads best friend' said Billy. 'I am not surprised at that' I said, 'Have you seen your dad yet? He was sneaking about earlier like a rat with his new wife and kids' Billy said. I might have walked past them for all I knew. 'Was he at the funeral?' I asked, 'He never bothered. You are better of sticking with your hermanos' he said. 'What is hermanos?' I asked, 'It is Spanish for brothers, I am bi lin gerry these days' he replied. I laughed, 'You mean bi-lingerie these days, don't you?' he looked at me curiously 'Oh aye yes that is what I meant, I am bi-lingerie in two countries'. I tried not to laugh too much as I explained 'Are you sure it is bi-lingerie?' he asked. I was not sure, knowing two words in a different language did not really count, 'I promise it means speaking two languages'.

Back at the bandstand, the mood had picked up. It seemed as if the towns folk were all getting a bit of courting done. I kept looking all the rest of the night, but my little white goddess was gone.

Waking around, I was a touch stiff in places, but I still felt good considering all the hits I had taken. There was one thing on my mind, well person that is. My head was still in the clouds. Suddenly, there was banging on the side of the wagon, 'Are you there? There is some riff-raff asking for you' shouted Betty, 'Just a minute' I shouted back. There they were, the seven riff-raff from the night before. I should have known this by the noise Patch was making.

There was an eighth person with them this time 'It is me, your dad Frank' the one at the front said, 'and' I replied, 'It appears you have done my friends here an injustice, all they want is their horses back, with an apology of course' he said. I sighed loudly, 'Let's hear the apology first' I said, I could see they were getting angry at this, 'Let us just have the horses then we will call it a day' he said, 'You pay your friends what you owe me dear old daddy, that way we're all sorted'. By this time Betty had her crew ready for action.

They were outnumbered as it was, then Billy with his brothers in tow turned up, 'Last chance for you lot to get out and stay out' Billy said as he took large strides towards them, the crowd jeered and heckled them as they left.

Breakfast was on my tummy's mind, the rumbling needed satisfying soon, 'Bring your tankard' said Billy. I noticed Billy and his brothers all had their tankards, 'Soup with a roll, proper scotch broth at that, my hermanos'. A tankard of soup, brilliant, 'Mind and wash your tankard out for the beer later, my hermanos' Billy said. This new hermanos thing was starting to grate on my nerves already.

Billy had the day planned out for us. I just wanted to relax and rest. 'First thing's first. I have a surprise to show you, my hermanos' we all followed as he strode out in front. When he reached a fancy looking wagon he stopped 'What do you think?', I was not sure what to think, was he referring to the fancy wagon or the terrible sight that sat up front with a newborn baby in her arms. She had dark wild unkept dirty hair, a hideous face that was made worse as it was covered in spots, 'Oh she is a good-looking wagon Billy'. Billy took the baby, 'Come see my little boy Billy and meet the wife'. Scarlett was right, he was not coming back to her.

The baby was a baby and I had no interest in it to be honest. I still felt bad about how Billy had treated Scarlett and little Jamie. What else was there to it? The anger was growing within me, 'What about the army?' I asked, then she spoke. 'He is not going back; he is with me now'. Her voice was a faked Glaswegian accent, very grating, she went on speaking, but I was too busy planning my escape, 'That soup is stirring, I need to go do one, I will not be long' I said as I left the company.

A grey start to a grey day, the clouds still hung low, fifty-one shades of dark grey. Mike was getting his fire started, 'Hello there Mike' I said, he looked up from what he was doing, 'Well good morning, good to see you again, the captain told me yours was on the house. It will be an hour at least' he said. Normally a free bit of food would be great, but today it was just grub, who cares, 'So how do you like married life?' I asked hopeful of answers, 'Oh it is fine' he replied, not as much information as I hoped, 'I will be back later' I said slowly walking off.

Once back at the wagon I went straight to bed, I wanted to sleep the day away. Perhaps she would return to the bandstand tonight. The moment I closed my eyes, a voice came, 'Come on hermano, we are going boating' Billy said. Turning my back on him I said, 'My guts are not right, just let me be for now'. He was now standing over me 'Cheese, that is what you need, cheese will settle your guts', he was not going to give up. 'Give me a minute' I said, then he started banging hard on the base of the bed, 'You should have pulled my Pa's old gun on them, the panel sticks sometimes', I rolled around to look just as a panel of wood fell off the bed. 'Look, this would have shown them!' Billy said.

There was not much to see, with the barrel of the gun pointing at my face.

The six of us marched along towards The Caul steps, 'Here get some cheese, they got all sorts at this farmers stall' said Billy, plain old cheese was good enough for me, it was nice fresh cheese, and it tasted great.

There were ten rowing boats all in different colours, and all had their own name painted on the sides. There was a pink one, Daisy, 'Three boats good sir' Billy said to the vendor, two to a boat. I was an experienced rower when compared to Billy and his four brothers. We rowed under the bridge arches, and we all shouted rude words at the echo, then screamed, this was followed with the blowing of large raspberries which caused a lot of hilarity.

We must have laughed the hour away when a whistle drew our attention 'Time to come in you lot' the vendor shouted 'Last one back is a big fart' Billy shouted then rowed like mad. Thom and Warren were last, Billy was not overly pleased that myself and Alex had beat him by a whisker, 'Come on you two farts' Billy said, helping his brothers out the rowing boat.

We headed back down to the bandstand and saw that a crowd had gathered. Instead of a band there was a strongman, 'Who will fight Hercules the world's strongest man?' the ring master shouted, 'I fancy that prize' said Billy. He slipped me a gold sovereign, 'Put that on me to win' Billy said confidently. Billy was standing up on the bandstand and before I knew it, the crowd taunted and laughed at him. Was Billy the only person that thought he could win?

I found a guy taking bets. The gold sovereign had been swapped for a penny, 'Hurry back for your winnings' he said mockingly. If the strongman tripped and fell, I would have some explaining to do to Billy.

It was show time. The strongman started showing off his strength and large, muscular physique, while Billy tried to show off with some fancy footwork and a bit of shadow boxing. The pair of them certainly were entertaining the crowd.

The fight was the funniest thing the crowd had ever seen. Billy pranced around taking swings at the giant he was fighting, but the punches that did actually connect were nothing but laughable to his opponent. Then it happened. The big guy punched Billy on the chin, Billy went down, unconscious, it was over so quickly.

After a feast of lobster followed by a large pork pie each, me and the lads were stuffed, 'Let's get some ale boys' said Billy. We went into the first beer tent, it was half empty tonight, 'Here I will get the first ones in' I said before reaching the bar, Billy heard me clearly but ignored me, 'Six of your best ale sir' he said to the bar keeper.

There was a guy talking just over my right shoulder, it cannot be I thought. Right enough though it was Robert, still ranting about haggis, 'Right lads we will have an ale in each tent, last man standing competition' Billy said. The ale was slops, but strong slops nonetheless.

Beer tent five, The Globe. There was only three of us left. Another five ales later we were standing in The Joker beer tent, just me with Billy. The night got a touch blurred around the edges after that, 'Hello Susan, Jane' Billy said to a couple of girls he knew. I think that it was one of them that Billy was dancing with soon after.

It was a good night. I could drink like a fish on a full tummy. A fight broke out over on the other side of the bandstand, 'I bet that it was over some woman' Billy said. My eyes had not stopped looking for the girl from the previous night, 'Never mind her, she's gone' the drink said to comfort me.

The beer tents were closing up, 'Everybody out please!' the calls came. I'd had my fill, 'Get another quick one' the drink said. Looking around Billy was gone, so was the band, everybody was gone except a few romantic courters.

The heavens opened; the rain was torrential. The last of the revellers ran off but I was too drunk to care. Fastening up my coat top button, then raising my collar, I headed slowly back to the wagon. On the way I passed a couple of drunks staggering around, one of them singing very badly at the top of his voice.

Sleeping long and hard into late the next morning felt good, the getting up however was not. The wagon was spinning fast, the dizziness in my throbbing head was in control, my tummy wrenched, it was empty. Food was the cure, the cure that I could not stomach.

The rain had stopped, everything was wet. The clouds were still grey, threatening more rain. Stepping out, Dark Lord had company, 'Good morning sunshine' the cheery voice of Billy said. I wanted to crawl back into the wagon, only to emerge no less than two days later, 'Morning' I said acting chipper, 'Nice horse you got these days, where is Ned?' he asked. My mind went to the captain, I should have paid him the money, 'Oh he is having a little break from towing the wagon, he is down at the beach relaxing' I replied, I was not sure what was to be said about Scarlett.

He turned his attention to the wagon; The boys are asking who is getting this wagon now I have my own one' Billy said. I had thought they might, 'Which one are you giving it to?' I asked, he looked at the ground then said 'Well that is a problem with there being four of them', it was a play, he was wanting me to offer to buy it, 'I would make an offer but I woke this morning penniless' I said. This was not true, but it was always best to stay sharp when doing deals 'She is yours for a case of rum' he said. Looking at the wagon, I would have paid him two cases, 'It is a bit of an old banger, twelve bottles then, just seeing as it's you' I said, shaking hands on it the deal was done. 'Take these two for now, I will get a box to put the rest of your bottles in' I said. Looking pleased with the deal he wandered off.

Mike was busy preparing to leave when I got to him, 'Is the captain still around?' I asked, he shook his head 'I have no idea where his is, where he has been or where he might be next' he replied. Mike did have a point; Evelyn was the only person that seemed to know when he was going to turn up.

Wagons had been packing up all morning. A large proportion had already left, 'Well that is another Rudeboy done and dusted, where are you heading now?' Betty asked. 'I am not sure, I might head back to Galloway with Billy and the others for a while, what about you?' I asked, 'We always go to Moffat horse show after this, here is your money' she said as she handed over a handful of coins along with the empty case.

Ready for the off, I headed down to catch Billy, then I remembered he was with his wife and kid, 'You heading back Galloway?' I asked him, but before he had time to answer, his wife butted in 'Yes we are, we are lead wagon', she said. Oh the joy, my plans of travelling with Billy changed the instant she spoke 'I am going the coastal route, here is the rest of the payment'. Before Billy had the case in his hands she spoke again, 'Just you get that over to me, after last night it will be a long time until you deserve a drink', pathetic as it was he did what she had told him to do. I thought she had finished talking 'Do you know where he was all night, he only turned up an hour ago' she said. I just shrugged my shoulders, and shook my head from side to side. I honestly didn't know where Billy had been.

DEAD MAN'S BAY

Watching as everybody dispersed with their wagons, apart from the horse manure, there was no sign that we were ever there. Two adventurous seagulls were scavenging for scraps of food and so was the young girl from the previous day. As she got closer a clear view of her face revealed a swollen shut eye, black as the night sky, 'Spare some change kind sir' she said. Life was hard for the young girl, how bad must it have been before she lived like this I wondered. Pulling a bottle out of my inside pocket, 'There is a quarter left if you want it' I said proffering her the bottle, Her poor little face lit up, her craggy smile revealing the mouth full of broken teeth 'Not half, anything you fancy mister?' she said as she pulled her skirt up to reveal her bone white legs protruding out the bottom of her dirty grey bloomers, 'Not today thanks' I replied, not any day if I was being honest 'Suit yourself' she said tossing her hair and walking off.

Standing at the bottom of a street named Bank Street was Robert. To kill some time, I wandered over to talk with him, but in the blink of an eye he had disappeared into one of the buildings. That was when I spotted the Royal Bank of Scotland.

The polished brass door plates gleamed as I walked up the steps, my heart racing at the sight of the classy establishment. The doorman had been opening the door as customers came in and out, not for me though. Instead he put a hand across to block my way, 'I think you are lost son' he said, turning around then taking one step away before turning again to face the door, 'It is a bank is it not?' I asked, although he may have had his fancy uniform, he was no better than me, he nodded me to enter.

Unlike the other customers I was left to open the doors for myself. Inside was so swanky, with its expensive looking fixtures and fittings. Looking down to the polished marble floor, it was so shiny, I could see my blurred reflection.

Several people looked at me in disgust as I stood in the doorway unsure where to go. I now had the doorman and a security guard on my flanks, the doorman pointed over to a desk where a young man stood waving us over, 'Take a seat, now what is your business today?' he asked. 'Can I exchange my cash for gold sovereigns?' I asked, this gave way to sniggering that quickly stopped as I started emptying out my cash on the desk, 'Have you two not go jobs to do?' said the bank clerk snootily to my chaperones.

The Clark busied himself sorting the money into piles, 'Do you have an account with us sir?' he asked, 'No' I replied, 'We can only do this exchange if you have an account with us sir, I could open one today if you would like' he said. It was a trap to get my money, but I left with three shiny new gold sovereigns, along with a bank account. Better than that now I had a status, I was a Mr, entering the bank as a ragamuffin was daunting, leaving as a Mr with a bank account I was a somebody. 'Good day sir' the doorman said as he opened the door for me, 'Good day to you good sir I replied, feeling quite pleased with myself.

There were two problems with the coast road. New Abbey and of course what to tell Scarlett. Telling her nothing would be wise, but would she want to know? As New Abbey appeared on the horizon, I got myself ready. The gun from the secret gun compartment was sitting on my knee, just for show. Sure enough, there they were in the grounds of Sweetheart Abbey, the same five as the last time I passed this way, along with the thing that was once married to the thing that was my mother.

It was all unwelcoming stares, except the one called John. He had had enough, and I could not blame him. Billy now sported a bandage on his burnt hand. They were a pathetic bunch, Betty was right, nothing but low life riff-raff. Aiming down the gun barrel I shouted 'Bang' as I pretended to shoot, then laughing away to myself I left the riff-raff to their own misery.

Stopping of at Colvend for the night, discussing my plans with Patch, 'If I go through the town after dark or first light, I will not see Scarlett' I said to him, he looked back at me, listening to every word. 'I should call in, it is only good manners after all', he refused to give any help whatsoever.

Just as I turned off Dalbeattie High Street, there he was, little Jamie with his unmistakable blonde curly hair. To my surprise he was with a gentleman to whom I had not been introduced, swiftly I returned to the High Street, if there was a new man in Scarlett's life I would not intrude.

Patch was no longer sat beside me on the wagon, 'See that dog' I murmured to myself, turning once more to head along the back street, there he was getting cuddles from everybody, making sure he had not missed any cuddles he went round each person two or three times.

The group of happy people were all pleased to see me, even Mike, 'Hello' I said to everybody, 'Nice to see you again' said Mike. Scarlett was now standing next to him, looking rather cosy. 'You two have met then?' Scarlett asked looking slightly puzzled, not as puzzled as me though, 'Yes dearest cousin, we are all friends with The captain' Mike replied, I smiled at my own silly assumption.

We travelled back to Galloway together, frustratingly he gave no clues to whom his wife was. 'So, you worked on my uncles farm, if you want you can work the harvests on my farm' Mike said. A bit of honest graft would keep me out of trouble. 'Yes, that would be good, where is your farm?' I asked thinking the location might help narrow down whom his wife was, 'Just outside Glenluce' he replied, almost exactly halfway between Port William and Ballantrea.

The wicker man still stood tall as we passed, pointing at Mike with my index finger as a local walked past us, 'He is a witch, burn the witch' I shouted, the local was not amused, I was in stitches with laughter. Mike laughed a little, perhaps a bit of a nervous laugh, that was one thing about Billy, he had a brilliant sense of humour, matched by my own.

Waiting at the outskirts of Gatehouse of Fleet was Billy, with his entourage, 'You took your time, did you not?' she said. Looking behind me, I pretended to look for who she was talking to, 'It is you I am talking to' she said, 'How is it going lads?' I said as I completely ignored her, 'My man is the king, show me respect you, I am the queen' she shouted angrily, 'Can you hear something boys?' I asked, we all laughed, but she did not, nor did Billy, 'Are you going to do something about him' she shouted at Billy, who was standing gormlessly wishing the ground would open and swallow him.

Billy wanted to talk business, but that was not going to happen when she was there. I kept my dealings quiet, only people that need to know need to know. She was a loudmouth; she did not need to know. What was Billy thinking? Spending the next few days in camp whilst waiting to get a private chat with Billy was excruciating, 'Our wagon should be over there, that is the best spot in camp' she bossily told Billy. It was where one of the older guys had their wagon parked, it was always on that spot. Billy did what he was told, moving the wagons around.

Finally, Billy stormed off into the woods after another episode of her ranting. After waiting five minutes before following him in, 'Nice day' I said to him, testing his fettle, 'She has got to go, I cannot take it, can you tell her?' Billy asked. It was difficult to keep a straight face, 'Can you not just go a trip, then forget to bring her back?' I asked, 'But she knows where we live' he replied, 'It will be winter soon, then in summer we will be on the move all the time' I said, he liked the sound of that.

The days in camp with Billy gone were long. If he could leave a lovely woman like Scarlett, dumping his dreadful new wife should be easy. With the last bottles of rum sold bar my own personal stash of two emergency 'for medicinal purposes only' bottles, I set off for Port William to see my old friend The captain.

There was no sign of the captain or Evelyn. With the wagon parked up behind the captain's house for shelter, I settled down for the rest of autumn, on into winter. Every morning, I would take a stroll into the village then in the afternoon I would ride the Dark Lord along to the Cock Inn. Walking back was essential after the first night of failed alcohol filled riding. The licensing act had cut public house opening times down to between 12 noon–2:30 pm and 6:30 pm–9:30 pm. This just meant spending from 2:30 until 6:30 in the snug playing cards with the regulars, Ali, Graham, Martin and Alan.

Port William was becoming my home. Only when spring had arrived did I have the urge to go anywhere. Even then I stayed, then one March day as I came home from the Cock Inn, there was smoke billowing from the chimney of the captains home.

Before I had knocked on the door a voice called out 'Come on in' it was Evelyn, 'Ahoy me boy' said The captain as I entered, 'I have been waiting with your money' I said, 'We always winter down in Devon' Evelyn said, 'It is warmer for me old bones' said The captain, 'Sounds nice' I said, although I really wanted to ask if it was just the two of them, 'It is that indeed, you looking for another bit of business are you?' The captain asked, 'Same again?' I asked in reply.

Back at camp sales were good, I did not want to be there though. 'Warren, any news on Billy?' I asked, 'Yes Alex says he is on his way back from Inverness' Warren said, 'Does Alex know how long?', Warren shrugged his shoulders then said 'No, but he left over a week ago, so not long now'. On the one hand returning to Port William was where I wanted to go on the other a travelling adventure was calling.

Mike's farm was surprisingly large, 'You timed that well, we harvest these new spring potatoes for the next two days' said Mike, 'The money will come in handy' I replied. Evelyn was approaching on horseback, but the horse was not Cookie. The closer she came the younger she looked, 'Meet the good wife, Cathie' Mike said, the resemblance to Evelyn was mind blowing.

The hard work felt good and honest, but the money was not so good, 'Come back next full moon if you want another few days' work' Mike said. I liked working, not for the money, for the self-pride, 'I will be here' I replied, some hard graft would explain were my money came from if ever questioned by the customs officers.

Billy was back in camp when I arrived, 'Come meet my lass, Alison' he said as he introduced a rather butch girl. She was not overly large, just a bit cuddly, but she was rather pretty for all that. A nice smile goes a long way. She fitted in well, one of the lads, she certainly drank like one, 'Have you got any gin?' she asked politely. It was something I had never thought about, branching out, 'I might be able to get some' I replied, as long as the government was putting a thirty percent excise tax and twenty percent sales tax on items, they would be good for my profits.

It was straight to business the next morning, somewhat subdued hungover business that was. 'We can supply all the inns and taverns in Galloway' Billy suggested, 'I do not think I can get that much' I replied. The risk was daunting. All my sales were kept to fellow travellers. Billy wanted to go further, it was a recipe for disaster, 'Nobody likes these taxes, everybody will benefit from our tax-free goods, happy lips are tight lips' he said. Billy's four brothers sat quietly, looking eager to be part of this enterprise.

It was a long morning. I finally agreed to his plan, this was under the agreement I would sell only to him, leaving him running the risks of dealing with outsiders, 'Do you want what I have in the wagon?' I asked. Billy's jaw dropped as I showed him the two cases, 'That is... what... you have been busy' said Billy, flabbergasted. My profits were down, so was my risk, 'I will square you up as soon as it is sold' said Billy, I knew that would unfortunately be the case.

The next visit to see the captain resulted in me purchasing two large cases of rum, a small case of twelve for myself, one bottle of gin for the lady Alison, one case of tea and a large sack of roasted coffee beans.

Rolling into camp, Billy and Alison were hard at it, shouting and bawling at each other, 'How is it going boys?' I said to Billy's brothers, 'Not bad, that pair are at it again, it will be all sweets and kisses tomorrow' said Warren, 'Our uncle John has gave up the travelling, the wagon is ours' said Alex, 'Maybe sort a wagon each once you get all this shifted' I said as they took a look at the new stock.

After a spot of dinner, I grabbed the bottle of gin. Billy and Alison were still at each other's throats, the brothers were all shaking their heads at me, 'No' said Thom. The devil was in me, banging on the wagon, 'Oh Alison, is this bottle of Gin going to drink its self' I asked, 'Just coming' came her reply, 'No you're not' shouted Billy, out stomped Alison in just her undergarments, 'Thanks very much' she said in a nice softly spoken manner.

Sitting around the camp fire with Alison, the brothers and a few others that were in camp, having a nice little quiet drink together, ignoring the sound in the background of Billy stomping back and forth in the wagon, 'Here he comes' said Alison bitterly, striding over then kicking embers into the air, 'What a big hardman' Alison taunted, silence fell on the group.

The only sound was of the crackling fire, it was an uncomfortable silence. Alison started rubbing her tummy, her face was screwed up, then she let it go, the biggest fart ever, it must have been saved up for at least a week, everybody burst out laughing, apart from Billy who was trying hard to keep in his foul mood, 'Watch that fire Alison, you might explode' I joked, keeping the laughter going, 'Give me a swig of that gin' Billy said grouchily, but with a hint of a grin on his face.

The months went on like this, buying whatever the captain had for sale, then selling in on to Billy. I helped out Mike at every harvest, 'Can you get more this time?' Billy always asked, 'It is too risky' the captain would say, Billy was fuelled with greed, but his brothers were happy, plenty money in their pockets, plus a new wagon.

Before I knew it, we were on route to this year's Rudeboy Fair. It was great to see some of the friends I had met last year, especially Betty with her convoy. I spent the nights watching but my mystery girl never appeared. On the Monday morning as everybody was leaving, I popped up to the bank for another exchange.

On the way back I pulled Billy to the side, 'This next load will be the last until next spring' I told him. He was not pleased 'We need this stuff, our customers all rely on us' he said, shrugging my shoulders I said, 'I will try but no promises, it will be the same every winter'.

Down at the port the captain had a random selection waiting for me, a large barrel of rum, a small keg of rum and a large case of stylish hats. 'Ahoy me boy, this is the last for now, see what next year brings' he said, 'What do you mean?' I asked, the captain chuckled 'You have bought the lot, these are my last', Billy was not going to be pleased.

Looking through the hats they were mostly too fancy or women's ones. The only one I liked for myself was a baker boys cap. It was so soft and light, made of pure silk, this will match my silk undergarments I thought chuckling to myself.

Alison chose herself the biggest most flamboyant hat of all. Billy's brothers all sported their new hats well, 'That is us out of pocket now' Billy said. There was nothing I could do or say to change this, 'My man will be back in spring, we just need to hunker down and keep warm until then' I explained to Billy, he paced about frustrated, 'I will think of something' he eventually said. I was not convinced.

By the time I got back to the port it looked like Evelyn and the captain had gone south for their winter warmth. After a few days spent at the Cock Inn, it felt like I never had been away, a nice little game of cards in the snug with the lads.

It was late one night after one such visit to the Cock Inn when I was trying to get to sleep, that the captains voice drifted in on the wind 'Ahoy me boy' it came, I ignored it. *The drink must be playing tricks on me again* I thought, 'Ahoy me boy' the voice came again, sitting up I listened, 'Ahoy me boy', I rushed out into the dark, to see an oil lamp swinging towards me.

It was indeed the captain, 'Come son, we got work to do' he said as he turned then rushed back to his boat that sat in the port, the drink got me onboard, then two minutes out to sea the drink decided to desert me. The night was wild, what was I thinking, the captain seemed to just skip and dance across the deck, I on the other hand, held on tight to the mast for the whole journey.

With all the wind, and the constant spray of sea water smashing into my face, the rain and darkness had left me almost blind. How the captain could navigate when I could not even see the fingers on the end of my hands was unfathomable.

As the sea calmed a little the captain let out a roar 'Ship ahoy me boy' he said. There was nothing that I could see until was banged into it side on. The captain was so swift on his feet, throwing a ropc onto the shipwreck before clambering onto it himself, 'Stay there' he shouted. Seconds later a large case was hanging over the side of the ship 'Grab this me boy' shouted the captain, I realised I had just become one of the captains wrecking crew, highly lucrative, highly illegal.

We worked hard in the dark, the boat was full along with the rowboat that the captain always had on tow, 'Just about done, me boy' was the call before he started throwing the rest of the ship's cargo overboard.

Although it had taken hours, the dark of the night still hung over us. Ten minutes later 'Anchors away, me boy' came the call. Taking an oar each, we rowed to shore with the first load of pilfered goods, 'Grab an end, me boy', and we rushed up the beach in the dark carrying a large case between us.

Suddenly it got even darker than dark as the wind dropped, 'Just lay it down here me boy'. I had to have a seat on the case for a breather, the captains footsteps stomped around in the dark, and the familiar sound of shells cracking under his feet echoed eerily.

Then as the captain lit a lantern, I realised I was in a cave, a cave with bones and skulls on spears that protruded out of the ground, 'Do not worry me boy, they been here since the caveman days', the skulls were small, children's skulls, my hatred of caves grew 'Bone Cave, they call it, nobody ever enters' he said. *No wonder* I thought.

Fifteen rowing boat loads later we were done, just in time to see the sun rise and signal the start of a new day, 'Let us get busy, me boy', I looked at the captain. 'Are we not done?' I asked, 'All this jetsam needs collecting' he said as he pointed along the shore.

Thirty-one crew members bodies along with the rest of the ship's cargo filled the deck of the captains ship by midday, 'If you look aft side you will see the ship, me boy, on the rocks of Ross Island'. Looking behind us there it was, with just the masts visible above water, with it now being high tide.

We were heading for Garlieston. 'The ship would have been heading to Kirkcudbright' said the captain. Other boats were now on the scene, Garlieston dock was crowded, 'Ahoy, were there any survivors?' the captain asked an official in uniform. 'Not yet, how many have you got?' the gent replied, 'Thirty-one plus some cargo' the captain replied. His hand was hanging strangely, almost like he had injured it, 'We will take it from here' the gent said as his men unloaded the ship. A rest was all I was interested in at that point.

Exhausted beyond belief I sat in a tired daze watching the captain. His hand was fidgeting nervously, the fly old dog had something in his coat pocket, 'This is payment for thirty-one bodies. My men will load your ten percent of the cargo. If only all men were as honest as you' said the gent, the captain was very humble, 'Just doing my duty for these poor souls' he said. We sailed of towards Port William in silence.

Back on dry land it was an effort to make it back to the captains home, 'Now you get some sleep, me boy, we got a lot to discuss', he said with his hand still fidgeting at that pocket. Patch looked like he had slept all night, and he lay there letting out a large yawn as I clambered into bed fully dressed.

Lying in bed exhausted, desperate to sleep, my brain was fighting it. What was in the captain's pocket? I wanted to know everything, the plans to sell our bounty, the reward for collecting the dead, there was a fortune in Skull Cave.

After two days sleep, I finally emerged, half expecting the old dog to be gone. It was a pleasant surprise to find him in his home with the fire blazing, 'Ahoy me boy', he beamed when I walked into the parlour. The first thing I noticed was the fancy little trinket box which looked very out of place on the raggedy old wooden bench.

The box was made of shiny wood of wonderful graining, imbedded with gold, 'The key is here' the captain said holding out a small gold key, 'Is that pure gold?' I asked him. He smiled 'Sure is me boy, open the box', the key turned easily, the box was lined with green velvet, 'A pearl necklace and a diamond ring' he said. 'It must be worth a fortune' I said, 'Alas not as much when we sell through a fence'. He was right, fine pieces like this were rare. We would hang if we were not careful.

The captain set sail for Devon a few days later with Evelyn by his side. The cash and jewels were his, the cave full of goods was all mine, along with the rowing boat that the captain had thrown into the deal.

OUR MEG

The aroma of burning coffee beans filled the wagon. The warm smell was pleasant, a homely kind of smoke. Our ten percent of the rescued cargo was going up in smoke, it burned well. The saltwater had ruined everything apart from a case filled with twenty-four bottles of sherry. My deal with the captain might not have been such a good one.

The days were getting colder and the coastal wind was relentless. Going to sea in a little rowboat was daunting but entering Skull Cave at night alone was a terrifying thought. After a few trial attempts I mapped my journey.

The cliffs hung high above, with millions of seagulls all perched on the smallest of ledges or swooping up and down on the windy drafts. Their constant noise blocked out the sound of the sea. This part of my journey was safer than my nighttime return would be.

Timing was everything. The tidal current helped push me towards Ringdoo Bay, and it was there that I waited for the tide to recede. At low tide I entered the cave. I was on edge, jumping at every little sound, the water dripping off the walls, the waves whooshing onto the small stretch of beach.

My own shadow made me jump several times as I moved in front of the lamp It was an awesome sight, fifteen rowboat loads, all piled high in the cave. Moving all this on my own was going to be impossible, especially with limited visiting hours.

Halfway through sorting the goods into perishable and non-perishable, the sound of the waves started getting louder, I had spent most of the night in the cave.

I could only watch, praying that the rowboat would survive getting knocked against the rocks, I would need to be back in that rowboat as soon as the tide had changed, otherwise I risked being seen.

Loading up with a sack of coffee, a case of tea and a keg of rum I set off into the night, using the lights that shone dimly in Garlieston as a reference I rowed to the far left. An hour or so later, the lights of Isle of Whithorn appeared, correcting my direction I headed north west.

My hope was to land on the shore at St. Ninians Cave, and lucky for me I did. There I waited until first light before setting of on the last part of my journey. The wind was against me all the way and by Monreith I was going nowhere. The tide had turned once more, and it was a struggle not to get smashed into the rocks.

The tiresome wait in the blustery wind at Monreith was the last straw, I would need help. Eventually the tide turned once more, and after securing the rowboat on the beach across from the captains home, I headed to straight to bed. Patch had other ideas however, and after a feed he took himself for a walk down the beach.

There were a few extra wagons in camp that winter, 'Billy is down the Rusty Hole' said Great Uncle Dougie. The Rusty Hole was the nick name of The Royal Tavern, so named as it was a complete dump, the roughest watering hole in Galloway.

Apart from the old timers everybody seemed to be there, 'Come and have a dram' shouted Billy as I entered the Rusty Hole. The ale was questionable at best, and the air was reeking of farts mixed with body odour and farm smells. Alison sat with Billy and his brothers. A new face was at the table and I had taken a dislike to him before I had time to even sit down. It was his weaselly look with the shifty eyes, 'Who is this?' I asked Billy, 'This is John, you remember his dad from the fair' he replied, I did remember punching the shifty rats face in.

I kept my business to myself, 'These lads are our new gang' Billy said introducing the five young men at the next table, they looked alright apart from John who now was Billy's little creep. Nothing good would come of having him around.

The drinks flowed well, and the mood was light, but this was about to change. A group of rough looking young girls had been drinking at the other side of the tavern, now they were getting rowdy, 'Well hello girls' Billy said. That was it Alison was on her feet in an instant. The four girls never stood a chance as Alison started throwing punches furiously. Her language was colourful enough to make a sailor blush and it took four men to hold her back as the girls made their escape.

Then it was Billy's turn. The verbal abuse raged on for ages before finally Billy laughed at her. Alison punched him square in the face, then stormed out, 'She loves me really' Billy said, returning to the table with the drinks, 'I only went for drinks, can a man no say a kind hello these days?' we all laughed. It was not funny, 'You need to sort her out Billy man, you're the boss' said John menacingly. *The nature of Alison and Billy's relationship was no business of his* I thought to myself.

Billy looked unsettled and suggested 'Let's get a few drams up the road'. The walk to The Lyver Inn was a bitter cold one. The rain was just turning to heavy snow and it was good to get back inside. 'Hello again girls, sorry about that, can I get you a drink to put it right' said Billy, the girls looked at the door uncertain of how to reply.

I stood by the fire getting warm as Billy took over drinks then promptly took a stool at their table. Before long the girls were laughing. John the rat sat beside him, but every so often he sneaked a look over at me.

I left them there, trudging my way back through the snow to my wagon, just in time to build the fire up for the night, coffee beans with a thick layer of damp tea leaves, a slow burner that warmed until morning.

The camp was dead when I looked out the next morning. My footsteps from the night before zigzagged a path across camp. There were no such footsteps to Billy's Wagon, they had both stayed out all night.

My porridge was interrupted with frantic shouts, 'Help! Help! Everybody help!' as small boy was running around camp, 'Come quick, she is dead' he shouted as people started appearing. A few of us ran after him, it was not far before he stopped then pointed to the ditch, 'The lady' he said. It was Alison, frozen to death with only a few hundred yards left to go. I must have staggered past her last night.

Alison was a great loss, everybody in camp liked her. The funeral wake was a silent affair. Billy blamed himself, we all blamed him, except his new best pal, John the rat, 'It was not your fault Billy' John kept saying, but it was. Billy was a buffoon.

Billy and John had sneaked out of camp in the middle of the night without a word to anybody. 'Right lads can you boys get me down Brighouse Bay in five nights time?' I asked Billy's four brothers, 'Yes, is Billy going to be there?' asked Alex. I hoped Billy would not be there, more importantly was that John was not there, 'Probably not son, but he will show up soon, I am sure of that' I replied, 'Will we bring that lot?' Thom asked, indicating towards the new faces, 'Just us, keep a lamp burning at just after dusk, I will be arriving by sea'.

Three nights later I landed at Skull Cave with an extra oil lamp for comfort. The journey had left me frozen, with fingers so numb I could not light the lamps. After five attempts I gave up, my brain was struggling to think straight too.

After struggling to cut the yarn that held the wool fleeces together, I kicked them around to form a bed on the sandy cave floor. Cutting another bale of fleeces open, I hauled all of them on top of myself, they stank to high heaven. Lying there in my wool cocoon, I was shaking like a leaf as I was so cold. Breathing my warm breath onto my hands felt good, but the numbness lingered.

Gasping for air I awoke, suffocating in the wool, frantically I tried to get the fleeces of my face but there was too many. I had to crawl out. The relief of feeling the cold air on my head and face felt invigorating, my body felt like it was in an oven.

The cave was dark. I was not alone. There was a face staring at me, a child's face. As I rushed out of my cocoon, the sound of running footsteps left the cave. On my first try the oil lamp was lit. I looked around but there was nobody but me in the cave, and the sea blocked the exit. There was no way I was sleeping in a cave ever again.

The heat from the two oil lamps and a small fire of coffee beans with tea leaves soon took the chill out of the cave and it was now bearable. Before dawn broke, I wedged the rowing boats nose as far in the cave as possible, then filled it with the first load of goods.

Most of the day was spent moving the goods to the front of the cave. The tide had gone out then returned once more. Digging in the sand was easy but the problem was that the hole filled with sea water. Burying the cases of alcohol was not going to work.

As I sat on a small rock I hit upon a cunning plan. Scraping the top few inches of sand into a large pile before making a makeshift wall approximately two feet high, thirty cases fitted into the space, a single case high. Once the sand had been shoveled on top it looked natural, and after hanging one oil lamp near the front of the cave, I checked over my handy work before setting off for Brighouse Bay.

The distance was not far, but far enough for the icy wind to start biting at the bones in my face and hands. There were two spots of light in the bay, wisely I chose the lowest one hoping it was at beach level. Instead of the expected four brothers with their two wagons, there were nine wagons comprising of the two wagons plus seven wagons belonging to Billy and his newfound followers. I was not pleased.

Billy organised the men, the rowing boat was empty in seconds. 'That is a good load, is there no drink?' Billy asked. I had to make up my mind quickly, give up the cave with all my goods or share, 'There are a few bottles, I will take your brothers with me to get them' I said, John stepped forward 'I will go with you' he said. Billy was about to agree with him, 'No there are enough rats in the cave' I said directly to John.

Staying in Skull Cave with a fire burning while the brothers took turns in twos to row back and forth from the bay to cave. On the fifth return, Thom had been replaced by John, 'Billy said Thom needs a break' he said. I wanted to punch him, perhaps his corpse would like to be buried here in Skull Cave.

The tides made it a longer night than it needed to be, it was breaking dawn when we arrived in the bay with the last load. John struggled to row; he was a useless little rat.

All nine wagons were almost full, 'We will set off after breakfast' Billy informed everybody. A sleep would have been more welcome, a strange inaudible sound was heard, 'Can you hear that?' asked Billy, we all listened, 'There it is again' Billy said, one of the new faces started shouting 'Look, look over there', he was pointing along the rocks that lined the bay.

It was Alex waving like mad with Thom was sitting screaming next to him, several of us ran towards them, Billy out in front, he was almost leaping from rock to rock. Billy took out his knife then severed the beast in two. Thom had passed out; the moray eel's head was still attached to Thom's knee. Billy bent over to rip the head off when a voice behind me shouted 'No, do not rip it off, you will rip his knee to pieces', Billy looked at him 'What am I meant to do Paul?', Paul rushed over, 'If you wedge the jaw open I will deal with the second row of teeth'. It was a monster, and it's razor sharp teeth had almost removed Thom's knee cap. It was a gruesome sight.

A couple of sticks were used for a makeshift stretcher. Thom was still out cold when we placed him in the back of his wagon, 'He will need a doctor' Paul said as he bandaged up the wound. 'Can you and Alex take him to the witch doctor?' Billy asked me. I looked at the rest of the guys, 'Yes of course' I replied. I did not want to leave my cargo with them, however nobody else would know where Meg lived 'He will need more than witchcraft' Paul said. Billy scowled at him 'Don't be daft, she can do more than that' he said. There was no better doctor in the land than old Meg.

It was going to be a long two-day journey to Meg's home, 'We need to hide some of this cargo. What were you pair up to anyway when Thom was bitten?' I asked Alex, 'Crab fishing. Thom was pulling a crab out of the water when the eel jumped out at him' he replied.

The first woods we passed were good enough for me. We dumped just enough of the cargo for me to get into the bed, 'I will take first sleep, have you got your lamp ready?' I asked, 'Yes, is Thom going to be alright?' Alex asked. 'Old Meg Merrilies will sort him out, we will travel all night if we have to', the quicker we got there the better, Thom was sweating in a fever already and did not look in good shape at all.

It was not looking good for Thom, he was ranting hysterically and beads of sweat covered his face, his hair was soaking wet. There was an odour coming from Thom's wound that set off alarm bells, the pungent smell of an infection flared his wounds, the smell of death itself.

The track to Meg's was quite well hidden and it was seldom used, unless you were looking for Meg you would not find it. She lived miles into the Galloway forest and was rumored to have once been a member of the travelling community but that was before I was born.

A beautiful young girl in a white dress answered the door at Meg's house, her blonde hair shone bright in the winter sun,

'Well hello again, put your friend on the table' Meg said with her back still facing towards us. 'Is that coffee I can smell?' Meg asked, there was no way she could smell it all the way from the wagon, 'Go get some coffee beans' I said to Alex thinking it was a hint, only to realise it was me that must be stinking of burnt coffee.

Alex entered with a whole sack slung over his shoulder, 'Give them to my niece Emerald, she will get the brew on' Meg said. Thom was delirious now, and as Meg prodded his wounds, he cried out in pain then laughed as if enjoying it. After a good prod and a sniff Meg announced, 'It will have to come off'. Alex looked at me, not quite sure what she meant.

We sat by the fire while Emerald boiled the large knife and realised that Meg was going to use it to amputate Thom's leg. Emerald set up a series of smoking herb burners around Thom, 'That will numb his pain' Meg said. We watched Emerald as she spooned a thick black liquid into Thom's mouth, 'They say my bonnie niece is spitting image of me when I was that age'. I nearly choked on my coffee, Meg was a strange looking old witch doctor, as old as the hills. Her eyes glazed over with the blindness.

Meg handed me the knife, 'Right son you need to do this as quickly as possible' she said, I was not prepared for this. Alex was looking squeamish already, 'You need to hold him down with all your might' I said to him. Meg's instructions were precise, it was all I could hear as I focused on cutting the flesh back from the bone, I felt faint as I started to saw at the bone.

Once I was done taking Thom's leg off, Meg with the help of Emerald packed the wound with a herbal compound of wet mushy vegetation, 'This will keep the chance of infection away'

Meg said, then she went into a trance, humming loudly as she chanted in a strange mumbo jumbo language.

As I washed the blood from my hands Meg wrapped up the leg, then passed it to Emerald, they never spoke. Emerald took of out the house not returning for some hours, 'She is a good girl, deaf and dumb since birth. She is learning to be one with nature' said Meg.

Thom looked terrible, like death warmed up, two days it took before the fever left and another day before he regained consciousness. Emerald cleaned his bandages twice a day, and now that he was awake, she spoon fed him soup. 'He is going to be just fine' Meg said. Alex and I did not think he was going to be fine about having his leg removed. We found that out as soon as he noticed.

The next few days Thom sat staring at his leg, well the space where his leg should have been that is. He never spoke, and he only ate his food if Emerald fed him. 'He is fine to travel. Did I hear you say you had some wool fleeces?' Meg said. It was worth a lot more than that, we had been fed and watered for almost a week or more, 'Go get the two fleeces, a bottle of port and a case of sherry' I said to Alex. Meg was sufficiently pleased, 'Give him one spoonful of this in the morning and the same at night before bed' meg said as she handed Alex a jar of the unknown black medicine.

It was a long trek out of the Galloway forest. Thom refused to come out of the wagon. 'Billy is going to make him stay with Ma, he won't like that', said Alex. 'I will have a word with him, the old timers are always there in camp, Thom should be fine there' I said. He would be a burden, unless he could show his worth he would get dumped with his Ma.

Parked up at the edge of the Galloway forest for the night we gathered wood for a fire, Alex produced a long branch, 'Can I borrow your knife? this will make a walking staff once the branches are trimmed' he said, Thom carved away for hours, it was a staff to be proud of. 'I just hope he uses it' I said. Thom had not spoken or left the wagon all day. After feeding his brother and emptying the slop bucket Alex joined me at the fire. The heat was fierce on my face while my back felt frozen in the night chill.

It got too cold not to keep moving. Taking it in turns we travelled through the night, only stopping for food the next day meant we arrived back in camp by dusk. There was nobody lurking around in camp, but all the wagons were there, 'They must be down at the inn, I will not be long' I said to Alex.

The boisterous roars of laughter as I approached the inn got my back up. While Thom was at deaths door they were partying away without a care in the world, 'Get yourself over here, the drinks are on me' Billy called as I entered. 'I am not thirsty; I just came to tell you we are back' I said. 'Come on, we are celebrating selling all our goods' said Billy, I was not too pleased to see the whole inn partying on my money, 'Good, I'll have my money in that case' I said. Billy laughed, 'We have all agreed to invest the money, we have fifty barrels of rum coming' said Billy, his sidekick John sat that close to Billy it looked almost like he was cuddling him. 'We are all going to be rich' said John, I swung a left hook smacking him on the chin, knocking him out.

Storming out of the inn, I had nowhere to go. I was fit to drop. It was going to be almost impossible to get my money now. Stomping off I left town heading towards Mike's farm to collect Patch, 'Fifty barrels at two hundred bottles a barrel, ten thousand bottles, minus spillage plus what they would drink would leave seven thousand five hundred bottles to sell' I said as I went over and over the maths behind this investment.

The farmhouse was in darkness when I arrived, a night in the barn was going to have to do. The straw was a great as insulation, sleep came swiftly. I slept like a log for the whole night, feeling totally refreshed by morning.

As I stood at the barn door watching Patch play in the field with the captain's granddaughter Eden. I wondered if he even missed me. Eden spotted me first, 'Who is that?' she said to Patch, who stopped running then pointed his nose high up into the air. A split second after looking in my direction he was on the move, and at high speed he came tearing towards me. He was going too fast, I braced myself just in time as he crashed into my shins, causing me to struggle for balance 'Hello my wee pal, did you miss me?' I said whilst petting his main of neck hair.

After a hearty breakfast at the farm, my little companion and I got moving. Dark Lord was going to be hungry but there was plenty of grass to eat. I had left him for far longer than I had intended, it was a full day's walk. The sleet showers that blasted into my face were torture, and I sought refuge in the Port William Inn so I could get heated up by the fire, with a few drinks to warm the blood of course.

It was a quick run along to the wagon. The fire was lit as quickly as I could manage, then I got feed of oats for Dark Lord. I searched for my oil lamp, 'Oh no I left it is in the cave' I growled at myself as I remembered the mysterious face in the cave looking at me.

I was not going back to Skull Cave if I could help it. I spent my winter days in the Cock Inn. The rowing boat was either still there or gone, that would have to wait until spring, it was the same faces at the inn every day.

Entering the Cock Inn on one extra blustery day it was Lauren that greeted me from behind the bar, 'He is in the snug' she said. Lauren was a nice girl, a real dog lover. I had to watch Patch did not sneak off with her. I looked around the Inn for jokers before pushing the door open, 'A small rum was it you wanted?' said the inn keeper looking rather pleased with himself, 'It is good stuff' said Ali, 'Cheers' said Allan, I reluctantly tried a dram, I had been in the day before, so Billy must have been sometime late last night or first thing this morning.

I drank it over in one, 'Which way did they go?' I asked, I was sure they had not passed by me, if they did, they must have sneaked by in the dark, 'They headed for Glenluce an hour past' said the Inn keeper. I ran in the opposite direction than they had went, back for Dark Lord, then rode after them like the wind.

There was only one track to follow, and I came up behind them in no time, 'Well hello, fancy seeing you here' Billy said. I was sure he knew where I had been staying, 'You got some money for me?' I asked. John was trying to avoid eye contact with me, 'We sold forty barrels, we split the profits once we get the last ten shifted. Your share will be the smallest, you never did the work after all' Billy replied. John disappeared around the opposite side of the wagon from me at this point.

I positioned Dark Lord in there way forcing them to stop, 'We need to talk about this' I said dismounting Dark Lord, 'Look it is for the best that we keep investing, we have a hundred barrels coming in a months' time' said Billy trying to talk me around, 'I want double what everybody else gets, then my investment back in full after we sell the hundred barrels' I said. Billy was not overly happy 'The rest of the gang will have something to say about that' he said, 'So you are not the king?' I asked questioning his authority, 'Come here you' I said to John, 'You are going to hit me' he said keeping his distance, 'Just get here, have you got a problem with my deal?' I asked, John looked at Billy, 'It is up to Billy' John replied.

John would clearly say something different as soon as I was gone, 'How is Thom?' I asked, Billy shook his head from side to side as he looked down at the ground, 'Not great, he is a very sad boy now his leg is gone' he replied, 'We left him at his Ma's' John said. This deserved a punch, but I held back, 'Am I talking to you?' I asked, I would visit Thom soon.

SMUGGLERS

The captain and Evelyn had not arrived back yet. They must be back soon I thought. I could not wait any longer as I was lacking funds. If I spent any more money I would be down to my precious savings, my gold sovereign.

Stopping of at Wigtown I purchased my next book 'The Pirate' written by Walter Scott. It felt like the right book for the position I was finding myself in. *Billy better have some cash for me* I thought.

Billy's Ma was awfully pleased to see me, 'Hello son, I am glad you came. Thom has not eaten or been outside since he arrived' she said. 'I have a new book I could read him' I suggested; Frankenstein would be a bad choice of reading material under the circumstances.

Thom lay with a cover fully pulled up over his head, 'How is Thom doing these days?' I asked, there was no reply, but there was significant movement however to signify he was awake. When I had finished the first chapter of the book a muffled little voice came from under the covers, 'Can I come with you' he asked. The answer was no, the travelling life was hard on the fittest of people 'Let me see you walk the length of the village first, then we will sort something out' I said. I never expected him to even try.

Back at camp there were more new faces with four more wagons and finding space for my wagon was not as easy as it once was. 'Squeeze in here' Great Uncle Dougie shouted to me. 'More new recruits, this is going to end badly' I said to Dougie. 'Word is spreading round the whole of Scotland, that does not bode well' he replied. Billy was with a group of strangers, with John hanging on to every word he said.

As I approached the group, they looked my way 'You are okay then, we were worried about you when we woke to find you gone' one of them said, I pulled out my knife as I recognised him from back in Ayrshire. 'Calm down everybody, we are all friends here' said Billy as he stepped in front to keep me back, 'You got your wagons back' I shouted over Billy's shoulder.

Billy pulled me to the side 'What is this bother all about?' he asked, I proceeded to tell Billy all the ins and outs of our first meeting up in Ayrshire, 'We need them, one hundred barrels is a lot to transport in one night' Billy said. He was right of course, we needed as many hands as possible, if anything we needed even more.

There was a week to go before the shipment arrived at Carsluith. *I will spend time along the road at Creetown* I thought, waiting for me was Thom. 'Watch this' he said with staff in hand he hopped his way up the street then back again, 'Come on then, I have a job you could help me with' I said.

The road to Brighouse Bay was blocked off with a barrier. 'We need to search your wagon' one of the guards said. I wasn't worried as there was nothing illegal inside my wagon apart from a few wool fleeces. 'Where are you going?', I was reluctant to tell him anything, 'Just travelling around for a few days' I said, 'Don't try to be smart, we need to know' he shouted, 'Just getting the lad out the house for a few days I replied calmly. The guards both looked at Thom who was sitting cuddling Patch while looking sorry for himself.

A few miles on we stopped once more, 'Well hello Robert, so you are a customs and excise man?' I said upon recognising him, '"We'll mak' our maut an' bre our drink, We'll dance, and sing, and rejoice, man, An' monie thanks to the muckle black De'il, That danced awa' wi' the Exciseman' he replied before letting us through.

I set to work with a good length of rope making a slipknot. Thom took of across the bay surprisingly quickly when he realised what I was doing, 'You are not putting that hangman's noose around my neck' he shouted looking terrified. I was laughing at him, the thought of hanging others crossed my mind, not him though. He stumbled over landing on the soft dry sand. Helping Thom up into a sitting position I slipped the noose around his waist then tightened it, 'There we go, come I will show you' I said as we headed back to the rowing boat.

Throwing the other end over a sturdy looking tree branch, before tying it to the front of the rowing boat, 'When I pull this end you will go up, then you can swing onto Dark Lord' I said then started hauling like mad, he was heavier than he looked, 'Ride him a few steps, keep going, stop' I instructed, the boat was now floating around in the air, I quickly secured the rowing boat to the back of the wagon.

We then spent the night inside keeping warm with a bottle of sherry each. I want to travel the whole of Scotland' Thom said, unless we all chipped in money for him it would be impossible. 'You will need to learn some skills first. You might do better with that stupid fishing rod than I ever did' I said laughing.

I had slept on the wagon floor, with wool fleeces under and over me, I was sweltered in there, ill prepared for the shock of the bitter cold outside next morning. The road was clear, with not a customs and excise man in sight.

It had taken two days to get here. *It would take that to get back* I thought. 'Can we go to camp?' Thom asked, I had to take him even if I did not want to, 'Yes why not' I said, it was on the way after all.

There was an eerie silence when we arrived in camp, only the old timers were there, 'Dougie, where have they gone?' I asked, he looked around before answering, 'They all pulled out this morning, there is trouble afoot' he said. He was right, the customs and excise were onto us.

There was no sign of Billy or the gang on our journey to Creetown the next day, 'You get some practice with that walking pole, Billy will be impressed' I said to Thom. His ma was watching as he hurtled down the street and back, 'Oh you two have been busy, well done both of you, come get a bowl of soup, I've got fresh rolls just out the oven' she said, We did not need to be asked twice.

The sky was filled with glistening stars, the moon was full, and visibility was almost as good as it was in daylight. I could see for miles in all directions, any ship travelling along the Solway coast would be easily watched by the customs and excise officers. The sea shone a rippling white with the reflection of the moon, the air was biting cold.

Thom insisted he came along, 'You drive the wagon. Once loaded hide it behind your Ma's' I told him. We arrived at the meeting point just as the ship appeared around the point, 'What is he doing here?' asked Billy showing his annoyance, 'What is he doing here?' I replied as I pointed to the toddler being held by

John. 'Ah that is our insurance against being caught by the law, it is the lairds lad' said Billy. I could not believe my ears, 'It will get us all hanged, who had the stupid idea to kidnap a child?' I asked. Billy looked at John then walked off.

It was a climb to get down to the beach. Billy was organising the men, 'Wagon's filled first then the cave, once the wagon has three barrels on board the owner goes to deliver to his allocated customer' he said, 'Yeah' the men cheered. 'You can deliver to the Cock Inn he knows you are coming' Billy said to me.

Six rowing boats from the ship were now coming towards us. The tide was also on its way. I grabbed one of the four ropes that hung down the face of the cliff. As soon as the first barrel hit the sand, I quickly tied a barrel hitch knot, then yanked the rope to signify to the guys at the other end to start pulling the barrel up. 'It is quicker if you do a barrel sling' the stranger next to me said, it did not look as secure, definitely quicker though.

With only four barrels on each of the boats it was going to take four trips plus a single boat load, 'Can you squeeze five on next time' I said to one of the rowers. They just looked at each other blankly, 'They do not understand, we are Dutch, there is no room in boat' came a voice from another boat. I watched as the first of the wagons went along the coastal track, the driver was on the right-hand side, as always in this country. On the second wagon there were the glowing eyes of Patch as the moon reflected in them.

I felt better as Thom and Patch went out of sight. The ground shook as a clap of deafening thunder rumbled through the air. Looking up the sky was still cloudless, 'Run!' came the shouts as guns started firing above. It was every man for himself. Out at sea a navy schooner was firing cannons at the Dutch vessel.

Above the cliff top the guns were doing some killing. A group of men with lanterns were heading alone the beach towards us from the west. There was but one choice, I ran along the beach to the east. When the sea blocked my way, I climbed the rocky cliff. I didn't want to risk going over the top of the cliff, so I climbed sideways. My hands were freezing as they hung to the ice-cold rock, the warmth of my own blood from cuts caused by the sharp rock was of no comfort.

The cannons stopped, the guns let out their last shots in the distance, the only sound left was the crashing of the tidal waves into the base of the cliffs that I clung to for life. While standing on a small ledge, I looked around. The Dutch ship was fully ablaze. The ledge I was on provided a good resting place. I was getting colder, and the stiffness was setting in. I needed to push on before it was too late.

The climb was getting harder, every limb was aching. As I came around a corner I recognised the place, Dead Man's Cove. My misfortune had driven me back to this unfortunate place. The tide was right up into the entrance of Skull Cave. I had no choice but to lower myself down into the choppy waves.

The cave was cold. Kicking around the sand with my feet I found the wool fleeces. The feeling of hope returned, and I threw off my saturated heavy clothes, before crawling under the smelly fleeces. I lay there shivering naked, to die here would end it all I thought. The nights events kept me awake, and the warmth was building up quickly within me under the large pile of wool.

Waking some time later my bleary eyes focused on a face, the whites of their eyes staring at me. I stared back. Without losing eye contact I slowly pulled a fleece over my head, I struggled to breath. All my internal organs felt like they were going up inside my chest ready to burst up my throat and out of my mouth. The fleece started to move, as if it was being pulled down by something at my feet.

My head was now uncovered once more, I rolled over fast before sitting suddenly upright. In the dark there was nothing but black. There I sat until a small glimmer of light shone through the entrance.

My oil lamp was still here, where I accidentally left it. My wet matches were in my wet clothes. I sat there wrapped up in the warm fleeces. There was one thing for sure, I would leave here naked and freezing before spending another night in this terrifying place.

The cold damp cave was not the place to dry wet clothes. I had no choice but to put them on. The weight of the wet clothes was too much, especially with the sand clinging to them. I grabbed the lamp. Furious about getting into another fine mess I smashed it down onto a rock in the middle of the cave, the glass smashed, oil splashed everywhere, a spark must have lit the oil, a ball of flame blasted into my face, burning off my eyebrows and lashes.

The fleeces were spread out all over the cave floor, all ablaze, producing an oven temperature heat, along with a nasty smelling smoke. My clothes were steaming, and at this rate they would be dry and in flames if I was not careful.

The smoke was overpowering, I had to get out of there. The flames were licking along the roof of the cave, then out of the entrance. The climb was steep, my clothes were only partially dry, and my hands were pained, with cuts and blisters. The flames chased me high up the cliff, then something grabbed hold of my leg, pulling me down, yanking me hard. Boom! came the sound exploding from the cave. My leg was free. As I lay on the grass at the top of the cliff, it came to me, I had just blown up the rest of my wreckers cargo.

I had lost all my fortune; the greed had got us. Laughing to myself for a few minutes before the realisation of the situation dawned on me, looking out to sea there was the wreck of the burnt-out Dutch ship, the large schooner, along with a few smaller boats. They must have seen the flames. Hearing the explosion must have alerted everybody for miles.

Running to the tree line as fast as my legs could carry me, the sound of jangling sovereigns in my pocket was fantastic to hear and lifted my gloomy mood. The sound of running horses, dampened my mood once more, mounted armed guards patrolled the area.

A group of people had gathered to watch as the guards sorted the dead bodies, all fifteen of them. all of them were the newer recruits. Ten wagons were clustered together, rum was dripping out of all of them, 'Wooow' the crowd said as the wagons were set alight, what a waste.

The crowd started to titter and laugh. When I realised it was at my expense I set of for Creetown, sneaking firstly round the back to check if Thom had made it. They were there, the wagon, Dark Lord and the tasty barrels of liquid gold. 'Have you seen my brothers?' Thom asked as he approached from behind, 'Not yet, they will have escaped' I said, not very convincingly, 'Ma blames it all on Billy' he said with a smirk on his face. 'What is so funny?' I asked, 'Oh it is your face' he replied, feeling my face I remembered the blaze of heat melting the hairs off my face.

After changing into dry clothes, I set of to find news of the others, my silk hat pulled down over my missing eyebrows. I rode Dark Lord fast, Patch chasing along just behind, the crowd has gone, the wagons had been reduced to a smoking pile of ash.

On the outskirts of Gatehouse of Fleet an unmissable poster had been displayed:

WANTED!

BILLY AND HIS FOUR BROTHERS

FOR THE FOLLOWING CRIMES

HIGH TREASON

PETTY TREASON

KIDNAPPING

DESERTION

SMUGGLING

LARCENY

VAGRANCY

REWARD 500 GOLD GUINEAS

Billy had got himself into a proper mess this time, he had got his brothers into serious trouble too. Petty treason might have been to do with the laird's child, high treason, what had he been up to in his absence? Up the street a commotion was happening outside the town hall, there lay more bodies, John was there too though very much alive.

Like the rat he was, John was talking to the customs and excise officers. He was too busy pointing and blabbing to notice me. I rode off to camp, hoping I had not been seen. Three wagons and three old timers was the sum total of occupants at the camp.

For the first time the old timers looked pleased to see me, then I remembered my eyebrows, 'I told you Ted, these young ones would mess up sooner or later' one of them said with joy, 'You were right there Gary, young fools'. I let them enjoy their moment of fun, that was when I noticed there were no horses. No wonder they never travelled.

Dougie was walking away from the other two, 'A quiet word son' he said. I followed him 'What news do you have for me?' I asked. 'Take Billy up some supplies, he is in the granite cave' Dougie said. My loyalty was being tested once more.

THE LONG WAY

Life was at rock bottom once more, and it was about to get even lower. The bakery was boarded up, my wagon was gone, so was Thom and his Ma. My heart sank, 'They are getting tried in Dumfries court' a voice came from the building adjacent to the bakery, 'Thanks' I replied, what was I meant to do now.

Taking stock of everything I had, three gold sovereigns, silk hat and undergarments, they must be worth a few bob. Dark Lord would fetch a good price, and Evelyn still had old Ned on her friends land. My first mission was finding Evelyn.

The captains door was open, it always was. The fire was struggling to fight away the cold, there was a blanket on each hammock. I needed them both, how anybody would choose to sleep in a hammock was beyond belief, on my fifth attempt I made it in.

I woke after punching myself in the face, 'Aw silly boy' said Evelyn who had been tickling my face with the ends of her hair, she kissed me on the forehead then giggled, 'You need to get up the captain will be home soon'. Getting up was just as difficult as getting in, stupid thing hammocks.

Evelyn had built up the fire and set the water up to boil, 'Ned's days are numbered' she said, he was getting old, over thirty at least. 'I will come see him' I said, it was only right, old faithful Ned.

In he came 'Ahoy me gang, I only got the two lobsters, plenty to share' he said, I was hungry indeed, I could have eaten old Ned I was that hungry. 'So, to what do we owe to this pleasure?' the captain asked, 'Just heard you were back, thought I would call in to visit' I replied, 'I have some bottles of the finest rum if you are interested' he said. I was, but without a wagon it was pointless.

It occurred to me that the captain never mentioned the cargo in Skull Cave. 'Have you been to the cave?' I asked, 'No me boy, the place is swarming with the law' he replied. He was right, 'See in the cave, did…' I stopped half sentence, feeling silly, 'You saw the red lady, did you?' he asked, I still was not convinced I had seen anything, 'Perhaps' I replied, he chuckled, 'That be Gilli Moon. The legend says she jumped to her watery grave after being jilted on her wedding day, others say she swam into the cave where she lived for years, enticing young sailors to their death' said the captain chuckling again. I had seen the last of her, had I mistaken the laugh of a young ladies laughter for that of a child.

After saying goodbye to old Ned, I headed straight to camp. A wanted notice was pinned to a tree just on the perimeter of the camp. They had added highwayman onto the list of charges, it was not his style, desperate times required desperate measures I thought.

Dougie was coughing and spluttering in bed when I went to see him, 'You are not looking great' I said pointing out the obvious, 'Have you got a bottle for me?' he asked. Dougie looked like he had knocked on deaths door and was waiting for the door to open. A nice bottle of rum would finish him off, 'What about if I hitch up your wagon, then I can take you to the rum?' I suggested, he gave a feeble smile 'That would be good of you son' he replied, this would be his last journey I thought.

Once in Creetown I kicked the door in, then escorted Dougie to bed. They had smashed everything inside when they had taken

Thom and his Ma. The race was on, I needed to catch the captain before he set sail. Halfway there I came across Evelyn out riding Cookie, 'Has the captain left?' I asked hastily, 'Yes, he will be back tomorrow he is only going to Carsethorn and back' she replied, that was a relief.

There was no false bottom on this wagon or secret removable panels in the bed, the walls I thought, then headed back outside, the shape was different, I pulled then pushed, even tried sliding, the wall panels would not move, there was something I was missing, I was sure of it.

Right on schedule the captain turned up on first tide, 'Ahoy me skipper' he shouted from afar, I waved back. 'Have you got those cases of rum you mentioned handy?' I asked whilst tying of the boat, 'What do you think is under here me boy' he said with a wink. Under a large tarpaulin were three large cases. Three small ones would have done.

The deal was done, and the cases of rum were loaded into the back of the wagon. I was feeling regret already; I knew I was going to get caught. The road was clear all the way to Creetown. After parking the wagon around the back, I delivered Dougie a bottle of rum, 'Here I got some cheese and bread to line your stomach' I said. He looked like he had not eaten in some time, 'No just the rum' he grumbled, the drink perked him up greatly. 'I have another if you want it, even more for you if you let me borrow your wagon for a few days' I said, he looked at the second bottle, 'Okay, make sure you bring more rum' he said, 'I will, how come the outer walls are a different shape to the internal walls?' I asked. This got a smile on his face, 'If you stick your fingers in the holes the wall lifts up' he said, before downing an extremely large swig from the bottle.

The walls slid up revealing a large cavity that was split into segments, the bottles fitted in nicely, stuffing in packing straw, not only stopped the bottles from clinking together it provided some much-needed insulation, all bar five bottles fitted in neatly.

I was Dumfries bound at last. Just after Carsluith a crowd had gathered once more, 'Halt' came the cry of a guard, I had a bayonet poking at me from both sides, 'I will deal with this one' came the welcome voice of Robert. 'Hello good friend' I said, he ushered me round the side out of sight. 'Have you got a wee dram of that rum that I might get a taste of?' he asked, I looked at him trying to size up the situation, 'Yes sure, what is all this about?' I asked, as I produced a bottle from my inside coat pocket, 'Oh it is a funeral pyre for forty-seven Dutch smugglers. Where are you travelling to now?', swift justice for them poor lads. 'Back to Dumfries' I replied, 'If you tag along behind us you will get safe travel all the way' he said, at a cost to me no doubt.

Betty was parked up on the Whitesands, a solitary wagon. 'Hello son, glad to see you are safe, all the men have headed north with the fear' she said. I was about to speak when my eyes caught a glimpse of a familiar face, it was John the rat. I hid as he walked across the old bridge, watching as he came closer, 'Do you know this one?' I asked Betty, she watched as he walked by, 'It looks like the guy who has been hanging around the courthouse these last few days' she replied, 'I will be back soon' I said as I walked off to follow him.

John was a man about town with money to burn it would seem. I watched patiently as he splashed out money to buy drinks for anybody that was willing to give him company. He was almost back at the old bridge when I grabbed him, pushing him to the edge of the river, 'So you like to spend our money do you?' I asked. He tried feebly to run off, I held tight making him lean over the edge, 'Please no, it was not me that grassed' he whimpered. He had denied something that he had not been accused of, the plea of a guilty grass. I dragged him back to the wagon, then gave him an all mighty punch, knocking him out.

When John regained consciousness, his hands and feet were bound, then the crying started. 'Was it you that grassed up Annie and Thom?' Betty asked before spitting in his face, he denied everything, 'I will take him to Billy see what he says' I said to Betty, John cried even harder. 'Poor Annie was found guilty of vagrancy, along with the charge with stealing eighteen cabbages and running off with them down the street' Betty said, both charges were made up, how could anybody run while carrying eighteen cabbages. 'What about her son Thom?' I asked, 'Oh found guilty son, they got deported for Australia yesterday' she replied, the chances are they would not even last the journey.

I set off for Moffat. Dark Lord had a loose shoe that Frankie would be able to fix. John was walking beside me 'Please! I will disappear, You'll never see me again' he said, it was just one of the many pleads that would come from him on the long journey.

By Beattock I was sick of him. After tying his arms to the front axle then his ankles to the rear, I went to relieve myself behind a tree. I had only just started when I noticed a young woman all in black walking towards me, I quickly covered myself, then acted like I was just taking in the scenery. She was good looking, with long dark hair, 'Come here you' she said as she gently slipped her hand around my waist. This alone sent tingles through my body, then she kissed me, it was my little angel from the Rudeboy Fair. 'Is that it' I said as she pulled away. She gave me a shy look before saying 'No', then she cuddled into me for the longest of hugs.

With a future date set to see her again, I went on my way. My head was so high in the clouds I felt like I was floating alone. Frankie was quick to fix Dark Lord's shoe; the cost was a bottle of rum.

John was gagged but the groans of pain as we banged over humps and bumps could still be heard. Each night I let him down for a few measly scraps and a drink of water. This went on for a week as we travelled down the Dalveen Pass then back up into the hills that surrounded Moniaive. From there it was a trek to Carsphairn where we entered the Galloway Forest.

The smell of John was getting too much to bear, a sniveling rat of a human cesspit. I made him walk up front, if he slowed, I poked him with a long stick that I had picked up. The trek through the forest was long and slow from this side, at least I knew there was nobody following us.

John crawled up nightly under the wagon. He had not spoken a word since Beattock when I tied him to the undercarriage of the wagon. It was strange how Patch had paid him no notice, not a bark or even a look. The last night that he slept under the wagon it rained what seemed like all night, but the rat was lying there half drowned in a puddle unwilling to move.

With the rope tied to the back of the wagon I started on the last few miles to the granite cave. The going was wet. John lay on the ground in refusal, Dark Lord plodded on regardless, it was not long before John got up onto his feet.

The damp air brought the midges out. They swarmed around John the pungent aroma attracting them, feasting on his blood like miniature vultures. It must have been the rum in my blood that saved me from the attacking menaces.

Patch sniffed the air; he had picked up the scent of something. He looked at me, it was as if he expected answers. A few more sniffs then he took off, racing straight towards the secret cave, well not so secret cave perhaps.

The welcome committee came out to great us as we approached. The four of them looked a bit raggedy, certainly well fed though, 'So you brought the rat' said Billy. 'Please Billy, I never grassed honest, I swear on my dad's life' John said, Billy sniffed the air, 'You are a stinking rat, I watched you grass, then claim you had rescued the child' Billy said, before kicking him to his knees.

John lay there silent with a vacant stare in his eyes, 'We escaped on foot, did anybody get through with the rum?' Billy asked, 'Do not think so, here you need a drink, you all do' I told them, then I explained about their Ma and Thom.

We drank in silence in the small cave, the fire was starting to burn low, when Billy stood up, 'There is only one thing for it I will hand myself in, if I confess that it was all me they will need to drop the charges on Ma and the boys' announced Billy. 'They were shipped over a week ago, it is too late' I said, Billy sat back down deep in his thoughts.

Leaving them to think of a plan I went back to the wagon. John lay where we left him in his own filth. I had done all I could, my own life had to be sorted out. I needed to earn some money for new clothes. I would need to look and smell on top form for my date. I would impress her with my silk undergarments, but I would definitely need to give them a good soak and wash first. I drifted off to sleep that night with a happy glow as I thought about her.

When I rose the next morning John had been stretched out over the boulder that capped the cave roof, 'We will leave him there, a slow death for the rat' Warren said, He got what he deserved, but I would have done it quick, he will suffer in hell soon enough.

They were looking set to go, 'Where are you all going?' I asked, 'There is nothing for it, we are going into the navy, we can give false names, they take anybody' Billy said. He was right they did take anybody, if they hung about near the dock, they would more than likely get press ganged anyway.

With only a week to go until my date I made haste, It was a two-day trek to get out of the forest. Dougie was gone when I checked in on him, nobody at camp had seen him, he would turn up, 'You boys need a drink?' I asked the two old timers. 'Just one bottle, we can share' one of them said. Sales were bad, I had given away more than I had sold.

Time was running out. I had to make it back to Beattock. Betty was still on the Whitesands, but at least she had company this time. Good paying customers they were too. I spent every last penny on a set of brand-new clothes. The sales assistant gave me a bit off the price due to me just being few pennies short. My rainy-day bank account was safe for another rainy day.

I spent the last day before we met in the river Annan, first washing my silk undergarments, then following on with a naked swim with a good wash down.

I took her to the top of the hill above Beattock. The view from there was superb, the Moffat hills, the hills to the north and of course Moffat itself. We laughed and smiled the whole day through, it felt like life had only just begun, 'Would you like to come in the wagon for a few days travelling along the coast?' I asked, 'Yes' she said with the most beautiful of smiles. Arrangements were made for a months' time; I hardly could deal with such a long wait.

THE NEW NEW

The camp was a shadow of its former self. If the two old timers go, there will be nothing to hold on to. 'Dougie passed son, paupers grave, up behind the church' said Ted, 'He passed the way he wanted, with a bottle in his hand' said Gary, by the look of them they would follow him soon.

I cracked a bottle of rum open then poured a drink on the ground for great uncle Dougie, the two old timers joined me in a small drink to say goodbye. 'He was in the army when he was a boy, your grandad on your dads side was his batman' said Gary, 'He was that, he travelled the world, so he did, in the merchant navy' said Ted, I knew nothing about him, there was a lot of things I would never know.

Dougie's battered old wagon was now mine. Sales of rum were so low that I was drinking more than I was selling. Mike had no work for me until next month. A week at the beach was in order. The captain's boat was sitting in the port, 'Ahoy me boy' came the usual greeting as I arrived at his home.

The captain looked the wagon over, 'It needs a touch of attention, I have some varnish and glass paper if you are interested' he said. It was old with a few dents and chips, 'That sounds good' I replied, foolishly thinking he was offering it for free. 'If you don't have the money you can work for it' he said. I looked into his cunning eyes before answering, 'Alright' I replied, the sea still scared me a little, how bad can it get.

My first day at sea was an experience to say the least, 'This is the sleeping area, it is also the kitchen and eating area' the captain said as he showed me around. There was not much to see, 'Just hang your arse over the stern if you need to go, no pooping on the poop deck' he said chuckling away. Patch sat up on the bow, relaxed, just watching the horizon.

A large ship was heading up the Solway Firth, 'We will follow that cargo ship to the bigger port, there we will pick up cargo to deliver to the smaller ports' he explained, we were not the only ones following.

After passing the Isle of Whithorn, Dead Man's Cove appeared in the distance. My heart pumped a little faster, the closer we got the faster my heart seemed to go. I wanted to look the other way, but the draw of the cave had a grip on me. The smoke blackened entrance made it look spookier than ever. Once we were a long way past the cave my heart calmed.

Kirkcudbright harbour loomed, the cargo ship had docked ahead of us. The whole place was bustling, the ship's crew rushed around unloading the cargo, 'Right me boy, come meet the merchants' the captain said, 'This is my son' he said as he spoke to various merchants. I just went along with it, it actually felt good to be wanted as a son.

It was a struggle for me to figure out what exactly was going on, Within the hour there was a load of the cargo sitting on the dock next to the captains boat, 'Once we get this lot loaded, we will be on our way' he said. Something about him told me he was in a hurry.

The boat was loaded to the maximum, 'Let us get going' he said. I was just about to untie the mooring ropes when a woman's voice shouted, 'Cooee Gilbert dear', the captain seemed to not hear it, 'GILBERT AUGUSTUS MACINTOSH' came her voice loudly shouting, the whole harbour stopped what they were doing to see what was going on.

The captain looked bashfully at the lady, 'Aw mummy, you are embarrassing me' he said, that got him a good cuff on the ear. He looked like a small bearded boy, looking at the ground huffing 'EMBARRASS YOU!' she shouted.

Gilbert's mother was a tall slim woman, from a well to do background. Gilbert took after his father, short, slightly rounded with a nautical background, 'Give your mother a hug me boy' she said smiling at her little boy.

The conversation was minimal once we were back at sea. I thought about his name with amusement, Gilbert Augustus Macintosh. He had lost his dodgy status of captain grey beard, I chuckled out loud, then stifled it quickly.

Kippford was our first call, 'Ahoy captain' a young man said, 'Ahoy' the captain said still a bit humbled after encountering his mother, the young man paid the captain for delivery, 'We were anchored for the night. Do you fancy a small drink in the local tavern?' he asked, 'Too right I do' I replied. After a hearty meal, washed down with a few beers, the captain was back to his old self, 'The truth is there is no truth in half the lies I tell' he said laughing, well that was true indeed.

All the locals knew him well 'Give us a song captain' one of the fishermen said, 'Oh no not tonight' he said, 'Come on captain' I said. I had never heard him sing, all the men started clapping stomping of banging their tankards on the table. The captain obligingly burst into song, the dirtiest song I had ever heard, something about a beautiful young maiden, once started he would not stop, the fellow drinkers kept him going by supplying us both with drink.

It was not only the boat that rocked from side to side, the whole world did as we staggered around trying to navigate our way back to the captain's boat. The captain was in his hammock quick as a flash, I however swayed around on my feet, 'Just jump in all in one go' the captain advised. I ignored him, managing to get myself securely in eventually. The snores of the drunken captain were like a lions roar, the drink along with the gentle rocking of the boat soon sent me off to sleep.

For the next few days we worked our way back to Port William, port by port. Passing Skull Cave was still very unnerving, she would not get me away out here I told myself recalling the face looking at me in the cave. The cliff was almost vertical at places, it was a feat to have managed the climb.

The captain was good to his word, 'Now rub it down good, right back to the original wood, then give it three thin coats of this' he said. The large tin of varnish had a brush with it, 'Thanks' I said. 'You will need to varnish it indoors, if you like you can nip up to my boathouse at Ballantrae' he said, I was not going back that way in my life if I could help it, 'I will see, I have a thing to do first' I said, my date with my little angel was coming soon.

After stripping out the wagons interior, I washed it down with soapy water. The fresh smell was a great improvement, but the covers looked worse for wear. I had only sold 6 bottles of rum that month, almost all of the proceeds went on new tartan blankets.

My angel arrived in Dumfries just minutes after me. The euphoria was intense. I thought it best to avoid New Abbey with the gang of riffraff that lurked there. Kirkcudbright beach was our destination, we had not made it to our destination when one of the wooden wheel spokes broke.

The night looked like it was ruined, for hours we sat as several people struggled to get the wheel off. The darkness fell, bringing the cold air with it. Under the light of the oil lamp, the wheel was finally fixed, 'Here's a bottle of rum for your help, you are a life saver' I said to the stranger, 'No problem I could not see anybody stuck' he said. The journey to the beach was still a few miles away, and once there we cuddled up in bed falling asleep very quickly.

The next day was warm. We had the beach to ourselves all day, the tide came in then drifted away in constant motion, the time drifted by fast, the star lit night appeared quickly, 'There is Aries the ram' she said pointing at a group of stars. 'So it is' I replied cluelessly, 'That constellations over there is Leo the lion' she said, 'That is so wonderful, my friend captain Gilbert must use them to navigate his sea voyages' I said, although I doubted it very much.

Our time together was almost over, and taking her back to Dumfries was a drag, 'Can we meet again?' I asked, 'Of course' she replied, saying goodbye was easier now I knew we would meet again.

After a hard day's work on Mike's farm, I was ready to be on my way, then I had an idea. 'Can I use your barn for a week or two?' I asked, 'Feel free, it is almost empty until the hay harvest' he replied. The relief was nice, no need to use the boathouse at Ballantrae after all.

The next two days was spent sweeping out the barn, then it was time to begin the restoration. Everything that could be removed or be dismantled, was. The internal wall was taken out, the stash of hundreds of bottles of rum made the barn look like a distillery.

Sanding down the wood was harder than I thought. It was a far longer job than I had anticipated, and it took the whole two weeks just to do that part of the job. 'You're getting there now' Mike said, 'I'll start the varnish tomorrow after a good wash down' I replied, 'The captain says if you interested there is a week's work for you'. Unfortunately, what I wanted to do was different to what I needed to do. The wagon would need to wait, as I needed the money.

The captain was on board when I arrived on Dark Lord, 'Ahoy me doggy' he said to Patch who had jumped onto the boat to see him, 'Give me two minutes' I shouted. I rode Dark Lord hard, then ran back after leaving him behind the captains home.

Patch was already in his favourite spot up front, 'Almost left without you' said the captain. We set of in a westerly direction, 'So where we heading today?' I asked, 'Up north me boy, stop of to see the wife and Sara on the way by first' he replied. I liked Ballantrae, just not the horrors of that nights memory.

Ailsa Craig was a lot larger than it looked from shore, 'Over there is where Sawney Bean lived with all his family' said the captain. It was not as if I needed any reminders, the poor little ones, never coming out of the cave except in the days before there execution.

It was just after dark when we docked. Patch went with the captain, relieving himself as he went. I spent the night stretched out in the hammock. I would have been happier if my guard dog had been a bit more loyal, but the sway of the boat got me to sleep before I knew it.

Sara and Patch woke me first thing in the morning with a nice cooked breakfast, and before long we were off. 'North me boy, have you been up to Glasgow?' he asked, 'Not yet' I replied. I was still very respectful of the sea, the vastness, the depth, wondering to myself if Thom and his Ma had made it to the end of their journey.

There was nothing I had ever experienced in my life before that felt like this, complete freedom, at one with nature as the boat rocked and rolled with the natural tempo of the water, the wind blasting, the sails fluttering. 'Have a look at that me boy' the captain said pointing to a strange boat. There were no sails, just a smoking chimney, 'It's got a good pace on' I said, 'It is a Clyde puffer, they will do me out of a job' the captain said. What a great piece of engineering I thought but thought it best that I kept my thoughts to myself in front of the captain on such matters.

There were ships and boats as far as my eyes could see, men hard at work loading, unloading, making deals, there must have been over a hundred horses and carts all coming and going, 'I will be back in five minutes' the captain said. He took a lot longer than that, not that I minded. The place had a lot of interesting things to take in, 'Still not interested mister?' came a young woman's voice, turning I got a right eyeful of what she was selling, with one foot up on a bollard, dress held high and no undergarments to be seen, 'No thanks' I politely declined, 'Suit yourself then' she said walking away, she had got around since I saw her last at the Rudeboy Fair.

The captain arrived back with a covered cage, 'Let's go me boy' he said, I was curious as we left to head back south, 'So what is in the cage' I asked, 'Oh that is a special delivery for the big house, two cockatiels, have a look' he replied. They were beautiful little things, one white, one grey, both with little orange cheeks, 'Speak to them, they can talk'. I looked at the captain, 'How are you liking the Scottish weather?' I asked to no reply, 'No like that' came the laughter.

As we sailed down the Clyde a puffer noisily followed us, dense black smoke billowing out of its chimney funnel. It was not hanging around as it zoomed up behind us, 'Toot' came the sound of its horn, I waved back at the puffer captain as they whizzed by, captain Gilbert turned his back on him. 'They might be faster, but they cost a lot on coal, look at the reek coming out of it' he said. He did have a point, wind was free, though rather unpredictable. The puffer could also travel directly into the wind, with no need to zigzag like the old sail boats.

The puffer was off into the distance already, 'Look, they are docking at Lochranza, I used to get cargo for there, first the railways now this' the captain said. There was nothing I could say, progress will stop for nobody, 'Glad I am due to retire' he said, he was the last of his kind, it took a real captain to single handedly skipper a sailboat.

Our first stop was Portpatrick 'Now you watch yourself, there is two girls that will, check out your manhood with one hand and your money pouch with the other' the captain warned, 'They not going to get much I am skint' I said. The port was alive the watering holes even livelier, 'Tell us a tail of your adventures captain' the inn keeper said, 'Well I suppose I could tell you about the time the lady in red almost got me' said the captain, was I going to be telling tales in my older years I wondered.

There were a couple of women having drinks in the corner, their eyes were keeping a close watch on the men as they made purchases. They were both rather well dressed for this establishment, the younger of the two was quite pretty, the older was rather peculiar looking with a long face, bigger teeth than Dark Lord and a short boyish hairstyle 'Keep away from them pair' the captain whispered in my ear.

Leaving Portpatrick harbour was hard going. The sky was blue, the heat was beating down on us, and it was a rare occasion that the costal wind had dropped to a light breeze. 'Come have a look through my spyglass me boy' said the captain as he pulled out a brass telescope, 'If you look over the bow, that island is the Isle of White, tax free there' he said, but I was more interested in the sea creatures. 'What is that?' I asked pointing over to just short of the rocks, 'That be a seal me boy' he replied, 'No that' I said passing him the telescope, 'Ah that be a harbour porpoise' he replied, the journey today was a long slow one.

The wildlife was everywhere I looked, 'There is a whale off port side' the captain shouted, it was colossal, and the telescope gave me a really good look at the amazing creature from the deep. As we started to turn left at the Mull of Galloway the captain pointed out again 'A basking shark', its mouth was wide open as it swam along, it was the strangest looking of sea creatures I had seen.

We had to wait for the tide before sailing into Wigtown harbour, 'They are not here again, blast them' said the captain, 'Will I run up with them?' I asked, 'You perhaps better' the captain said, before I had a chance to leave the boat a young man ran towards us, 'Sorry I am late sirs, here is your money' he said as he passed a small pouch to the captain.

The captain was somewhat quieter as we sailed the last part of our journey. When we reached Port William he said 'Me and the wife are heading up north for a while, island hopping. Feel free to use the house while I am away', he seemed quite deflated. Change was bothering him, 'Thanks, see you when you get back' I said, I was in a hurry to get a coat of varnish on the wagon.

Three days later the wagon looked splendid with three fresh coats of varnish, a good layer of beeswax finished it off nicely, 'Looks like new' Mike said, 'Thanks for the use of the barn' I replied. After a few days of hard work on the farm I headed the long road to Port William, this allowed me to stop off at the Cock Inn on the way.

The inn was busy with the usual faces, plus a few newer ones, 'What will you have?' asked Lauren, I looked at the shelves behind her, 'What is with all the different drinks?' I replied. The shelf had every drink I could think of plus a few more, 'Lower tax nowadays, come on what will it be?' she asked. I did not know what I wanted, 'A beer please' I said, the changes were hitting us all, the rum stashed in the walls of the wagon would bring little return on my investment now.

Whilst I was making enough from working Mike's farm to survive, it was not enough. Even with regular pots of rabbit stew I had little money half the time. Steady jobs were low paid, with long hours and constant misery. I needed a new business venture, preferably a legal one.

Dating was going well; we were meeting up almost every second week. Earning enough to keep us both was my priority, and with

Billy gone I had no distractions. The quiet life was good. Then one evening after a hard day's work, Evelyn met me as I rode back to the captain's home. 'The captain is not coming back; he has sold his boat. The house is for sale too' she said, it seemed our adventure at sea together would be our last, 'Where is he?' I asked, 'He has settled in with his wife at long last' she replied. Ballantrae was calling once more.

The potato harvesting lasted another two days. As soon as I finished, I set of immediately for Ballantrae. It seemed rather strange that neither Mike nor his wife had mentioned the captain. I thought it best not to interfere. The short journey was quick, though it was still dark after I arrived, 'Ahoy me boy' came the shout as I pulled my wagon up in front of the boathouse. It was the captain standing on the harbour wall, looking out to sea in the darkness, dreaming of a life that once was.

I took him out a bottle of rum, 'Thanks son' he said, the sadness was hidden but still very visible. We drank in silence for a bit before the captain said, 'That is Sara married, Evelyn too come next spring', I had never realised they had even been courting. 'That's good news, congratulations' I said, not sure why the father gets congratulated at these things. Perhaps it is for successfully getting rid of his daughters and the financial responsibility for them.

The subject of his home was a difficult one to raise, 'I hear you are selling your home down at the port' I said. 'Well yes, I have no need for it now' he replied. He never really needed it before. If you can wait until I go to the bank in Dumfries and back, I will make you an offer' I said. This was very agreeable to him, I just had to sell as much of the rum as possible on the way.

Midafternoon the next day I rolled into the camp at Gatehouse of Fleet. The old timers had company, the family that I had met at Bladnoch, plus one more wagon, these were strangers to me. 'Well hello, what brings you here' I asked, 'We are getting put off the land, they want rid of all the travellers' came the reply. I was about to say they cannot do that, it was pointless though, the greedy landowners seemed to do whatever they wanted. 'Would you be interested in a cheap bottle of rum?' I asked, after a bit of chat with their wives they bought three bottles. The profit was very marginal, getting my money back on my investment was my main goal.

Old Ted was coughing and spluttering, 'Nice new wagon, you must be minting it in' said Gary, I looked at the wagon with pride, 'Just getting by, how long has he been like this?' I asked, 'Near the two months now, he is just going to get worse' said Gary. There was a half full bottle of rum sitting in my wagon. After fetching it I handed it to Ted 'Here, for medicinal purposes' I said. He took it in his frail hands, then glugged down a large mouthful, 'You two need to go stay at Billy's, for a bit, he is away the now' I said, they were overjoyed, the last few years had been hard for them, soul destroying.

After hitching up Ted's wagon we were ready to go, 'Away lie in your bed' I said to him, 'I will be fine. I want to sit up front' he replied; Gary sat up with him. Dark lord made short work of the trek, Gary helped Ted inside while I parked the wagon around the back, 'I will bring your wagon first thing in the morning' I said to Gary, Dark Lord raced back to camp like the wind.

Gary was out front waiting for me when I arrived next day, 'Would you be having any more of that medicinal rum left? Ted is in a bad way' he said, 'If you got the money' I replied, his face said it all, 'We are a bit short, he has not got long to go' said Gary. I had to get moving, 'Just the one bottle, make sure you give Ted some' I said. Silly old fools.

The journey to Dumfries was unlucrative, there were plenty of traffic, just nobody I knew. I hoped to see Betty or somebody on the Whitesands, but alas there was nobody.

The doorman at the bank opened the door with a polite nod. With my silk hat in hand I entered; the young man I had done the business with before was not there. I scanned the sea of faces before choosing the attractive young girl sat at a clerks desk to my left. Under the desk I could see a small section of her lower leg and ankle, her sheer silk stockings were mesmerising. I fantasised about seeing more as I approached the desk, 'Hello again, how can I help you today?' came the dainty sweet voice. It was Elizabeth. A posh job for a posh girl I thought, 'Can I get all my money out please?' I asked, 'I see you want to make a withdrawal sir' she said, 'Yes all of it' I said, she smiled nicely at me, 'The interest rates are good at the moment, you should think about leaving a little in' she said as she started counting the money. If she said leave it all in, I would have, 'Alright, I'll leave a quarter of it in' I said. The interest had been good, but I still do not trust banks.

The sun was out when I arrived back at Creetown, so were Ted and Gary. They must have spent their whole lives outdoors, why stop now, 'How are you doing lads?' I asked, 'Not bad' Ted spluttered, 'Have you got a spot of rum for us?' Gary asked. Like Dougie, the drink had taken over their lives. Drink came before food, before everything in fact, 'You two got any money?' I asked, 'Well not at the moment, but we are good for it' said Gary. They would drink me dry for free given the chance, 'Free lodgings for six months plus a case of rum each, in exchange for your wagon' I said to Ted, 'Now hold on a minute, we need to have a tete a tete' said Gary. I left them to it for a moment, the way I clinked the rum bottles in the wagon, was just a little clink of encouragement.

Their faces said it all, drooling at the prospect of a hearty drink, 'A year lodgings' said Ted, 'Make it three cases, a case and a half each' said Gary. With the deal done I gave them a bottle each 'I will bring the rest when I pick up the wagon' I said. Ted's wagon needed some of the wood replaced with new, who knows who the building belongs to now Billy was on the run.

The rain came for three days and three nights. It was heavy, and it looked as if it was never going to stop. The trek to Ballantrae was a muddy slow one. I wanted to get there badly so I trundled on regardless. On the fourth day the clouds broke, the sun had returned at last.

The familiar coastal wind blasted straight in my face, 'Ahoy me boy' came a faint distant sound, I thought I was imagining it at first, 'Ahoy me boy, over here'. Just offshore there was a sailboat with the captain on board waving, 'Ahoy me boy' he shouted again, the sea was his home, now with a boat less than half the size of his last one, he was at home once more.

The captain was waiting for me at Ballantrae harbour with the look of a mischievous little boy on his face. After a discussion I was now the owner of my first home, well the amount was agreed at least, and a quarter payment was made.

We sealed the deal with a few drinks 'So are you a real captain?' I asked, 'Of course' he said with a bit of a scowl on his face. Can you do me a favour?' I asked, of course me boy, anything you like' he replied, I explained my plans, to which he agreed.

The next day I went to the post office, where I wrote two postcards, 'Can I send this one to Dumfries and this one to Dalbeattie please' I said to the post clerk, 'They will be delivered Tomorrow' she said. That was quick, the plans were now in motion.

THE DANCING BEAR

Dressed in our Sunday best, the captain and I set sail up the Solway Firth, the tide helping us on our way. Our first stop was Dalbeattie harbour, where I was glad to see Scarlett awaiting our arrival, 'Ahoy me girl!' the captain said as Scarlett climbed on board, her even larger than I remembered bosoms now jiggling close to my face as I helped. 'So, what is this all about? where are we going?' she asked whilst holding me in a warm embrace, 'All will be revealed soon enough, come meet the captain' I replied. The captain was a total embarrassment, his eyes were fixated on Scarlett's bosom, not that she minded, she seemed to revel in his attention.

Once in the mouth of the River Nith, the Glencaple harbour was visible in the distance. A ship was docked blocking our view, my nerves were getting to me, the closer to the harbour we got the more my heart raced. Suddenly I was cold, so I took a seat as my knees went weak, then I spotted her. She was wearing the same white dress that she wore the night we met.

The captain was busy showing off to Scarlett. She was a keen helper, and he was even keener watching her. There's nothing like an ample bosom to control a man's mind. My mind however was on the angel waving at me from the quayside, her smile was radiant, 'Come on board we are not stopping' I said, she slipped twice as she attempted to board, the soles of her boots were not made for slippery wet wood.

Brief introductions were made as we turned around for open waters, she too had a good look at Scarlett's impressive bosom. 'Come see the picnic I have prepared' I said. She looked impressed when I pulled out a bottle of champagne that the captain had gifted us for the occasion.

Scarlett and the captain were busy chuckling together, my nerves were still giving me the shakes. The captain was now watching me, giving me the *go for it* nods, perhaps it was the *hurry up* nods, 'See over there, a porpoise' I said, although it might have been a dolphin, 'Aw he is so nice' she said. I grabbed her hand, pulled her into my body, 'Will you marry me?' I asked, her face lit up with a glowing big smile, 'Yes' she replied, we sealed the deal with several kisses, 'Ahem, shall we begin' said the captain bible in hand, 'You mean marry you right now?' she said in surprise.

The ceremony was over quickly, in legal terms it was as legal as a tinklers wedding, to us it the most romantic moment of our lives. We made arrangements for her to move in with me down at our new home, down by the sea.

The next two years were the happiest I had ever been, life was simple, the money I earned from working Mike's farm went to the captain as payment for his home. My angel wife spent her days beachcombing, returning empty bottles for the half penny deposit was quite lucrative. What was the world coming to when people would just throw money away? At least the stupid ones that threw money down a well got the joy of hope with a wish. The garden was large enough to set up a good-sized vegetable patch, the products of which went well with rabbit stew.

Patch was getting on a bit in years, preferring a more relaxed run along the beach to his old ways of racing everywhere at top speed. Even Dark Lord was a notch slower in his pace. Ted was no longer with us, Gary struggled on, still desperate on the drink.

I was now the proud owner of three renovated wagons. Gary's was so neglected some of the wood had to replaced due to rot. The money from selling them would square off my debt to the captain but finding a buyer at this time was impossible. Greedy landowners kicking us off the land was not helping the future of the travelling people.

The captain was a frequent welcome visitor, always with a story to tell, always with his pail of water containing three living lobsters. It was on one such visit when he asked, 'Have you pair been to see the dancing bear that is travelling the region?' I was getting looks, smiles and nods, I knew she was wanting to see it. 'So where would we find this bear?' I asked, 'It was last seen heading to Stranraer, after that probably heading to Dumfries. They will be passing through every town and village that is near the main route' he replied. With a glance at my angel, I knew it was settled, we were going bear hunting.

We were organised by morning, our travels in search of the bear had begun. The talk was rife, the bear was heading for Castle Douglas and so were we. On the second day just before dusk we came upon a group of wagons. Patch was barking like crazy; he was silenced by the sudden ear busting roar. He scampered inside the wagon to hide, he was not the only one that was scared, I put my arm around her shoulders, holding her tight, then giving her a kiss on the side of her head.

A group of angry men started shouting, I was clueless to what they were saying, it was not a friendly welcome, 'Well, well look who it is, just ignore these Ukrainians, they not to happy when strangers invade their camp' a scruffy looking man said. His beard and hat did not fool me, 'Billy what are you doing here?' I asked, others would recognise him, even though the wanted notices were ripped, faded or gone. He was still a wanted man, the reward was still a very large and tempting amount, 'Just passing through, come meet, Ruperto the sloth bear' he said. Ushering us over to the poor creature that cowered away from us, his snout strapped shut, a chain was attached to a mouth ring, that went in the bears mouth then out of its lower jaw. This poor bear had lived throw cruelties that only humans were evil enough to inflict.

We stayed there with Billy and the Ukrainians for the night, 'Where are the lads?' I asked, 'We joined the navy, the boys are still in, sailed to the west indies about six months gone' he replied. We talked into the night. Billy once again was a deserter, 'Meet Zlata' Billy said as a young female sat beside him. She was a pretty enough girl, her affection towards Billy seemed strangely false, I could not put my finger on what it was.

We parted company the next morning, the poor little bear getting dragged along. One of the Ukrainians seemed to enjoy poking the bear with a long wooden pole, it was a struggle not to intervene. They headed in the Dumfries direction, we opted for a visit to Dalbeattie.

The Wolfs were pleased to see us as always, 'I am about to get married, Joseph the town clerk proposed a month past now' Scarlett said, 'Nice, he is a lucky man' I said. Jamie lay on the floor with patch, they were playfully hugging. In six months', time we would be back for the wedding.

The weather made the journey back slow. There was an absence of traffic. It was not until we were at Gatehouse of Fleet that we heard the news, 'Read all about it, Billy the kidnapper trial starts on Monday' said the newspaper boy, 'Give me a copy son' I said.

There it was, front page news, the reward had been collected by a group of Ukrainian travellers.

The gossips had found him guilty with a thirst for a hanging. I made haste, travelling alone to Dumfries. It was not until Monday afternoon that I arrived, and the court hearing had begun. Outside the courthouse there must have been at least five hundred people gathered.

The stories circulating were getting worse as time passed 'I heard he kidnapped a young boy then ate him, disgusting I hope he hangs' one of the crowd said, even without the wild accusations, he was going to hang.

A strange feeling came over me, 'Hello again' it was the unmistakable foreign voice Zlata. The Ukrainians had me surrounded, 'Hello' I said back, not sure of the what or why of this situation, 'Billy is a good man, this is his share of the reward, you need to share with brothers' Zlata said, I was bowled over with surprise. Not only had Billy done the right thing by his brothers, he had also found some trustworthy friends, a task I thought impossible.

I stood speechless looking at Zlata, her round freckled face was almost completely covered with her long curly hair, 'We good yes' said Zlata, I nodded 'Yes, we good' I lied. There was no way we were going to be good as long as they still neglecting and abusing that poor little bear.

Three hundred gold guineas, it was a fortune. I left the crowd, opting to put the share that belonged to Billy's brothers in the bank awaiting their safe return. 'Can I deposit two hundred guineas please' I said to Elizabeth with a touch of suave in my demeanor. She looked impressed, but she did not need to know who or where or even the what behind this handsome amount of cash, 'Our manager always deals with our larger depositors' she said with a wink and a smile.

The bank manager was a slimy looking little fellow, with greasy slicked back hair. The antimacassar that sat on the head of his leather chair must have took some washing. After listening to his drivel about being a highly valued customer, I left with a free cigar in my hand.

Back at the court the crowd were still prattling on about nonsense, all things that they would never say to his face given the chance. The night was drawing in on us, as the doors swung open, 'The defendant has been found guilty on all counts, the sentence of death will be carried out this Wednesday at seven in the morning' said an old man. This was it this time, Billy's version of being on the straight and narrow had ended badly.

A group of wagons were on the Whitesands. There was nobody that I recognised, and conversation was kept to a minimum, 'I hear Billy pleaded guilty and that his brothers were not involved' said a voice that came from outside my wagon.

On Wednesday morning I was up early. Queensberry square was already starting to fill, the Midsteaple clock struck six, the executioner was busy making adjustments to the rope. If the length of rope was too short, he would slowly choke to death, possibly taking some hours, too long and the head might be decapitated, the executioner had to get it correct in order to snap the neck.

Almost every minute that went by I found myself looking at the clock. Queensberry Square was now overflowing, with thousands of people all thirsty for death. The local militia had been called in to control the swarm of excited revellers.

The death drum started to bang a beat, several young kids marched to the beat, laughing as they did so. The side door of the Midsteaple opened, the crowd cheered and booed in a frenzy of hate. To my surprise Billy stepped out with a hood covering his face, the spectators close to Billy were taking their turn to spit on him as he passed.

As Billy walked slowly up the steps to the platform, a barrage of rotten fruit and veg flew at him. The same man from outside the court started to address the crowd, but I was too far away to hear his words over the noise. One of the guards punched Billy in the side of his ribs, this made the crowd go wild, the cheers were deafening. 'Give him one from me' a screeching voice sounded above all the noise, Billy's ex-wife looked happier than I ever seen her before, I made sure not to be seen by her. This was not hard; she was far too focused on celebrating his death.

The crowd fell silent as Billy took his final steps towards the hanging slipknot. The only sound was the clink of his manacles, what would have taken him three normal strides now took him nine restrained shuffles. The macabre crowd hung in silence as a priest read him his last rites, not that Billy would care about that.

The executioner fixed the noose around his neck, a whisper spread through the crowd. My hands were cold and sweaty. There seemed to be an unnecessarily long pause. I looked at the clock, the countdown was on, thirty seconds until the bells would chime seven.

I realised that all eyes were on the clock. As the sound of the clock striking seven rung out, the executioner pulled a lever,

Billy's body fell through the trapdoor, the crowd all gasped in unison, it was over in a split second, his lifeless body swung gently as the crowd cheered.

The square took all day before it was quiet. A solitary guard watched over the body. Two old haggard looking women used his lifeless hand to cure their warts, the custom of passing the wart onto a new corpse was well known, if it worked was a lesser known ailment.

After thirteen hours I watched as the body was finally taken down. There was no doubt he was definitely dead; He would be dumped in an unmarked undisclosed paupers grave. The king is dead long live the king.

There was no sign of life when I got back to the wagons. It was just as well, as I was in no mood for talking. After a few swigs of rum, I turned in for the night, there was so many ifs and buts going through my head that I could not sleep. All I wanted was to be back home with my faithful friend Patch and my angel.

I set of for home at first light. My small detour to Dalbeattie was interrupted by John senior 'I am not wanting trouble' he said with his bare hands raised. His friends stayed back at a good distance, 'What's up with you' I asked. I was fully expecting him to ask for his son, 'It is your dad, he died last year' he said with his head hung low. As next of kin I would have expected somebody to have the decency to have informed me a lot sooner than this.

I thanked him for the information then travelled on. Not a word was mentioned about his son, he was in the navy was the lie that I had prepared. The truth be that he could not care less about his son. John senior was too busy with his new gang of low life fools.

Scarlett was looking glorious in a glamorous red dress, 'I have heard about Billy, how are you feeling?' she asked. It was a good question, one that I had no answer for. I stood there pondering, 'I am alright' I finally said. I was alright really, there were no feelings whatsoever, the only feeling was the longing to get home.

Jamie was sitting quietly with a puzzle of sorts. His face was full of disappointment when I arrived without Patch, 'What about the little one?' I asked discretely, 'What he does not know cannot hurt him' she replied. That is true, unless he finds out later in life.

Mrs Wolf supplied a more than ample feast for the trek home, enough to keep me going for a week it seemed, all delicious. A call in to see Gary was my next stop.

It seemed Gary had visitors. A wagon was out front, another around the back. It was Edward and Donald with their families, 'How are things going?' I asked, 'Just fine, no so good for Gary though' said Donald. 'Is he not keeping right?' I asked, 'Well you could say that, he passed away a week past' said Edward. I was in a hurry last time I passed, not that it would have made any difference if I had stopped in.

I could not but help notice how settled in they were, 'So you owe a week's rent then' I said, Edward and Donald looked at each other before Donald answered, 'Well there was a lot of cost involved with the funeral and all that'. A paupers grave cost nothing, they were trying it on, 'If you have taken responsibility for Gary you owe his months' rent' I said. The wives and kids appeared, nicely timed for a sob story.

I walked off around the wagon that was sat out front, then a glance around the back got me suspicious, 'Where are your horses?' I asked. Again, they looked at each other before answering, 'Well money has been tight lately, we have a bit of work sorted for next week though' Donald said, 'I will be back, money or you are out' I said, they both agreed to this.

Only one more night to go before the last small trek home. I stopped off at the same spot that I met Elizabeth, setting the traps regardless of her brothers. It was dark, and by the time the light came in the morning I would be gone without a trace.

The tide was on its way in by the time I arrived at Port William. It looked like the captain was too, a spy glass would be handy I thought. He was well out, a good two hours of sailing at least. I had plenty of time to go see my two angels, Patch came running up to me first, he was waggling his back end just as much as his tail, it was great to be home.

Right enough it was the captain, we walked along the beach to greet him, 'Ahoy me shipmates' the captain called as he sailed into port, 'I have something for you' I said as I handed over the last payment. Both my companions gave the gold guineas a good old stare, 'I had a bit of luck on the horses' I said they both knew that was not true, they never questioned it though. I had always tried to keep my life with them and my other life with Billy separate.

The captain spent the day with us as he awaited the next tide. The lobsters went down a treat, so did the rum along with Mrs Wolfs scones. I was happy when the captain left, some precious time with my precious one. We sat holding each other on the beach for hours after he had sailed out of sight. I had found my place in the world. It was not much but it was everything.

For me life was complete, no more chances, no more dodgy get rich quick schemes, I was rich in my heart. For the next five months we just enjoyed the beach life, with the odd day visit to the Cock Inn, 'What will you be having?' asked Lauren, 'A rum for me, what do you fancy?' I asked my angel, 'We have some French wine or Italian wine, red or white, medium or large' Lauren said. 'She is only five foot five, a small glass will do' I said laughing with Lauren, not everybody was amused.

Life had been so dreamy that I almost forgot about the freeloading squatters. A trip up there on Dark Lord revealed they were still there, 'Still here then, you got the rent money?' I asked Donald, 'Well no, things have been hard' he replied. 'Get your wagon hitched to my horse, you have six months to pay or it is mine' I said. They were taking liberties, I was expecting him to argue or at least say something, but he just hooked up the wagon.

I now had three wagons to sell. They were sitting gathering dust, so was my wagon, that is when I got the idea 'Do you fancy a trip all around Scotland?' I asked. My wife smiled, 'Yes!' came her swift reply, 'Next spring we will set off' I said, confirming the plans with a kiss.

Our travels took us up the east coast then back down west. The summer was a good one, the sun lasted for weeks at a time. We met some great fellow travellers, along with my old friend Betty. There were no troubles with anybody we met. The seven months was spent sightseeing, most of our time was spent on one splendid beach or another. The best thing of all was being together, it was still nice to be home.

The postman came a knocking one frosty November morning, 'I have been told this is for you, it is addressed to Billy and Jamie, Gatehouse of Fleet' he said. 'Yes, I will take that' I said, I also had to pay for the pleasure of receiving the post card, 'Sailing for home tonight, see you in about one to two years, Alex' was all it said. The post mark was Jamaica, the date it was stamped had been worn away.

My thoughts were on the three young men returning, looking for wagons perhaps, looking for there now long-gone brother Billy. It occurred to me that they may still be on the wanted list.

After another trip to Creetown I found out the tenants had gone, without a trace. They had left a few of their things behind, not that they had much in the first place. A week later I checked again, there was still no sign of them. Their belongings were still sitting in exactly the same place. There were however two empty whisky bottles on the floor, somebody had been here.

The next day I was up first thing. I rode Dark Lord hard and fast. There was nobody there, the bottles were gone, replaced with a half full bottle. I kicked it over spilling the contents onto the wooden floor, 'I will return tonight at dusk, catch them sneaks' I said to myself as I thought to myself it must be the family of squatters being fly.

There was no sign of life inside, I hid Dark Lord around the back, he blended in nicely with the dark night. Easing the door open just enough for my body to fit I squeezed in, there was nobody there, just as I sat down on the bed the sound of the door closing gave me a fright, the heavy footsteps were coming my way.

There were two sets of footsteps, their candle flickered as they came, sending shadows dancing around the wall. I made myself ready with knife in hand just in case. Two ghostly faces appeared, the ghost of Billy with the red lady, come for me once more,

'Keep back' I shouted waving my knife at them, they both got the fright of their lives. The red lady screamed then passed out, 'Calm down, what has got your dander up?' Billy asked as he lifted the red lady up before laying her on the bed.

Silently I watched as Billy blew in her face, some strange attempt to resuscitate her, the even stranger thing was it worked, 'Nice to see you too' Billy said sarcastically, 'It is not every night you see two ghosts' I said. Billy explained it all in great detail. It did all make sense apart from the part about laying low and still managing to find himself a woman.

Billy was after his money. I had a better plan for him, 'How would you like the pick of three wagons of the greatest condition?' I asked, 'Well yes, but I will still be needing the money' he replied. 'Did you hear your brothers are on their way back?' I asked, 'That is the best news, when?' he asked, 'Sometime between soon and a years' time. I put their share in the bank', Billy looked a bit displeased at this. 'I do not trust thieving banks' he said, the conversation ended in me agreeing to give him fifty gold guineas plus a wagon, It was a small fortune, his companion in the red dress looked more than pleased.

Before I left them to it, I had one more question to ask, 'So where did the squatters go?' they both laughed at this, 'Well it seems you are not the only one scared of ghosts' Billy said, they both laughed again. 'Three nights we spent haunting them until they fled' his companion said, it might have been funny if I had been on the drink like them.

It took the best part of a week to purchase a horse. Billy was happy with my choice, and he was even happier when I showed him the wagons. It was Ted's wagon he chose; he was none the wiser of its last owner, 'So where you planning to go?' I asked,

'Well I should be pretty much unknown up in Aberdeen for now' he replied, 'I am happy anywhere' his companion said, Billy hid in the back as they set of towards the coastal road to Ayr.

I was glad to see the back of him, peace to live my own life, a good honest life, a happy content life. Unfortunately, he had other plans. Six months later he was back, penniless, with a new lass on his arm.

We went for a quiet ale in the Cock Inn, 'This is my wife Davina' Billy said, she seemed nice enough, perhaps sacrificing a goat was making it too easy for Billy to get out of these marriages. 'Your brothers are not back yet' I said, 'That is a shame, I was looking for them to chip in with this new investment I have planned' he said. I knew what was coming next, he was wanting his brothers share of the money.

A month later we set of for the bank in Dumfries, I had used every excuse I could think of to put this day off, but Billy was persistent, all the time. 'Let's go get this sorted' he would say daily. He travelled up front, no longer was he afraid of who would see him.

A wave of embarrassment came over me as he followed me into the bank, 'This way sir' the bank manager called as we entered, 'You will need to wait here, I'll only be five minutes' I said to Billy.

Once out of the bank I gave Billy the one hundred gold guineas, 'That is me out, it is not worth all the risk' I said. 'We done good so far' Billy said as he proudly clinked the coins in his pocket. Knowing when to quit while you are ahead is something Billy would never learn; he also would never learn how much I was still squirreling away in that bank.

It was a full seven months later before Billy's brothers turned up. 'Here lads, two wagons. I will sort you out with a couple of horses' I said. It was more than they expected, 'Aw thanks, have you seen Billy?' Alex asked, 'He will show up soon enough' I replied. They all looked up to Billy, far too much for their own good.

THE END END

As I lay drifting in and out of memories, I felt a disturbance next to me. It was my wee angel, she must have sneaked in beside me, her arm around me, with her body cuddling in tight, the best feeling in the world. Mind you her presence did little for my throbbing hungover head. 'Paarrpp' went the rusty trumpet next to me. I could hear a stifled *Teehee* as a warm spicy smell filled the bed. I screwed up my face and pulled away, seventy-one years old still giggling at her own flatulence.

I was going to get no peace now, 'You need to get up' she said. I gave a low growling 'Hmmm, I'm not going'. I wanted to stay there in bed for two days minimum, 'You are expected, plus you need to say goodbye'. Who cares, it's not as if Billy will know I thought. 'Hmmm, I suppose' I muttered, she kissed me on the head then slipped away without a sound. Peace. I closed my eyes desperate for a few more moments sleep, the noise outside was bothering me though. A crowd had started to gather, and I started feeling a lot worse. My head throbbed even more, the room was spinning, my tummy cramped, 'Oooooh' I muttered to myself. As fast as I could I kicked off my covers, I jumped out of bed, grabbing the pale just in time to fill it with the last of my tummy's contents.

I was up but still half blinded by the light, then grabbed my Sunday best. I struggled to dress; my balance was not at its best this morning. I stumbled and half fell onto the bed where I sat half dressed with my trousers still bellow my knees, head in hands. I wanted to just cry, there's nothing worse than the hangover blues on a big day. I breathed in through my nose deeply until my chest was at full capacity, then exhaled slowly through my mouth, after the third breath I stood up, and quickly hauled up my breaches before slipping my boots on. 'Here we go' I said to myself.

Stepping outside I was blinded again, I stood stretching with the biggest of yawns. As my eyes got accustomed to the glare, I felt unsteady as the world wobbled. I recognised the face coming toward me 'Whis...' I stepped forward knocking the drink out of his hand, I never drank whisky, everyone knew that. It was young Brian. I looked at his dad Collin, he looked away quickly, they had both always tormented me, but my actions had made them think twice about it today. Brian had never known his Uncle Brian from whom he was named after.

The camp was awash with faces, some familiar some complete strangers, 'Must be a good couple of hundred here' I said out loud to nobody in particular. 'The streets are starting to fill already' said a voice beside me, I turned to look at the chest of a giant of a man. Squinting up to look at him I said, 'Well hello little Tony' he looked back shaking his head 'You look half dead' he said I nodded a *yes* 'Just half dead, I feel more like death warmed up'. I laughed with effort, 'Here, some elixir of life' I looked at the bottle he proffered me, hesitated, then winked at him, taking the bottle I glugged down a good drink, 'Ahh, that is better' .

I strode over to the horse drawn hearse, 'Let us make a start' I shouted out, looking up to the hearse driver giving him the nod. On a good day it would take 30 minutes to walk, but today was not a good day, I guessed there was two to three hours before the church service, it would take that today.

What followed behind were cousins of Billy or well-wishers from the travelling community far and wide. The streets were all lined with well-wishers, and it seemed like the population of the whole world had come to say goodbye. It was more like a party parade than a funeral march. The crowds cheered as the coffin passed them. The bunting flapped in the breeze; the children waved their little flags frantically. Some had the saltire flag, this was the official flag of Scotland first introduced by the Pictish king Angus MacFergus, others had the Lion Rampant flag, a fitting tribute for rampant Billy, King of the Randies.

This was a completely different atmosphere from when he was hanged, with no spitting or rotten food this time. In the preceding years, Billy had managed to go from being despised to being regarded an upstanding and much-loved pillar of the community. His death was a great loss to everybody in the land, from the poorest of the poor, to the richest of the rich, most noticeable was the Caird of Barullion.

Even as we walked out of town the route was filled with well-wishers. The walk was uphill all the way to the graveyard. The rum was knocking at the door. Drinking on an empty stomach had two effects, instant drunkenness, closely followed by the sudden need to relieve one's self, there was nowhere to go, uncomfortably I trudged on up the hill.

Turning the corner into the graveyard there were guards posted. Only family were permitted past the guards. Beyond the guards stood Billy's offspring. Seventeen marriages had produced a sizable brood, not to mention the children born out of wedlock. There was not a dry eye to be seen, from Billy's children to grandchildren they all were weeping.

My bladder was now in pain, I had to go. I moved quickly, taking a spot hidden from view by a large bush. It was a long one, and by the time I had finished I had company. Almost all the males had joined me, 'Ahhhh I was about to burst' said one of them, this was followed with a volley of 'Me too', the wives all had faces like fizz when we reappeared.

The ceremony was long-winded, a few family members had a few words to say, 'May Billy rest in peace, at one hundred and twenty years old he has deserves a rest at last' said Jamie, his first son and heir. We had started our life in the same year, yet Billy had squeezed an extra fifty years into his life, the man was a legend.

The drink was flowing like water once we made it back to the campground. Myself and my angel had agreed to get out of there after having a feast and one drink. Unfortunately, I had more than just the one before we had even reached camp.

There was going to be trouble tonight, more than the usual fist fight. With Billy gone a new chief would need to take his place, there were plenty of contenders. 'Let us get out of here' I said, my angel smiled, 'Yes let us go before it erupts' she said. I sat on the top of the wagon stoop letting her do all the work, it was for the best with the condition I was in, three days of drink was showing.

When we came to a stop at Kirkcudbright beach the sound of the revellers could still be heard, the sound was being carried on the water, 'Do you believe all them tales Billy told us?' she asked. We were always in touch with Billy, he had often told us bizarre and wild stories, some of which he had used me as a witness, 'There was me stalking this stag deer for four days, through the forest, over the highest of peaks, then when the opportunity arose I sneaked up behind him, with a mighty leap I jumped onto his back, quickly I slit its throat, for almost a whole day after that I trekked down from the hills, carrying the biggest buck I have ever seen on my shoulder' he had said. I remembered the day well, although it was a pig not a deer, his version was slightly exaggerated to say the least. 'Yes, some of them, come cuddle in, I will tell you the truth behind them' I said, well some of the truth. Some of the truth was harder to believe than the fiction.

24949539R00142

Printed in Great Britain
by Amazon